BONEGRINDER

Also by John Lutz

Buyer Beware

BONEGRINDER
JOHN LUTZ

G. P. PUTNAM'S SONS, NEW YORK

Copyright © 1977 by John Lutz

All rights reserved. This book, or parts thereof, must not be reproduced in any form without permission. Published simultaneously in Canada by Longman Canada Limited, Toronto.

SBN: 399-11990-6

Library of Congress Cataloging in Publication Data

Lutz, John, 1939–
    Bonegrinder.

    I. Title.
PZ4.L977Bo3   [PS3562.U854]   813'.5'4   77-3312

PRINTED IN THE UNITED STATES OF AMERICA

To My Mother and Father

ONE

The horizon was red-rimmed, tall cedar and pine trees standing out in sharp relief like black notched arrowheads against the glow. In the dark sky above the glow no stars were visible, but directly overhead in the smokeless sky were several pinpoints of wavering yellow light, like tiny eyes watching what was going on below and blinking occasionally in disbelief. The reddish glow might have been the trailing glory of a brilliant Ozark sunset only the time was 10:30 P.M., and the glow was on the northern horizon.

Sheriff Billy Wintone stood in the dusty main street of Colver and watched the crimson glow, one hand resting lightly on the holstered .38 that lay on his right hip, the other hand clenching and unclenching empty air in an unconscious nervous gesture he'd lately acquired.

"Hell's own," old Bonifield observed beside Wintone. "Worst forest fire this country's seen." There was a trill of excitement in his voice, like that of a young child at an accident scene. Old Bonifield owned a little truck farm some ten miles out of Colver, but he seemed never to farm it, choosing instead to inflict his presence on Colver and Sheriff Wintone. Bonifield was a whipcord-lean old man, well into his sixties, with surprisingly young pale blue and eager eyes and a cantankerous soul and tongue. He liked to harangue. And since he was alone and had no one to harangue, he harangued everyone.

Wintone didn't answer Bonifield, hoping that the old man would leave, knowing he wouldn't. The August heat made a man sweat even at 10:30 at night, and Wintone moved out farther into the street, away from the buzzing glare of the half-lighted neon sign above Mully's tavern.

"Been burnin' some two days now," old Bonifield said, following the sheriff. "Burnin' out thousands of acres up there, all them resorts an' tourist places. Serve 'em right up there, maybe. They been rich too long."

"It'll burn some while longer with this drought," Wintone said, still gazing at the low-lying reddish glare that was miles away, on the other side of Big Water Lake. He thought of how the fire must be dancing in the dry night breeze, crowning in heat-blasted explosions of flame through the tops of the drought-thirsted trees. He had seen a few forest fires close up. A few had been enough.

The front screen door of Mully's slammed, reverberating like distant rifle fire, and Wintone heard footsteps on the hard ground. Luke Higgins, owner and operator of Higgins' Motel, walked toward Wintone and Bonifield through the neon glare, walked none too steadily.

"Still a'blazin' up there, ain't it," he said, looking toward the northern horizon. The red glow was caught for a second like candlelight in his thick, wire-rimmed spectacles, lending his round, unshaven face an almost angelic appearance.

Wintone saw the pint bourbon bottle sticking half out of his hip pocket.

"You be careful goin' back to the motel, Luke," Wintone said.

"Sheriff ain't about to arrest you for drunkenness," old Bonifield said. He spat chewing tobacco skillfully and carefully onto the street, as if aiming at something.

"What I come out for," Higgins said, "was to tell you Mrs. Plumber phoned to see if you were at Mully's, said Jack Allen's hound is givin' her fits again with his yowlin'. Wants you to shoot the dog . . . wants you to shoot Jack Allen."

"There's plenty I'd shoot before Jack Allen," Wintone said. Now that he was listening for it he could hear the lonely howling of Git, Jack Allen's coon hound, from the other side of town though the wind was carrying it away.

Higgins moved off toward the back of Mully's where his ten-year-old Dodge was parked, and old Bonifield followed him or the bottle. Wintone ran a hand over his damp forehead and set off walking toward Jack Allen's.

A tiny night insect struck Wintone's face, buzzed for a second about his nostrils. He swiped at his nose, brushed his coarse mustache with the backs of his knuckles. He drew a handkerchief from a pocket of his tan sheriff's uniform and wiped his forehead and cheeks, the back of his neck. It was simmering hot still, as though the heat of the northern inferno were somehow rolling over the lake's black surface to Colver.

Git's howling was louder now, and Wintone could understand how Mrs. Plumber would have trouble sleeping. Most likely she did want him to shoot both Jack Allen and the dog, knowing that if he shot only the dog Jack Allen would howl.

Wintone turned down a side street, walked awhile longer, then turned in through a wooden gate needing paint and crossed the hard ground, ground that seemed it must be packed dry to bedrock, to Jack Allen's front door. Behind the small, cedar-plank house the hound took up its mournful howling in a more serious vein, as if to impress the sheriff. Across the way, lights burned in the Plumber house.

Five minutes passed before Jack Allen, sleepy-eyed, hair mussed, wearing only a torn T-shirt and boxer shorts, opened the door some six inches. He squinted hard at Wintone.

"Gotta keep Git quiet," Wintone told him. "I got complaints. People can't sleep."

Jack Allen rubbed his eyes. "Keep what? . . . Quiet? . . ."

"That howlin'," Wintone said. "It's keepin' some folks awake who don't want to be."

"Howlin'?"

"You're used to it, Jack Allen. That's how you can sleep. Listen, there's some that ain't."

"Uh-huh!" Jack Allen nodded as if for the first time he heard the sirenlike wailing rising from his backyard. "Some bein' that Mrs. Plumber, I'll bet."

"She's got a right to sleep," Wintone said.

"Old bitch'd rather be up all night lookin' into other people's affairs, is what."

"Take Git inside. Calm him down."

"If'n I don't?"

Wintone sighed. "I'll have to take him out somewhere where he's not botherin' anybody."

"You'd take my dog, would you?"

"If it came down to it, which I hope it won't."

Jack Allen opened the door wider, looking silly with his massive upper body and skinny legs. "Never threatened to do that before, Sheriff. It's like you're pushin' things with that badge of yours lately, ever since . . ."

Wintone's left hand clenched, unclenched. "Since what?"

"Since, is all."

The two men stared at each other, conveying what words would have given shape to, made actionable. But no words were exchanged. The dog howled louder, inspired by Wintone's presence.

"He ain't et," Jack Allen said by way of explanation.

"You feed him, why don't you. Make him quiet." Wintone walked the short distance to the back of the house into sudden silence. He untied the rangy spotted hound and led it around to the front door. Jack Allen hadn't moved.

"He smells coon, maybe," Jack Allen said.

"Maybe." Wintone dropped the thick rope and the dog wedged between Jack Allen and the door frame to get inside the house, where it remained quiet.

There was a crash inside the house as the dog knocked something over. Jack Allen glanced back into the darkness, then stared at Wintone with resigned anger.

"You keep him in now," Wintone said. He turned and walked the hard ground halfway back to the dirt street that was just as hard.

A big dark station wagon, fairly new, seemed to appear like a magician's illusion in the street before Wintone. Four men sat in the air-conditioned interior behind rolled-up windows, all middle-aged, dressed casual-expensive. As the power window on the passenger's side glided down, Wintone saw that one of the men was wearing a gold chain and medallion like a necklace.

"You know where there's a passable motel around here?" the driver called to Wintone. "Near some passable fishing?"

Wintone noticed the fishing gear in the back of the wagon, rods and reels, hip boots, tackle boxes. "Higgins' Motel'd do. Keep goin' like you are, make a right when you can't go no farther and take that road on up along Big Water Lake till you come to Higgins' place off to your left."

"Straight, right, left," the driver impressed upon himself.

"Thanks, scout," one of the passengers said, and the window glided upward as the big car accelerated, raising dust invisible in the night air.

Wintone watched the wavering red taillights until they disappeared, then he walked on toward the street.

"Since, is all . . ." Jack Allen repeated loudly behind him.

When Wintone looked back after a few steps, the door was shut.

TWO

"We shoulda know'd the tourists'd be comin'," Mully said from behind the bar. He was a large man, though thin and a bit stooped in middle age, and his tanned face behind dark-rimmed glasses was lined like old folding money.

"Takes a real ass to have that kinda hindsight," Frank Turper, who ran Turper's Grill, said to laughter up and down the bar.

Mully smiled to show Turper he wasn't riled and started wiping the smooth bar top with a tattered but clean white rag.

It was dim in Mully's, and though the old brick building wasn't air conditioned it always seemed cool compared to outside, maybe because of the old wide-bladed ceiling fan that was always slowly revolving as if it might just continue to do so as long as the earth revolved. The floor was rough-sawn plank, and the red vinyl booths and some of the bar stools were so patched with smooth electrician's tape that they were more tape than vinyl. The bar itself was grand, twenty feet long and of fine mahogany with a solid brass foot rail. Mully laughingly refused frequent offers from tourists who wanted to buy the bar. Behind the bar, hung high on the wall, was an illuminated beer ad, a faded picture of a heavy-antlered stag poised atop a rise and looking back over his shoulder as if at his pursuers. There was a broken electric clock beneath the stag, its coiled cord plugged into a wall socket, but its ornate black hands had indicated 11:59 for as long as Wintone could remember. Above the front door was a mounted trout upon the belly of which a taxidermist had skillfully attached rabbit fur. The few city fishermen who had ventured into Mully's had been amused.

Mully set Wintone up another beer.

"Ain't an empty cabin in my motel," Luke Higgins said beside the sheriff.

"It's an ill wind . . ." Wintone said.

"Ain't nothin' ill about it," Frank Turper said from down the bar. He was a heavyset man with soft padded cheeks and small dark eyes that seemed harder and sharper for being set deep in all that inflated flesh. "Every business in Colver's picked up like we never believed. Only wind I can see in it at all is the one fanned those flames that burned out all those tourist traps on the north shore."

"That big new fancy one built last year," old Bonifield said, "it burned clear flat level, Seth Orson told me. Serves the bastards right; they done made enough money."

"Amen," Luke Higgins said beside Wintone.

Turper bought Bonifield and himself another round. "Thing is, once the tourists start comin' down here for their fishin' an' boatin', they might keep on comin' even after the north shore's built back up in a year or so."

"Except for one thing," Wintone said, tilting back his beer mug and taking a pull while Turper waited. "The south end of Big Water Lake ain't nearly the resort an' fishin' kind of water they got up north. This end is wild, shallow an' reedgrown. There's places nobody's set foot in for years."

"And with good reason," Mully said. "If you don't get lost or snakebit, you'll drop your hook in an' all you'll bring up is weed or slime. Lynn Cove an' the bank down near the dock are the only decent fishin' spots on the shore."

"City fishermen are funny sorts," Higgins said. "They'll go someplace where nobody's set foot just to get their lines tangled."

"So's they have to buy new line," Turper said.

"Which the Colver General Merchandise store'll sell 'em," old Bonifield said, raising his beer mug to Wintone.

"Still," Wintone said, "this water ain't clear like off the north shore, an' it's too overgrown and shallow for a boat to get around for some hundred yards off the bank. A little shallower and it'd damn near be swamp."

"Sheriff'd bitch if you hung him with a new rope," old Bonifield said, lifting his mug again. "He oughta be glad prosperity's come to Colver."

"Amen," Higgins said.

"Mayor Boemer might not like you talkin' like that, Sheriff," Frank Turper said with the burlesque of righteous indignation that was all he could muster after five beers.

Wintone shrugged. "Piss on the mayor. He's lucky I don't arrest him in his office for loitering."

"Ain't you techy," old Bonifield said. "Been techy on to . . . six months or so."

Wintone's fingers whitened on the dark beer bottle as he poured.

"I will say the sheriff didn't arrest me when I got glorious jug-bit last Saturday a week," old Bonifield went on. "I will say he ain't that techy, to arrest a man drunk but not so drunk as to be a nuisance."

"You're a nuisance sober," Wintone said.

"A nuisance," old Bonifield said, "ain't exactly a menace . . ."

"Sheriff's right about this end of the lake, though," Mully said at the right time, as was his way. "Ain't nothin' but miles of bad water, wild growth an' copperhead snakes. We fish this part of it 'cause we live here an' we're used to it."

"Fish is a fish," Bonifield said with a shrug of his thin shoulders.

"If mudcat, crawdad an' bony carp are your fare."

"Good eatin' if you know how to cook 'em!" Bonifield snapped.

"Tourists don't know," Wintone said calmly.

"Them that don't know comes to my restaurant," Frank Turper said.

Bonifield cackled.

Wintone saw that the talk was caught in a circle, a hoopsnake conversation bound to bite its own tail. He finished his beer, slid off his stool and walked out into the brightness and heat of midday.

He crossed the hot street slowly and walked toward his office, thinking of Lil Higgins renting cabins and making money while Luke sat in Mully's. Thinking of Velda, the henna-haired waitress at Turper's Grill, dealing out hamburgers to the ring of the cash register. The hordes of tourists that had invaded the south shores of Big Water Lake meant added business for most everybody, and Wintone knew that sooner or later he'd get his rightful share of business. Only he was likely the solitary one who didn't want it.

Wintone waved to Web Hooper, passing in his red pickup, then he opened the door in the frame street-front building that used to be a sweets store but some twenty-five years ago had been converted into the sheriff's office and "temporary" jail. Wintone remembered the sweets store from when he was a boy, the taffy in the winter, still hot, that would steam some if you dropped it in the snow and taste all the better after you dug it out. He was just turned forty-one now, and that time seemed long, long past, only a dream more vivid than most.

In fact, it seemed years since Etty had died, but old Bonifield had set the time right: six months and nine days. The sheriff could tack on the hours and minutes, if you wanted, to a hair.

Wintone shut the door behind him quickly so the old window air conditioner wouldn't have to strain to catch up. The office itself was small; scarred wooden desk, green file cabinets on one wall, a few hickory chairs with seat cushions on them, a cork bulletin board with the usual curled and yellowed memorandums and wanted notices attached like mounted long-dead butterflies that had faded. The back room, where Wintone had a cot, was larger than the office and held most of the furniture, and beyond that was the room containing the three eight-by-eight cells, most often empty.

Wintone ran the back of his wrist across his forehead and slumped in the swivel chair behind his paper-strewn desk. The office was the coolest room right now, but if Wintone decided to spend the night here he'd set up a small fan to blow the coolness from the air conditioner into the back room. It worked. Cool air pretty much went where it was pushed, and where it was pushed was cooler than the small set of rooms Wintone leased from the Lalprin family, who had left the rest of the house empty two years ago to move to Springfield.

Etty regarded Wintone from her portrait on his desk corner, a dark-haired, dark-eyed woman in her mid-thirties, with beauty but no hint of mystery in her slight smile. The smile was simply something that belonged about the generous lips; the thing about Etty that stayed strongest with Wintone was the smile.

Wintone leaned back in the wood swivel chair, a big man, nearly big enough to be called huge, with a barrel chest, oak-trunk thighs and large hands that were surprisingly quick and dexterous. He had angular, fine-chiseled, almost haughty features and a boyish thatch of curly, brown, unruly hair that looked too innocent for the face below. When he moved, it was with a lightness and balance and a deceptively lazy cast to his eyes. With a certain sadness, he knew from occasional shortnesses of breath, from lapses of reflex and aches in the mornings that he wasn't near the man he'd been at thirty-five. He was a man beginning to feel the burden of time.

That was what made the thing about Etty all the more persistent. If only they'd had some few years together instead of the few months. . . . He remembered Etty's father, Henry Card, a hard Baptist rock of a man, and his endless biblical philosophizing after the accident.

Wintone tilted back his head and stared up at the finely cracked ceiling. "The Lord taketh away." The Lord had taken Etty and her softness from Wintone, taken what had given a joyous pattern to his life, taken the only future that meant anything. On Route 44 the Lord had been an over-the-road tractor-trailer with diesel stacks; on Route 44 the Lord had slammed down His fist like a sledgehammer. On Etty, not Wintone.

As in a relentless TV news film he was forced to watch, Wintone again saw the flames, again heard the screams that had meant so little to him at the time as he stumbled about the highway shoulder. An intersection collision, impossible to say whose fault. A hand, an arm, supporting him; Malloby, a state trooper he vaguely knew; Malloby staring hard into his face. "Listen, Billy, I ain't gonna ask you . . ." And Wintone had been drinking before the accident; Wintone and nobody else knew that for a provable fact, and nobody including Wintone knew if he'd been drunk enough for it to affect his driving. He had nodded numbly, hadn't had to take the inhalator test to determine if he was legally drunk, legally and morally responsible for Etty's death. "Jesus . . ." the dazed truck driver had repeated over and over, "Jesus . . . Jesus . . . Jesus . . ." And a county sheriff hadn't had to take the test that any other driver would have been required to take, that would have fixed responsibility or innocence; and Wintone wished to Jesus now that he had taken the test, wished now that he could know one way or the other, so eventually he might forget.

Wintone hadn't seen or talked to his father-in-law since the funeral.

The swivel chair squealed as the sheriff dropped his weight forward, rested his elbows on the scarred desk top. What he'd had the crazy urge to do after the funeral was to take his shotgun, knife and fishing gear and disappear into the deep woods along Big Water Lake, simply disappear, from himself, from everyone. There were dark places there, shady and cool, where nothing in this world could find him. But he hadn't done that; he wasn't a man to surrender to senseless impulse.

So Wintone sought his escape in sleep; he dreamed less often now. He lowered his head into the cradle of his folded arms on the desk, and in the morning he awoke on the cot in the next room, neither remembering nor caring how he'd got there.

The cedar frame of the cot groaned like something dying as Wintone rolled onto his side and sat up, raking his fingers lightly over his sleep-swollen features as if to check for changes. After a brief, cold shower and a quick shave, Wintone felt better. He felt good enough to put on a fresh uniform and to walk down to Turper's Grill and have scrambled eggs and gravy biscuits for breakfast.

There were several fishermen breakfasting at the counter at Turper's, dressed in expensive city-bought outdoors clothing and talking about the insurance business. A vacationing family—man, wife and teen-age daughter—sat in one of the booths by the window, eating in silence. The place where Wintone customarily sat at the counter was taken, so he ate at one of the small tables near the door. From time to time he'd look up and watch Velda's bubblelike henna hairdo moving back and forth behind the tall serving-shelf from the kitchen, much like a balled-up artificial animal in a shooting gallery.

It was nine o'clock when Wintone ordered a cup of black coffee to go and carried it back to his office.

Things to do. Nate Graham had claimed some city fishermen had trespassed to fish his private lake, and after he'd chased them off in none too friendly a fashion one of his milk cows had turned up dead of a bullet wound. He'd managed to find out the name of one of one of the fishermen, and though they'd gone back to Saint Joseph the next day, Graham had filed charges. Paperwork for the state, enough to keep Wintone occupied for over an hour hunt-and-pecking on his old Royal typewriter.

After that Rufe Davis, proprietor of Colver General Merchandise and Colver's postmaster, came by with the day's mail and sat for a long chat, talking mostly about how his business had picked up and how hellish hot it was getting outside. When he was gone, Wintone leisurely opened his mail with his pocketknife and scanned the various colorful ads and form letters with disinterest. He had no need for a new anything, really. The tools of his trade were basic.

It was just past noon when old Bonifield crossed the street

toward the sheriff's office with his curiously agile, limping gait. Sweat had streaked his grizzled, lean face and he was walking fast, bent slightly forward, nervously shifting his usual large wad of chewing tobacco from cheek to cheek behind set lips.

He threw open the office door with a suddenness that startled and momentarily angered Wintone.

THREE

Wintone sat and listened. Craziness here. What old Bonifield was yammering about couldn't be true. The sheriff decided to let the old man talk until he ran down.

Lazily rubbing a forefinger along the side of his nose, Wintone speculated that maybe it was the combination of afternoon heat and morning alcohol that had ignited old Bonifield's imagination.

Quite a story he was telling, about a boy who'd been attacked at the lake by something that sounded as if it came right out of a late-night horror movie. Wintone had heard this sort of almost incoherent ranting before from Bonifield when the old man had been drinking hard. What did worry the sheriff was that a boy might have been hurt badly somewhere in some other fashion. Though even that part of Bonifield's tale was probably so much wind.

"It be true, Sheriff!" Bonifield shouted, sensing Wintone's doubt.

"Ain't always easy to know what's true," Wintone said.

"You'll be knowin' when you see the body." Bonifield opened the front door for a moment, rattling the blinds against the window, and spat an amber arc of chewing tobacco into the street.

Wintone resented him letting the heat in against the hardworking air conditioner. "I wish you'd left the body," he said, not knowing himself if he was trying to humor old Bonifield. ". . . Make things easier."

"He were still alive when we found him, I told you, screamin' on about what come up outa the lake an' attacked him. When he quit screamin' an' closed his eyes we didn't know if he be dead or not, so we figured we oughta bring him on in to Doc Amis."

"Uh-hm. If he's as tore up as you say and wasn't dead at the lake," Wintone said, "he's bound to be now after the ride over rough road in Joe James's pickup truck. You shoulda sent somebody in to get the doc."

What passed over old Bonifield's lined face unsettled Wintone. A kind of fear and shame that suggested that maybe none of the men had had the courage to stay at the scene of whatever had or hadn't happened to the boy. And Wintone knew that none of them were cowards. Old Bonifield's wild story, in those few seconds, gained a certain chilling credibility.

Brakes squealed outside and a tinny-sounding door slammed. Through the slanted blinds Wintone saw the dented black roof of Joe James's rusty pickup truck. Car doors slammed. Old Bonifield had already shuffled his stooped, whipcord figure out the door, leaving it hanging open for Wintone like an unfriendly invitation.

As he stepped outside, the heat hit Wintone like a soft hammer that continued to press. He was reminded again that he was forty-one and tilting to overweight.

"See here now, Sheriff!"

Bonifield was leaning over the bed of the old pickup and pointing, a look of triumph on his creased and stubbled face, a glint of wildness in his surprisingly alert blue eyes.

Joe James, a heavyset man with a red face and no eyebrows, stepped aside for Wintone to move in close. "He were dead when we hoisted him into the truck, Sheriff," James said with a sad tension. "Figured it best to stop here first."

"Figured right," Wintone said, staring at what was in the bed of the pickup. Wintone had seen a lot. He looked away. Bonifield had said the boy's eyes were closed. The eyes of the dead thing in the pickup bed were open. Maybe the jarring ride had done that.

"Boy about twelve," Sonny Tibbet said. He had been in the truck cab with Joe James and was with him when the screams had led the men to discover the boy on the bank of Big Water Lake. "Wonder what did that to him, did all that an' took his leg near off? . . ."

"Somethin' bad," Bonifield said, "real bad. . . ."

"Animal?" Joe James ventured.

Bonifield spat. "Animal, hell! Boy said it come up outa the lake at him, said that 'fore he died."

The sun seemed to be getting hotter by the second, and already an unpleasant odor was rising from the bed of the truck.

"Take the remains on to Doc Amis, Joe," Wintone said. "Take Bonifield, too. Sonny, come on into the office. Cool in there."

Sonny Tibbet was a shade over Wintone's six foot two, even a shade huskier, but not as hard a man. He owned the sawmill his dad had owned before him, and he had Wintone's respect. They went back a way together, back to when they were in school.

Sonny squinted and yanked at a lock of curly black hair.

Old habit. "Is cool in here," he said, settling down into the hickory chair opposite Wintone's desk.

Wintone sat and rolled a ball-point pen back and forth between his thumb and little finger over the scarred mahogany desk top, trying not to think of what he'd seen in the pickup bed. He leaned back in his creaking wood chair and got right to official business. Cold facts were best for burying nightmare images. "What all happened down at the lake, Sonny?"

"We was goin' down to inspect our trout lines we put out last night. Old Bonifield had some lines out, too, an' me an' Joe James met him on the path to Lynn Cove." Sonny bunched his body in a way Wintone didn't like. "That's when we heard the screamin', an' another sound, like splashin' an' a kind of groanin'—real low, not the boy groanin'. We run there fast as we could an' found the boy pretty much like you saw him but alive. He was ravin', said he was fishin' an' somethin' come up outa the lake an' got him, somethin' big an' dark. Joe pulled me aside, said he figured the boy wouldn't live long enough for us to get Doc Amis an' bring him back, so we decided to bring him on in with Joe's pickup. We put an old blanket an' some rags in back so's to soften the ride, but I knew the boy was dead when we loaded him in—too much blood lost."

"Know who the boy was?"

Sonny shook his head, yanked unconsciously at his hair. "Wasn't any identification on him. We thought he must be the son of somebody in that bunch stayin' at Higgins' Motel."

Wintone's insides seemed to twist and he cringed. He would have the unpleasant task of checking that out and notifying the boy's family. "What was it you think got him?" he asked.

Sonny shrugged. "That comin' up outa the water business'd be the boy's imagination. He was ravin', busted up the way he was."

Bonifield had come back from Doc Amis's and was standing leaning against the wall near the cork bulletin board. "Doc Amis says he ain't seen nothin' like it . . . jaws an' claws, is what he says . . . boy been put through a grinder."

Wintone thought about running Bonifield out of the office but decided against the effort. Besides, he might have some questions to put to the old man.

"Tell the good sheriff 'bout the footprint," Bonifield said. "Though it weren't no footprint, nor paw, neither."

Sonny nodded. "There was a print, Sheriff, leastways one clear one, on the bank near where the boy was layin'. Rest of the ground was soft an' all churned up."

"So," Wintone said, "what kind of print?"

Sonny hesitated and shook his head. "No kind I ever seen."

"Big, though," Bonifield said. "Six, eight inches across. An' deep, like the thing were somethin' heavy."

Wintone grunted. "How 'bout goin' back up there," he said to Sonny. "Make sure nobody messes things up around where it happened. I got some people to talk to an' I'll be along."

After a moment Sonny nodded. "I'll get Joe James to go with me. We'll take his truck."

"I'm goin' down to Mully's an' get a drink," Bonifield said.

Heat rolled in before Sonny and Bonifield slammed the door behind them, rattling the blinds. On the warm windowpane a bluebottle fly crawled across the loop of the R in SHERRIFF. Wintone picked up the phone like it was something slimy.

Lil Higgins answered the telephone, and Wintone had to wait awhile for Luke to come in from where he was working on one of the cabins. Then he told Wintone that the couple in cabin eight, the Larsens, had been inquiring since morning about the whereabouts of their eleven-year-old son, Dale. Higgins confirmed that the boy was blond—that was really all the description that Wintone could give him. Wintone told Higgins not to mention the phone call to the boy's family and said he'd be on his way up there shortly.

Wintone stood wearily and strapped on his holstered .38 revolver. He ran broad fingers through his brown curls, pulled the leather holster strap tight and adjusted the weight of the pistol on his hip. Then he went out into the heat, careful to shut the door tight behind him, and set out walking toward Doc Amis's.

He was in front of Lige Thompson's Ozark Used Furniture store and already sticky with sweat when a low red sports car slowed to keep pace with him. There were two men in it who looked to be in their middle twenties, each with a flowing dark mustache, and several fishing rods were lashed to a chrome carrier on the car's roof.

"Hey, Marshall," the driver called, "is there anyplace to buy bottle liquor in this metropolis?"

Wintone kept walking. "Colver Liquor and Tobacco Shop, three blocks over."

"How about that dive over there?" The man extended his arm from the car to point toward Mully's.

"No carry-out liquor there, nor hard liquor at all," Wintone said, "only bottle beer in mugs."

"Bottle beer in mugs . . ." the driver repeated as if in disbelief. The sports car suddenly seemed to drop six inches and the engine hummed louder as it sped away. It occurred to Wintone that there was no speed limit posted anywhere in Colver except where the little-traveled alternate highway cut through the town's center.

When Wintone arrived at Doc Amis's, he noticed that the twice-lightning-struck, huge cottonwood tree that shaded the low brick building looked as if it might be dying from the drought. Its leaves appeared wilted and had taken on a dull brownish hue out near the ends of the long branches.

Doc Amis's nurse and receptionist, Sarah Ledbetter, didn't look up as Wintone entered. A thin, almost skinny, woman with close-cropped blond hair, pretty in an intense way, she was busy at her desk entering something in a large black-bound record book, and her hands were unsteady. When she did glance up and saw Wintone in the small, comfortable anteroom, she smiled and laid the pen in the crease of the open book's binding.

"Didn't hear you come in, Billy."

"Didn't make much noise."

She gave him a flickering up-and-down glance with almost a mother's concern in wide blue eyes that were penetrating in their sensitivity. "You look worn down."

"Worn down's what I am. Doc keepin' you busy, Sarah?"

"Busier'n I wanted to be today."

Wintone smiled a bit of sadness and nodded. He was at ease in Sarah's company. They had gone together for over a year when they were in their teens, when touching each other had been a bona fide black-sky sin instead of something like shaking hands the way it was now. Wintone sometimes wondered which attitude was worse.

A horizontal frown-line appeared on Sarah's forehead, softened but stayed when she stopped frowning and looked up at Wintone. "I haven't seen anything as bad as that boy for a long time." She had spent three years as an RN in Kansas City after nursing school, and Wintone was surprised to see her upset. But then a person's capacity to endure a sight like the boy's remains probably lessened if the senses weren't kept dulled by frequent similar sights. Wintone could understand that; he remembered the dead return gaze from the back of Joe James's pickup truck and almost shivered.

A door behind and to the left of Sarah opened, and Doc Amis came into the anteroom and nodded a hello to Wintone. The doctor was a tall, hawk-nosed man in his late sixties, very erect and very gray. It seemed that every year he got some straighter in the back and some grayer, but never older.

"That boy looks like he's been put through a threshing machine," the doctor said. "What happened to him?"

Wintone crossed hamlike forearms. "Somethin' attacked him down at Big Water Lake."

"Something big, judging by the slashes and tooth marks."

"What do you figure it was? Pack of dogs?"

"Not dogs. Something bigger. Hard to say just what."

"What was the cause of death, Doc?"

Doc Amis snorted. "Take your pick, Sheriff. Without going into unpleasant details, it could have been anything from shock to loss of blood."

"The men who got there right after it happened said the boy told them somethin' came up out of the lake after him while he was fishin'."

Sarah, who had been intently following the conversation, looked questioningly at Wintone.

"Could it have been a bear?" Wintone asked Doc Amis.

"No bears around here."

"Cougar?"

"Definitely not. I've seen the work of cougar on a man. All I can say, Billy, is whatever it was had the tools to do more damage than a cougar. It's hard for me to believe the boy could have lived long enough to tell anybody anything, but it happens."

"And it's not good when it happens," Sarah said.

Wintone caught the undertone of helpless compassion in her voice, wanted to ease her mind but didn't know what to say. "See if you can do something with what's left of him,

Doc. I'll be sending his folks in from Higgins' to officially identify him."

"They know yet?"

"On my way to tell 'em."

Doc Amis shot him a gray look of understanding. "Don't let me keep you, Sheriff."

When Wintone stepped back out onto the street, the heat seemed to envelop him with an eager malice in a way that was strangely personal, as if the elements had conspired to infuriate him.

He tried not to think of where he was going, what he had to do, tried not to think about the heat. From horizon to horizon the sky was a shimmering blue without a single cloud, and without a single hope of rain.

FOUR

Wintone waited in the tiny, knotty pine–paneled office of Higgins' Motel while Lil Higgins went to see if the Larsens were in their cabin. The motel office was so cool that the abrupt change from the outside heat had brought a nauseous, hollow sensation to Wintone's stomach. An oversized air conditioner mounted in the wall behind the wooden counter hummed powerfully, and Wintone heard the steady drip of condensation falling into a half-full yellow plastic bucket beneath the air conditioner. There were faint spatter marks on the paneling from when the water level in the bucket had gotten too high.

The CB radio base unit on the desk was turned on, and somebody called Bulldog was laboriously giving somebody called Flatiron directions to a restaurant on the main highway. Wintone reached over and turned the unit off.

On the motel desk were a number of wire holders containing maps and travel brochures. Wintone didn't remember seeing them there before, and on the wall was a freshly painted sign with motel rules and a new and earlier check-out time. One of the knotty-pine walls was covered with dozens of photographs of both Lil and Luke Higgins smiling and holding up prize fish or large strings of smaller fish they'd caught. None of the fish had been pulled from the south end of the lake.

Wintone hadn't heard anyone approach, but the office door opened and the Larsens came in, fearful and eager. Lil gave Wintone a look that said she pitied everyone in the room and left them alone.

Paul Larsen was a tall man with straight blond hair neatly cut and parted to the side as if it had been flipped there to disguise a receding hairline. He had fine, elongated features and agonized blue eyes. His wife Beth was a narrow-waisted, tiny woman with dark and deep eyes that seldom blinked. Wintone wished she didn't have eyes like that.

"Why don't both of you sit down," Wintone said.

Beth Larsen sat in a chrome-armed vinyl chair, but Paul Larsen said he preferred to stand. He rested his hand on his seated wife's thin shoulder, as if posing for a photograph.

Willing the feeling part of his mind to be numb, Wintone told them what had happened.

Paul Larsen did sit down then, as if he'd been heart-shot. Beth Larsen's dark eyes went blank, rolled back, and she closed them and bowed her head, squeezing her slender hands together as if praying, squeezing both clasped hands between her whitened knees. Her thin body convulsed with her soft sobs, as if jolts of electricity were passing through her chair.

"It'll be necessary for one of you to drive on in to Colver," Wintone said. "Make sure."

"I am sure," Paul Larsen said in a flat voice. There was a

stunned expression on his face, an almost-smile of a leer that he wasn't aware of.

Beth Larsen regained control first. "We'll both go," she said, reaching out a hand and touching her husband's wrist.

"Mrs. Higgins has offered to drive you," Wintone said. "I think it'd be best."

Beth Larsen agreed. Her husband was still wherever he had gone inside himself.

Wintone nodded to them, feeling awkward in the curiously graced presence of their grief, and stepped to the door. The voice that stopped him was soft and controlled.

"Did you say an animal, Sheriff?"

With an effort he turned and looked at Beth Larsen's soul in her dark eyes. "Had to be. . . ." He nodded again and left quickly.

Lil Higgins was standing by the corner of the office. Wintone didn't say anything to her, was barely aware of her on the edge of his vision, as he strode to his parked patrol car.

He started the car and headed toward Big Water Lake, dwelling on the idea that his job was getting harder with the years. According to Lil Higgins, the Larsens had originally intended to stay at one of the motels on the north shore of the lake, deciding after a long discussion to drive their station wagon south rather than let the northern forest fire ruin their vacation. That was a discussion they would both remember for the rest of their lives.

Wintone slowed the car and steered through a curve beneath an ancient leaning elm whose lower branches had been axed to permit passage. Then he turned right onto the narrow dirt road that skirted the lake. Rocks beat against the insides of the patrol car's fenders and a plume of thick dust obscured rear-view-mirror vision. The green wildness that surrounded Wintone was in many places almost impossible for a man to move through, its interior guarded by brush and thick, upright sapling trunks like sturdy, impassable bars. Even ax and chain saw were insufficient to probe the woods' depths. Through the trees to his left, Wintone could occasionally glimpse the lake's surface, dull and flat and endless-seeming. It looked like a place that would keep its secrets.

Sonny Tibbet moved out fast from the shade of a blackjack oak and flagged down the car. He looked glad to see Wintone.

"Joe James had to go on back to town," Sonny said when the sheriff had rolled down the car window to the heat. "Up over that rise is where it happened."

Wintone got out of the car and followed Sonny over a small rise and down a flat stretch shaded deep by oak and maple to the bank of Big Water Lake. Insects flitted up at each of their footfalls in the bent, dry grass and mosquitoes and gnats swarmed about the two men. Wintone watched a large mosquito light on Sonny's sweat-stained shirt collar and crawl toward his red, perspiring neck.

The boy had died right at the water's edge, and Wintone stood for a moment and looked at the gentle lake water lapping at where blood had soaked into the churned mud. A cane fishing pole still lay on the bank, the homemade bait on the end of the line already covered with ants. The lake was shallow here, sloping out to the deeper area, and the water was dark green and broken by reeds and a rotting, half submerged fallen tree. Not much fishing here except for carp or mudcat, but an eleven-year-old boy wouldn't know that.

"Lookit here, Sheriff."

Wintone looked to where Sonny was pointing and saw a good, clear print up where the bank was less muddy. After his first glance he bent low to examine it.

Old Bonifield had been right. Whatever had made the

print must have been big, heavy. The impression was over an inch deep, almost round, with one edge of it deeper than the other and sort of gnarled.

Wintone stared at the print awhile and decided he should make a plaster cast. He'd brought equipment with him in the trunk of the patrol car, and he gave Sonny the keys and asked him to get that and the camera in the glove compartment. Wintone hadn't been sure he would want to make a cast of the print, but now he hoped that moisture hadn't gotten to the quick-dry plaster mix that had sat so long in his bottom desk drawer.

The plaster was fine, and while the cast was hardening Wintone looked over the rest of the scene carefully, examined the boy's fishing pole and bait and searched in vain for another clear print. He felt a chill like one of the damned mosquitoes was crawling up the back of his neck when he looked out at the lake and noticed that some of the reeds were bent or smashed in an indistinct path, as if something big had passed through them. When he turned to mention it, he saw that Sonny was up the bank away from him, standing with his hands in his pockets and gazing out at the lake. Wintone snapped his photographs, then walked up to join him.

"Figure out anything?" Sonny asked as they walked back to the dusty patrol car.

"Only that somethin' killed the boy there, most likely somethin' big."

"Find out who the boy was?"

"Dale Larsen was his name. He and his folks were at Higgins' place, here for a vacation. Lil Higgins is drivin' 'em into Colver so they can see what's left."

"That's rough."

Wintone slammed shut the trunk lid of the patrol car, leaving four long finger-streaks in the coating of dust on the lighter tan, smooth paint. The sheriff and Sonny got into the car at the same time, slamming the doors almost simultaneously. Wintone twisted the ignition key, fishtailed the car in a dust-spewing U-turn and punched the windshield-washer button once to clear the glass.

They had turned onto the main road back to Colver before Sonny spoke.

"I been thinkin' about that print, Sheriff."

Wintone was silent, watching the countryside, the gentle roll of green-wooded hills, like the soft curves of a reclining woman, the angled line of rough cedar-rail fence, the faded, miraculously standing outbuildings canted to the wind.

"There weren't any more prints," Sonny said, "up the bank or in either direction."

"Meaning?"

"It seems whatever it was must have come outa the water and gone back in."

"It does seem so," Wintone said.

The patrol car topped a rise and passed Sam Olfer's red-roofed barn. They were almost into Colver. Wintone hoped he could avoid the Larsens.

FIVE

Wintone detoured to drop off Sonny at his sawmill, then drove the patrol car the rest of the way into Colver and parked in front of his office. The heat had run everyone off the street except a couple of teen-aged girls dressed in shorts and halters and riding ten-speed racing bikes. Wintone didn't recognize either of the girls as they pedal-stroked the bicycles past him with graceful muscularity. Tourists.

Inside the office he sat at his desk and tried to work, but couldn't. He picked up a dull metal paper clip and bent it into various meaningless shapes, pricking his finger several times with the deceptively sharp wire end. Colver was changing, Wintone was changing, everything was changing. It was as if Etty's death had altered the meaning of it all.

The sharp ring of the telephone broke the oppressive silence of the office and Wintone's gloomy musings. He reached out and lifted the receiver from its cradle slowly, as if it were glued.

He was glad to hear Sarah's voice.

"I thought you'd be back earlier," she said.

"I had things to do at the lake."

"The Larsens made a positive identification of their son." Her voice told Wintone there had never been any doubt in anyone's mind; the formalities had to be observed.

Wintone thanked her.

"How did they take it?" Sarah asked. "When you told them at the motel?"

"Like you'd expect."

She sensed Wintone's reluctance to talk about it. "If Doc Amis comes up with anything I'll let you know.'

"Thanks, Sarah."

"Billy, you come by if there's any way we can help you find out what happened, any medical information, or for that matter any kind of help we can give you. You come by."

"I will, Sarah."

Wintone hung up the phone. He picked up the paper clip he'd been toying with from his desk top, deftly worked it into a kinked though reasonably straight piece of wire and tossed it into his waste basket. As he sat back in his chair and stared at Etty's picture on his desk corner, Wintone wondered if he really kept her face there—where he could look at it every minute—out of his dark suspicion of guilt. Probably, he decided. If his mind were opened like a walnut and all its contents examined, probably.

Wintone stood, started to put on his tan uniform hat, then remembered the heat outside and tossed the hat onto his desk. He left the office and walked down the street to Mully's, where he found old Bonifield still using his talk of the boy's death to milk the other customers for free drinks.

"Ain't it like I told you, Sheriff?" Bonifield asked in a voice a shade taunting. "We'ns was just talkin' about it."

"Like you told," Wintone said, taking a stool at the long

bar. It was cool in Mully's, and Wintone accepted a mug of beer and sat watching the soft shadows of the revolving overhead fan blades play on the rough wall near the ceiling.

Bonifield's heavy boots clopped on the plank floor as he came over to sit at the bar near Wintone. "Any ideas?" the old man asked, his face an eager, serious mask.

"No inklin' yet," Wintone said. He knuckled some foam from his beer off his mustache.

Luke Higgins settled down on the other side of Wintone. "A hard thing for that Larsen family," he said. "Lil told me the man cried. Doc Amis had to give him somethin'."

"Can't blame him."

"Guess not." Higgins stared at the backs of his hands on the bar. "Listen, Sheriff, it'd be best all ways if you didn't let some creature story out now, with the tourists an' all. Lotta money comin' in an' around Colver 'cause of the forest fire up north, an' some of these folks might come back next year—if they ain't spooked away this year."

"Nobody's sayin' anything about a creature except Bonifield here," Wintone said. "I ain't said anything cause I don't know anything yet, but I'm not coverin' anything up, either."

Higgins started to say something else, then lapsed silent.

"Higgins's got a point, though," Frank Turper threw in.

"Good point," Bonifield said. "Main point."

Wintone suddenly wanted shed of Mully's. He drained his beer and got off his stool. "You shouldn't have any trouble if you shut up old Bonifield," he said as he walked toward the door.

". Ain't been worth hog slop since his wife died in that car wreck," Wintone heard Bonifield say as he stepped out into the heat. Through the window he saw Frank Turper buying Bonifield a drink.

Wintone walked back toward the office with long strides,

slowed down when he realized he was working up a sweat that was making his clothes stick to him.

He wondered what it was curdled the soul in a man like old Bonifield. Age, maybe. Age coupled with loneliness. Something Wintone might be able to learn about firsthand.

Lately there'd been so much he wished hadn't happened. Etty's death . . . the Larsen boy's . . . the fire that had brought the tourist invasion of Colver . . .

Despite his slower pace, Wintone was sweating again.

SIX

After breakfast the next day Wintone stepped out of Turper's Grill into the comparative coolness of morning just as Sarah Ledbetter was passing.

"Billy," she said in greeting, with a smile of pleasurable surprise. She was wearing her white uniform dress, pulled tight with a sash about her lean waist.

"On your way to work?" Wintone asked her.

"Been an' goin' back," Sarah said. "Had to go out to buy some plant food for the office ferns." She held up a small, folded white bag. "Doc'd have a fit if those things died."

They stood for a moment, moving awkwardly out of the way as several breakfasted fishermen exited from Turper's.

"Walk me back, why don't you?" Sarah asked.

Wintone walked beside her, adjusting his stride to her pace. They were on the shaded side of the street, their own dark shadows merged with the stark black outlines of the buildings. Wintone felt good walking beside Sarah.

To the right, down Hawk Street, green hills rose behind shaded frame houses. It was still early enough for there to be wisps of vapor clinging to the sides of the wooded hills, like gentle night spirits longing to stay in the shelter of the tall, huddled cedars.

"You still think about the accident, don't you?" Sarah said.

Wintone slowed his pace and Sarah slowed beside him, as if they'd begun walking up a grade.

"Be unnatural not to," Wintone said.

"I don't like to see you blame yourself."

"I don't."

"You seem to."

Their steps fell out of rhythm on the cracked pavement.

"I wasn't even hurt. . . ." Wintone said.

Sarah was silent for a while, staring down at the ground as she walked. "You can have certain kinds of internal injuries," she said. "Any doctor can tell you that . . . any nurse."

"Maybe they take awhile to heal. Maybe they never heal."

"They'll heal if you let 'em. You can't go on an' on blamin' yourself, not forever."

"Maybe it'll be my fault forever."

"Even if that's so, it seems eventually you oughta swallow it."

"It sticks."

They turned the corner toward Doc Amis's office, into the face of the slowly climbing sun. The sudden warmth seemed to saturate the front of their clothes like heated liquid.

"Not likely to be any cooler today," Wintone said. With the sun's warmth had come the internal heat of his awakening anger. Sarah had no right to talk to him about Etty's death. It was a private, painful matter. Maybe too private and painful, but that was his business, not Sarah's.

Beside him, she seemed to sense his resentment. "Maybe it'll rain," she said with baseless optimism, "cool things . . ."

"I doubt it."

"Learned anything else about the Larsen boy?"

Wintone shook his head. "There aren't any solid facts to grab onto."

"The family took the body back to Little Rock last evening. I felt really sorry for 'em."

"They deserve your pity." Wintone was telling her that he didn't deserve it, and she seemed to understand even if she didn't agree.

"You think we'll ever know what happened to him?" Sarah asked.

"Don't know that it makes a difference; he's dead. It was one of those things that happen from time to time in this country an' nobody ever explains it. Remember the Iron Ridge man was found dead up in the fork of the tree some years back?"

"Lightnin', they said."

"Coulda been. Lightnin' does strange things. Probably we'll never know about that or the Larsen boy."

"Folks around here are more scared than they been in awhile," Sarah said.

"Time'll have to pass for 'em to calm down, but they will."

"Time heals most everything."

"Some things," Wintone replied, feeling another surge of annoyance. Why did she have to press where she had no business at all?

They had reached the doctor's low brick office and were standing in the shade of the huge cottonwood that seemed to be bracing for another day of unreasonable heat.

"Why don't you come on in," Sarah asked. "Have a cup of coffee?"

"Thanks," Wintone said, "but there's things need doin'."

He smiled at her as he turned to walk away. She saw that he didn't mean the smile.

Back at his office, Wintone settled himself behind his desk and engaged in some routine paper shuffling. The office was quiet and cool, illuminated by soft, slanting sunlight through the blinds. It was easy for Wintone to become engrossed in his work, so that the time passed unnoticeably.

Near noon the sheriff tossed his pencil onto the desk in a gesture of accomplishment and finality. He rose and poured himself a cup of strong coffee from the dented electric percolator on one of the file cabinets. Then he stood sipping the hot coffee, staring idly out through the blinds at the empty street.

Now that the morning's work was over he felt somewhat depressed, and he again felt resentment over Sarah intruding herself into the sanctity of his grief. There were private places in a man's life where what he did with himself was his own concern. That's how it was, even if Sarah was trying to help him. He didn't want her pity, or anyone's. If it came to a choice, he'd prefer her dislike.

When Wintone turned back to his desk, he saw protruding from beneath a stack of file folders Doc Amis's report on the Larsen boy. Wintone picked up the report and crossed the office to file it with his own scanty report on the Larsen incident.

As the long file drawer slid smoothly shut on its metal rollers, Wintone wondered for an uneasy moment just how the boy had died. Probably he'd never know. The incident would be one of those bizarre cases that would eventually fade into half-believed, half-remembered Ozark folklore. Like some of the stories his grandfather used to tell. And his great-grandfather . . .

During the next week, calm settled again over Colver, a slipping back into the time-worn way things were. Wintone had only minor problems to deal with, and at Mully's the talk turned to how good business was, to fishing.

Whatever roamed the darkness beyond Colver, where the night was blacker and things nocturnal stirred to the cacophony of frog and cricket, was fading from the town's consciousness as Wintone had hoped.

SEVEN

Two miles out of Colver a portable gas stove cast a faint, shadowy glow about a makeshift campsite. A blackened aluminum coffee pot sat off-center on the stove's burner, and while the three men about the stove waited for the coffee to brew, they passed a quart bottle of Jim Beam bourbon among themselves. Beyond the campsite, through a slope of thick woods, an occasional glimmer of moonlight on black water, like an eye winking through the trees, was the only sign of their proximity to the lake.

Brian Colby sat hunched on one of the folding cots. His two companions, Les Matson and Dave Larker, were crouched animal-like on their haunches.

Colby was a tall, lean-faced man with long brown hair brush-combed sideways in a careful arc across his forehead. He sat checking the small .22 revolver that he'd used that day to plink at squirrels from the boat.

"It's darker than I thought it could get," Larker said, gazing into the blackness of the surrounding woods and passing the bottle to Matson.

Matson was short and thick-bodied, with a round face that expressed his uneasiness while reflecting the stove's glow like a small, dissatisfied moon. He took a pull on the bottle and wiped his lips with the wrist of his plaid shirt. Colby had talked him into coming on this trip, and while Matson had enjoyed the day's fishing and the recent dinner of fried bluegill that represented the day's catch, the complete isolation and darkness of the woods seemed to dredge up all his boyhood fears.

"There are things moving out there," he said. "Hear them?"

"Of course there are things moving," Colby said reasonably. He was the head of accounting where the three worked at Vector Enterprises, and in a subtle carry-over from work, he considered himself the leader of the group. "There are day animals and night animals."

Larker grinned his broken-toothed grin. "You must have learned that from one of those television nature programs." He belched lightly, with almost a polite delicacy.

Matson took another pull on the bottle, passed it up to Colby.

"Think of it this way," Colby said. "The darkness wouldn't bother you if you were out here with some chesty blond."

Matson shrugged. "I look around, I don't see one."

"What I mean," Colby said, "is then you'd be thankful for the darkness." He raised the bottle to his lips and tilted back his head. "It's relative, like everything else."

"I'm a lights-on man, myself," Larker said. "What did you do with the remains of our supper, Les?"

Matson motioned with his thumb. "Threw it back there in the woods. Those night animals Colby talks about are probably feasting on it right now."

"You think you're kidding," Colby said. "That's probably what you hear."

Matson frowned. "I hear things from the other direction."

"What about that kid who was killed here last week?" Larker asked. "Supposed to have been killed by some kind of lake creature."

"Lay off the bullshit," Colby said. "The kid was probably mauled by an animal. These stump jumpers around here are superstitious."

"Pass me the bottle," Matson said. "I don't think I want any coffee."

"It's not ready anyway." Larker inserted a toothpick in his mouth, focused liquor-dulled gray eyes on Colby. "They say whatever killed the boy rose up out of the water."

Colby took another swig of bourbon and handed the bottle down to Matson. "They say!" he repeated disgustedly. "Half these yokels will say anything because they know the other half are dumb enough to believe them."

Matson raised his right hand for silence, like a traffic cop signaling *stop*, his moon face intent. "I hear something," he whispered. "I know I do!"

After awhile Colby said, "Coffee's ready."

"Don't turn the fire off!"

"Easy, Les. We'll light the lantern."

"There's something comforting about fire, though," Larker said. "Goes way back." He realized he'd drunk just enough not to be afraid and was enjoying his advantage. "Either way's okay with me."

"Fire then," Colby said. "And the only lake creature out there is the bass that snapped my line this afternoon."

Matson glanced up, catching the hitch of anxiety in Colby's voice. He licked his lips.

"Christ!" Larker said. "Three grown men—"

He stopped when he heard the loud snap of a branch behind him, from the direction of the lake. Every sound in the black woods ceased, even sounds the three men hadn't realized they were hearing.

"Squirrel, probably," Colby said, quickly raising his pistol. "Give me the flashlight; maybe I can plink him."

"Leave it alone if it's a squirrel," Matson said hoarsely. "You had enough luck shooting them illegally from the boat today."

"I'd have paid your part of the fine."

There was another sound now, the rhythmic thrashing sound of something moving through the woods, something approaching.

Matson's round face twisted with fear, and Colby stood up from the cot.

Larker suddenly pointed toward the darkness. Between themselves and the dull sheen of moonlight off the lake, something was moving toward them through the trees.

Matson started to say something, but with a sudden dance of black shadows from the stove's glow, the thing was upon them.

"Shoot it!" Matson cried. As he stood his foot caught on the stove, tipping the pot of scalding coffee onto Colby's ankles. "Shoot it, for Christ's sake!"

Colby yelled in pain. Larker bumped into him, backing away. The pistol cracked four times.

From the woods came a wheezing, enraged screech.

"Again!" Matson shouted. "Again!"

Colby emptied the pistol in the direction of the screech, at the darkest of shadows near the base of a tree.

In abrupt silence the three men stood still as the night, their breath hissing. Then Colby sat back down on the cot and clutched at his ankles.

"Jesus, my legs!" he moaned. "My feet! It went down my shoes!"

The other two men ignored him, their eyes unblinking and wide.

"Let's go," Larker said, still chewing on his toothpick. "Let's go see what it is."

"Maybe it's not dead," Matson said, following Larker toward the motionless shadowed form.

As if to accommodate them the clouds shifted from the face of the moon, and in the faint yellow light filtering down through dark leaves they saw that it wasn't dead. The one agonized eye that was visible rolled aimlessly, then lost expression and was still, as if fixed by moonlight.

"What was he doing walking around out here in the woods at night!" Larker snarled at fate.

"A man," Matson said in a soft, dumbfounded voice. "God, Colby's shot a man!"

"His name was Charles Jenkins," Wintone said, "from Joplin." He replaced the man's driver's license in his wallet and laid the wallet alongside the body. "Any of you know him?"

The campsite was illuminated by several gas lanterns now. A dozen or so men stood about with set, unrevealing faces.

"Of course not," Matson said. "None of us ever saw him before. We thought he was that lake creature you people talk about, that killed the boy last week." He glanced about and lowered his head, stuffing his hands into his pockets as if to hide them. He knew he sounded ridiculous now, in the light of the gas lanterns.

"He shouldn't have been walking in the woods at night," Colby said through his pain. He was still seated on the low cot, hunched over with his head resting on his knees.

"He shouldn't have been shot, either," a man near the body said.

"Jenkins was down at the lake giggin' frogs," Wintone told the three men. "He's got four of 'em in a plastic bag."

"How were we to know?" Larker asked. "He should have shouted, let us know who he was."

Old Bonifield stepped forward from the knot of men near the portable stove. "They been juggin', Sheriff," he said, pointing to the quart bourbon bottle.

"Less than half a bottle between us," Matson whined. "Nobody was drunk."

Bonifield looked at Wintone, worked his chewing tobacco.

". . . An accident, I swear it was!" Colby moaned between his knees. There was little conviction in his voice.

Wintone was suddenly sorry for Colby, stood for a moment watching him in the moth-shadowed yellow light. After telling the other two men to sit on the cot next to Colby, Wintone walked back to the patrol car and radioed the State Patrol.

When he returned, the three men were seated exactly as he'd left them. "State Patrol will be here soon," he said. "You can repeat your story to them."

There was movement, then voices nearby, and Doc Amis, wearing neatly creased slacks and a blue canvas jacket over an undershirt, stepped into the light. He was accompanied by Joe James.

"Dead over there," Wintone said, and watched as Doc Amis bent over Jenkins's body and searched futilely for vital signs.

After a while Doc Amis stood and looked questioningly at Wintone, his gaunt face younger but just as wise in the yellow lantern glow.

"This one's burned," Wintone said, motioning toward Colby.

Still without a word, Doc Amis went to Colby and knelt before him, slit his pants legs and skillfully worked off his shoes.

Colby's eyes were clenched shut and his lips were pale. Occasionally he let out a short, sibilant moan, as if to release some unbearable inner pressure. Doc Amis cradled Colby's bare feet one by one gently in both hands and examined them as if they were injured creatures with lives of their own.

Colby leaned back on his elbows on the sagging cot, opened his eyes to stare up at the night sky. He seemed to be searching for something that wasn't there.

"I'd better take you in to my office," Doc Amis said.

"Best let the State Patrol decide," Wintone interrupted. "He's the one shot the fella over there."

"How'd you get the burns?" Doc Amis asked Colby.

"Coffee . . . spilled on me when the pot tipped over."

The doctor had Larker and Matson stand. Then he skillfully swiveled Colby so that he was lying on the cot, covered his upper body with a light blanket. For the first time Wintone noticed that Colby was shivering.

"They'll get you to a burn clinic," Doc Amis told Colby. He quickly filled a hypodermic needle and injected something into Colby's arm. Then he walked over to Wintone.

"Second-degree burns from the knees down," he said. "Some of it went into his shoes. Why'd he shoot that man?"

"He thought he was the lake creature."

Doc Amis snorted with something like unbelieving contempt.

"He was scared," Wintone explained. "The three of 'em were."

"By the looks of the dead man, *he* didn't have time to be scared."

"Twenty-two-caliber bullets," Wintone said. "A couple of 'em hit right."

"Lake creature!" Doc Amis snorted again and shook his head sadly. In the unsteady yellow light his hair appeared almost blond.

Wintone looked through the trees to where gleaming

pools of moonlight lay like rich syrup on the water. He heard sirens, surprisingly loud in the clear night air, and he turned his head and within a few minutes saw a red flickering light winking through the woods. A car door slammed. Another. A man's voice sounded, made incoherent by distance.

The State Patrol had arrived.

Wintone felt some relief at having the sad affair taken off his hands.

EIGHT

Two days after the Jenkins death Wintone was forced to realize that a box of trouble had been opened.

"McKenna," the white-haired, heavyset man who'd entered the sheriff's office said by way of introduction. "Saint Louis *Globe Dispatch.*" He shut the door behind him without looking at it. "It always this hot around here?"

"It'll get hotter," Wintone said. "We been needin' rain for a while."

"You could have used some rain to prevent that fire up north. Hell of a thing."

"It was that."

"I wonder, Sheriff, if you'd give me a few words on the lake creature."

Wintone leaned back, gazed across his desk top at the man. McKenna was about fifty, with a face like a sackful of rocks and gray seen-it-all eyes. "Lake creature?"

"Sure. Whatever it was that Charles Jenkins was mistaken for and shot. I understand this what's-it killed a boy here on the sixteenth. I talked to the doctor, some of the people around town, and they said you might be able to help me further."

"I don't believe in any 'lake creature,' Mr. McKenna."

"Neither do I, necessarily. But something killed the boy."

Wintone couldn't dispute that. He sat regarding McKenna, listening to the distant, sputtering drone of a motorcycle apparently being ridden in circles. Against the otherwise complete silence the sound was somehow relaxing.

"Doctor Amis let me read the autopsy findings," McKenna said. "It took time; the boy was badly mutilated by something powerful. And they say some of the larger bones looked as if they'd been worked back and forth in a vise."

"Doc Amis could tell you more about that than anyone."

"He says he doesn't know what caused the damage."

"Neither do I."

"What condition was the boy in when you saw him?" McKenna asked.

Wintone knew the reporter was looking for an emotional response. "Dead."

"A lot of blood?"

"Quite a bit. I thought you already had the clinical details."

"Too clinical. Were people around here frightened?"

"Some. Mr. McKenna, I can't give you much information on what happened; nobody can because nobody knows, and probably nobody ever will."

"But according to Mr. Bonifield, the man who found the body, the town was gripped by curiosity and fear."

"Somebody oughta grip Mr. Bonifield."

"Oh? I found him cooperative." McKenna smiled a yellow-stained smile to let Wintone know he'd dealt before with the

Bonifields of this world. Maybe he and they had something in common. "What steps have you taken to try to solve the case, Sheriff?"

"The routine gatherin' of information, talkin' to whoever might know somethin'. There's not much to point the way."

McKenna was getting chilled now in the air-conditioned office, his perspiration-damp shirt turning clammy. He pushed up on his tie knot, which had been very loose, and straightened his diagonally striped tie. "What about the cast you made of the footprint?" he asked.

"You're pretty thorough, Mr. McKenna."

"My job. Yours, too. You were thorough enough to make a cast and I was thorough enough to ask about it."

"It won't tell you much, I'm afraid." Wintone walked to the file cabinets and pulled open a bottom drawer. From behind a short row of file folders, he withdrew the rough-textured plaster cast. When he'd laid it on the desk, McKenna stepped close and frowned down at it in such a way as to make his face even uglier.

"It was something big, all right," he said. "Ever seen a print like it?"

"No," Wintone said. "The ground was soft, though, and sometimes it'll play tricks."

"Not tricks like this. I've done enough hunting in my life to know. Mind if I send a photographer around later today to get a few shots of this?"

"I guess not."

The distant motorcycle engine continued to drone lazily as McKenna reached out a surprisingly smooth, unblemished hand and ran his fingers over the contours of the plaster cast. He glanced up suddenly at Wintone and withdrew his hand, as if he'd been interrupted with a woman.

"I'm interested in any ideas you have on the matter, Sheriff."

"My idea is that it's done and best forgotten."

McKenna smiled his lumpy smile and shook his head. "It won't be, though. Maybe it would have been, but Charles Jenkins was a well-known man in Saint Joseph, and his death brought attention to the circumstances of the Larsen boy's. You're dealing with news, Sheriff. Not big news, but news nonetheless. You might as well be aware of it. It might be good for the town."

"That's what some are sayin'."

McKenna contorted a chunky arm to tuck in his damp shirt at the small of his back. Wintone noted the play of muscle beneath the thin material. The reporter wasn't as soft as he first appeared.

"How long you been a county sheriff?" McKenna asked.

"Nine years."

"All here?"

"Every one of 'em."

"I suppose you're not used to all this activity."

"Things'll die down."

"Everything does eventually," McKenna agreed. "You hear of anything else, you call me. I'd appreciate it. I'm at the Rest Away Motel on the main highway."

"Sure," Wintone said, watching the heavyset man move toward the door as if reluctant to return to the outside heat. "You got any ideas yourself, Mr. McKenna?"

"Ideas?" McKenna clucked with humor and shook his head. "It's not my job to formulate ideas, Sheriff. It's facts that concern me. Our work is more similar than you might think."

After McKenna had closed the door behind him, Wintone stood at the blinds and watched the stocky form of the reporter make its way across the street, then walk south on the other side. Even some three feet away from the window, the sheriff thought he could feel heat radiating inward from the plate glass. The office seemed cool but confining, stonily silent. Wintone realized he could no longer hear the drone of the distant motorcycle engine.

Much as he disliked the idea, Wintone decided to talk to Mayor Boemer. A glance at his watch told him that it was barely past two. The mayor would still be in his office, where he'd taken to spending more of his time during the past several weeks. Mayor Boemer was only just beginning to discover his own political importance.

It was a short walk from the sheriff's office to the mayor's office, which was situated above an abandoned and boarded-up shop that had once sold harness ware. Wintone was sweating when he got there, but the office itself was cool; after a few minutes, uncomfortably cool.

Mayor Boemer pretended to finish whatever he was pretending to be doing. It was all an excuse to make Wintone wait and to establish an aura of importance about the mayor. The office was small, not clean but meticulously, symmetrically arranged. A chintz-shaded lamp sat precisely in the center of a round pie-crust table, and a row of books was aligned by height on a shelf behind Boemer's desk. The mayor himself was a plump man in middle years, with a ruddy complexion, a ski-jump nose and once-black curly hair gone white and grown long about the collar to lend him a revolutionary-era countenance that he no doubt cultivated. He had narrow blue eyes, calm and vaguely mean. The mayor's eyes were calm, Wintone often told himself, because there was little going on behind them.

"What're you up to, Billy?" Mayor Boemer asked with his wide and practiced smile.

"Man came to see me," Wintone said. "Reporter named McKenna."

Boemer leaned back, still smiling, and made a pink tent with his stubby fingers. "Yeah, I talked to him myself."

Wintone pulled a wood chair away from the wall, flipped it

to face away from Mayor Boemer's desk, then straddled it to look at the mayor, his folded arms resting on the chair back. "I'm thinkin' maybe we oughta play down these two deaths," he said to Boemer. "The truth's all that's necessary, without all this speculation an' whistlin' up a hollow log."

"I can't agree," Boemer said, "but there ain't any sense even discussin' it. The story's already in all the big-city papers." He reached beneath his desk and lifted several folded newspapers from the floor. "Look here, Billy." One by one he spread the papers out before Wintone, identifying them by city. "Little Rock, Saint Louis, Kansas City, Atlanta . . . even Chicago. The story makes good copy an' lots of it."

Wintone laid the newspapers in his lap and leafed through them. Mayor Boemer had all the pertinent columns outlined in red ink. The big-city papers were making the most of the situation. Many of the news items were full of inaccuracies and lurid descriptions. THE BIRTH OF ANOTHER GRISLY OZARK LEGEND, one paper headlined its account of the two deaths.

"I wish it'd die down," Wintone said, laying the stack of newspapers back on Boemer's desk.

"It will, Billy, but in the meantime we gotta make the most of it. Sure it's tragic, but because we got the cloud's no reason to turn away the silver linin'. This ain't scarin' people off. Tourists an' fishermen are flockin' down here thicker than before. There's truth, an' then there's public relations. We're damn fools if we don't make the most of what we got dumped in our laps."

Wintone looked past the mayor out the window at the leaves of a tall maple, green and motionless in the still heat. He didn't like the idea of capitalizing on the death of an eleven-year-old boy.

Boemer's ruddy, expansive features were flushed with the excitement of his glimpse of a prosperous future. "I think we need to construct some kind of display," he said thoughtfully. "Maybe a memorial to the Larsen boy on the spot where he died. That oughta be a future point of interest we could feature in our color brochures." Mayor Boemer looked at Wintone with sudden sobriety. "This really is beautiful country, you know."

Wintone and Boemer were in accord on that. The lush, wooded hills were beautiful in a primal yet gentle way, green and alluring and mysterious; it was a beauty that cloaked the grim struggle of nature with an aura of leafy and graceful tranquility.

And the country was a part of Wintone that he didn't want to see changed, neither its sunny places nor its shadows. That was where he and Boemer differed.

"Tourists an' fishermen can be the lifeblood of the Colver area," Mayor Boemer said earnestly. "That's the aim we oughta be workin' toward. Al Kingsford's thinkin' of openin' up a souvenir and antique emporium downstairs in the old harness shop. I think it's a good idea."

"Could be," Wintone said, in one motion standing and gently flipping his chair to where it had been against the wall. He could see any further conversation with Mayor Boemer would be useless.

Boemer stood also behind his desk. He seemed relieved and somewhat surprised that Wintone was leaving, as if he'd expected some sort of trouble or argument from the sheriff. Boemer was a retired government clerk living on a fair pension, and the office of mayor neither paid nor meant much. The influx of tourists and fishermen, with their money, might change all that and Wintone was the only one who seemed to look on the situation with disapproval. Mayor Boemer could always remove Wintone from office, but he knew that without a good reason that would be awkward. Knowing Wintone, it might even be dangerous.

"I'd be interested in any ideas you have, Billy," Mayor Boemer said as Wintone was leaving.

Wintone nodded and closed the door behind him.

On the walk back to the office, Wintone was stopped near the Colver General Merchandise store by Luke Higgins. Higgins's usually unshaven, round face was smooth and scrubbed, and he was loading some cartons and a shiny new wheelbarrow into the trunk of his old Dodge. The car had been recently washed, and flaking rust around the headlights and doors stood out like cancerous sores on the white paint.

"I admit it, I was wrong," Higgins said, tying down the trunk lid with a knotted length of brown twine. "I thought people'd be scared away by those creature stories, but instead they're flockin' like chicks at feedin' time. I shoulda know'd folks like bein' scared. Hell, they pay to go on roller coasters."

"They like to be scared only so much, though," Wintone said.

Higgins took off his rimless glasses and polished them on his shirttail. "Appears we scared 'em just right," he said with a grin.

"Work to do?" Wintone asked, motioning toward the wheelbarrow handles protruding from the lashed-down trunk.

"Gotta do some landscapin'," Higgins said. "Gotta pretty up the place so I can compete. Location ain't everything."

"Guess not."

"An' I can afford some things now, load of gravel for the parkin' lot, repairs on some of the cabins. It feels good to be able to afford things, Sheriff."

"You got a full house at your place?"

Higgins grinned. "Every cabin's full an' I'm booked through the month. I hear even a few of the places that wasn't too bad damaged on the north shore are makin' back some of their losses." He walked around and opened the car door. "Best make it while they can, I say."

Wintone watched the old Dodge drive away, rocking on its worn-out springs.

Instead of returning to the office, Wintone walked down to Mully's and had a cool beer. He didn't stay long. Old Bonifield was entertaining two men wearing business suits, probably reporters, in one of the corner booths. When Wintone noticed Bonifield lean across the table and lower his voice and the two men glance over at him, he quickly finished his beer and left. He'd had his press conference for the day.

But half an hour later the two men were in his office, asking the same questions McKenna had asked, getting the same answers. Only these two were more persistent than McKenna, and Wintone had to stand and almost bodily force them from the office when they began baiting him and trying to provoke him into a newsworthy statement.

More press people, more tourists and more fishermen descended on Colver during the next week. Though the drought held, and the heat, the streets were no longer empty at midday. Cars passed Wintone's office window several times an hour, and men and women in tourist apparel strolled Colver's "rustic" streets with cameras and asked questions about whatever had killed Dale Larsen.

Wintone was kept busy, though most of the inevitable trouble fell within the jurisdiction of the State Patrol. Still, he listened to his share of complaints, calmed his share of disturbances, worried over his share of paperwork.

The lake surface had never been dotted with so many fishing boats, nor the deep green woods invaded by so many campers and hikers. Yet the soft, yielding, but uncompromising countryside seemed to make room for them, to absorb them. When Wintone had reason to drive up to Hap Ferrill's place to investigate some vandalism, he'd looked down on the rolling green carpet of woods beneath where the gravel road dropped away. But for snaking roads and the rooftops of scattered buildings, he saw nothing to give a sign of human presence. Only when the patrol car had crested the hill and Wintone descended into the scene he'd admired, did he see the sometimes unpleasant marks of man.

Near Hap Ferrill's, off the side of the road, Wintone saw the dark, rusty ruins of a huge hay baler, its voracious razor-edged blades dulled by corrosion. He recalled the old story about the farmer who'd fallen into a hay baler during harvesting, of how a funeral was impractical if not impossible, so the family and church congregation held a service and burned the bale of hay. A tall tale, maybe, but no taller than some Wintone had been hearing lately.

Mayor Boemer continued to show Wintone the big-city papers, and the story based on the two deaths continued to run strong. Experts seemed to volunteer their weighty opinions from every corner, and the speculations grew more sensational. After reviewing the facts of the Larsen boy's death, the press had taken to calling the burgeoning figure of Ozark legendary fear Bonegrinder. Of all the epithets, that was the one that stuck.

It made for good melodrama, and it pleased Mayor Boemer.

But Wintone kept seeing McKenna's lumpy, practical face, marked by years of hard-nosed digging for hard facts, and he kept hearing McKenna's irrefutable words: "Something killed the boy."

What was beginning to bother Wintone was, with the continuing influx of people throughout the area, the chances that someone else might be killed kept increasing.

And every day brought more people, from farther away.

NINE

The Petersons lived in Saint Louis, over three hundred miles northeast of Colver. They made their home in a low, gray, brick-and-frame ranch house with an attached two-car garage, centered on a quarter-acre of weedless, mowed green punctuated by small trees and square-trimmed shrubbery. They had a tomboyish ten-year-old daughter named Melanie who wore glasses, and they had a Ford station wagon and a dented Toyota. Their house was in a sprawling subdivision that for a hundred dollars a year provided them membership in a club that made accessible a swimming pool, tennis courts, yearly club parties and a small playground which Melanie had outgrown.

Bill Peterson was a draftsman for an aircraft design company. He was thirty-nine, a year older than his wife Cheryl, who stayed home to tend house and child. In the past few years Cheryl had acquired a worn-at-the-edges sort of prettiness that made her more attractive, in Bill's mind, than when he had married her.

The Petersons spent much of their free time entertaining neighbors on their patio, working in the yard, going to movies, PTA meetings and grocery shopping together. They were unhappy.

Lately the low, gray ranch house had been the scene of desperate discussion.

"You're the one messing things up," Bill said with uncomprehending bitterness as he sat at the Spanish-styled dinette set after dinner. He'd had an unusually troublesome day at work and didn't know if he really wanted the argument he was instigating. But he couldn't restrain himself; it was as if some pressure were being exerted on a nerve that brought about an automatic response.

"No one's messed up anything," Cheryl said patiently, with a resignation that showed plainly she thought she'd never be able to make her husband understand. "Things just got messed up by themselves. Nobody's to blame."

"Maybe that's your way of justifying what you're considering." Peterson studied his wife with careful objectivity as he spoke. She was still an attractive woman, with a lean, supple figure, small in the bust but with perfect long legs. Impending middle age had given her sallow-cheeked face, framed by still grayless black hair, a vaguely noble beauty. Peterson was hurt, physically hurt, by the possiblity of losing her. The only person he wanted even more to hold onto was Melanie. And if he lost Cheryl . . .

Cheryl poured herself another cup of coffee, drank it standing up as she began to gather the dishes. She drank more and more coffee lately, black coffee, as if to maintain a state of nervous superalertness.

Peterson gave up waiting for her to answer him, sat and watched her as he smoked a cigarette. Contrasting her quick, sure movements refined by time and thousands of tables cleared after thousands of meals, her face was tranquil and unreadable, the face of a woman who masked things.

It all made Peterson wonder what had gone wrong. He was still not a bad-looking guy, with most of his hair and the same clean-cut, squarish features; gone a little to overweight, but who the hell hadn't? He was faithful, reliable, and had given Cheryl more than she had a right to expect. And until recently their sex life had been more than satisfactory—at least he'd thought so. He still was, in most respects, the same man Cheryl had chosen to marry.

It occurred to him that maybe that was the problem; she had changed and he hadn't. He snubbed out his half-smoked cigarette in the saucer she'd left him for an ashtray, listening to the dying ember hiss briefly in the muddy brown residue of coffee.

Damn it, she *hadn't* changed! Not gradually, anyway. Not until the last few months, when words between them became forced, and her features had taken on the cast of a stranger's.

Stranger though she'd become, Cheryl was candid with Peterson. She had told him about Carl Bauer, even though he hadn't remotely suspected anything was going on behind his back. Carl Bauer, his ex-drinking partner, ex-fishing buddy, ex-friend. They had more than ever in common now. It disturbed Peterson that he couldn't work up the proper fury toward Bauer. He knew that was because he believed Cheryl when she'd told him she had initiated the affair. Carl was a few years younger than Peterson, divorced, ruggedly handsome and an unabashed fun-lover. No surprise that a bored woman would choose him, and that he wouldn't resist that choice. If it weren't with me, it would be with someone else, was the old rationale. There was truth to it.

Carl was basically a shallow person, unstable, not Cheryl's type. Eventually the infatuation would pass, Peterson knew, and Cheryl would be his again, maybe more firmly than ever. The pain was in the waiting.

"Where's Melanie?" Cheryl asked when the dishes were

cleared and the chugging, watery labor of the dishwasher sounded faintly from the kitchen.

"She's swimming," Peterson answered.

He touched his lighter flame to another cigarette, got up from the table and moved toward the family room, aware that Cheryl was following him. He no longer felt like arguing, wanted only to settle into his recliner chair and read the newspaper, read about other people's problems. The newspaper was becoming an increasingly frequent escape for him.

"I've decided to go away with Carl," Cheryl said.

How simply and matter-of-factly she spoke the words that drove the breath from Peterson. There was no quaver of uncertainty in her voice, making the blow all the more lethal. Peterson didn't answer her right away, couldn't. He settled into the vinyl recliner chair quickly because he had to.

"It's what I want," Cheryl said.

"It's what you think you want." His own voice was high, choked, but he drew a deep breath, swallowed and knew he'd regained control at least of his vocal cords. "It's not unusual for a woman, an attractive woman like you who's been married a long time, to think the grass might be greener somewhere else. It's an infatuation, a temporary infatuation that will pass within months . . ."

She shook her head slowly; there was anguish in her mascaraed eyes. "It's not only an infatuation, Bill, it's a need."

"For Christ's sake, a need for *what*? For Carl Bauer?"

"Not only for Carl Bauer. There's a part of me that's never come to life, that I need to give a chance. At least that's how I feel . . ."

Peterson appeared puzzled, frustrated, the look of a man in a maze. "What could you possibly want within reason that you don't have or can't get?"

Cheryl shook her head with a serene sadness that infuriated him. "It's nothing material. I feel I have a potential for life that I'll never realize the way things are now."

"Potential that needs to be realized? . . . What do you mean—artistic?"

"Maybe . . . I don't know."

"For Christ's sake, you take ceramics!"

Cheryl began to laugh then. The bitter laughter came bubbling up from dark unexpected depths within her, and she could no more stop it than she could stop water bubbling from a deep well. It was subterranean laughter, alien, and it scared her.

Peterson stared at his wife, his face reddening, a faint tremor in his hands that gripped the arms of the vinyl recliner. Then he saw the expression on Cheryl's face, the tears tracking down her cheeks, and he didn't know if she was laughing or crying. He didn't know what to think, didn't know what he should feel.

"Think of Melanie," he said.

The muted, broken sounds gradually stopped bursting from Cheryl, and she was calm again, wiping her cheeks with stiffened yet graceful long fingers. Her knuckles were gnarled, the tendons on the backs of her hands prominent. Her hands had aged before the rest of her. There was a soft sadness in her eyes, as if she realized what the hands foretold.

"Think of Melanie," he repeated

"I am . . . I have."

"You can't do this to her on some whim, some illogical, transitory crush that will soon pass."

"You could see her anytime you wanted, Bill, you know that."

"Don't you care what you'd be doing to her?"

"She was the thing I cared about most, thought about most, before I made my decision."

He hadn't wanted to hear that, another cold penetration to the heart. "Have you talked to her yet?" he asked.

"No, I thought we should do that together. I thought that's how you'd want it."

Peterson pressed his head against the soft back of the chair, closed his eyes. His face was pale. "I don't want it at all. Eventually you'll realize the mistake you've made, but by then the damage will have been done."

"Something like this happens," Cheryl said, "you do the best you can. That's what I'm trying to do." Her voice was controlled now; she'd slipped back behind her mask.

"When do you plan to leave?" Peterson asked.

"I don't know. Soon."

"Don't go," Peterson said, "please."

"We've been through that."

The flesh around his closed eyes danced as if he were in pain. "But I'm begging you now. Really begging you."

She was surprised that he'd beg at this point, surprised also that she was embarrassed for him. "Don't, Bill . . . " She recognized her growing pity for him as a weakness, fought it.

"A week," he implored. "Give it a week before you do anything else, say anything to Melanie."

"It won't make any difference, Bill; we both know it won't."

"It might. A week . . . You owe us that."

She did owe him something; at least she thought she did. "All right," she agreed, "but I don't see what difference seven days will make."

"The earth was created in seven days."

Cheryl smiled at him, sighed. "It was at that. But not by you and me."

Melanie came into the house the back way, through the garage, slamming the door hard enough for china in the kitchen to rattle.

"A towel, Mom!"

But Cheryl was already on her way to get it.

"Nice swim?" Peterson called to his daughter.

"The water was cold, and I scraped my chin on the bottom." Her speech came haltingly from the cool kitchen, through chattering teeth and rigid jaw muscles. He heard her thank her mother as Cheryl tossed her a bright red beach towel.

Within a few minutes he watched Melanie's bikini-clad, gangly young form cross the family room to get to her bedroom and some warm, dry clothes.

What was the threat to his married life? Where could he direct his rage? It wouldn't be hard for him to hate Carl Bauer, but he knew Bauer was only a symptom of the problem. Cheryl had as much as told him that. There was nothing here for a man to come to grips with, to understand and fight.

Peterson watched his wife across the room. She was absently picking up a clutter of magazines Melanie had read that afternoon, fitting them one by one into the wooden rack by the sliding glass doors to the patio.

It was impossible to tell what she was thinking.

Peterson picked up his evening newspaper, opened it full-width before him to block out his view of the room, of Cheryl.

He sought solace in the sorrows of others, in the precise black-and-white world of newsprint.

TEN

"You seen the latest batch of outa town papers the mayor's got?" old Bonifield asked Wintone from down the bar at Mully's.

"Not yet," Wintone said, swiveling slightly on his bar stool to turn away from Bonifield as a signal that he didn't want to talk. What he really felt like doing was telling Bonifield what he, Wintone, wished the mayor would do with his out-of-town papers, but there was little point to that.

"They're all interested in Colver now," Bonifield went on. "Not long ago they never know'd we was alive, an' now they're askin' how to spell our names. An' I told plenty of 'em how to spell yours, Sheriff."

Wintone didn't thank him.

"I was careful not to mention nothin' else, though. They was all interested in your personal life an' all, how reliable an' such you was. 'No comment' is what I told 'em."

"Ain't you got someplace else to go?" Mully asked Bonifield.

The old man curled a tobacco-darkened lip at him. "Sure, you can afford to drive off customers now."

Mully chuckled hopelessly and shook his head. "I don't see nobody in here but the three of us. This ain't the kind of place tourists take to, not when they find out there's no hard liquor."

"Then you oughta serve hard liquor," old Bonifield said. "Cater to 'em. This here's your golden opportunity."

"Opportunity for what?"

"Didn't I say golden?"

"Nothin' I need gold for." Mully began to wipe down the bar, though it was smooth and dry. "I promised Cora there wouldn't be no hard liquor served in here, after her brother got killed in that fight. Don't see any reason to break that promise now."

"That's all been fifteen years ago!" Bonifield said in exasperation. "An' Cora's been gone five."

"Don't make no difference," Mully said calmly, but his face seemed darker, the fine-etched lines deeper.

"Don't you ever hear ice crackin' under you?" Wintone asked Bonifield.

Bonifield was finished with his beer. Turned on his stool, he leaned back against the bar and bit off a chew of tobacco from a brownish mass in a wad of crumpled wax paper he'd drawn from his pocket.

"Maybe I did speak hasty," he said. "A man's wife is never really dead to him, in a manner of speakin', that is."

Mully continued to wipe the bar, Wintone to stare into the disappearing foam of his beer.

"All I meant," old Bonifield said to Mully, "was that maybe you oughta pretty up the place some. Maybe even get some entertainment. Then maybe folks from outa the area would take to comin' here."

"I got business enough to meet my needs."

"Reserve," Bonifield said. "I'm talkin' about somethin' you know you got an' don't have to spend. A cushion's what I mean. Fer that rainy day folks talk about."

"Ain't never gonna be another rainy day around here," Mully said.

Wintone cupped his hands around the coolness of his half-filled beer mug. "Not today, anyway. Not accordin' to the weather bureau."

"In the middle of a financial boom," Bonifield said with contempt, "an' you two're talkin' about the weather."

"Lotta farmers around here ain't havin' a financial boom," Wintone said. "Weather's about all they talk about." He wished Bonifield would leave, go to one of those prettier places he'd mentioned.

"Things other'n crops is growin' just fine here," Bonifield said. "Like, every business in an' around Colver. Or ain't you noticed?"

"It'll calm down," Wintone said.

"Maybe not. Maybe it ain't even peaked out yet."

"You want another beer before you go?" Mully asked Bonifield, by way of invitation to leave.

"Nope." Bonifield held firm on his stool.

Wintone didn't want to go back to his office, or outside into the heat. Earlier the heat had made him nauseous; there seemed to be a dusty, noxious film over everything in Colver that needed a steady, cool rain to wash it away. So Wintone had come here, to Mully's, where it was cool without the sealed confinement of his small, air-conditioned office.

But in Mully's he'd found Bonifield. Maybe the old man had sought refuge here like Wintone. Even Bonifield could get too much of the press, who were congregated mostly at the modern, air-conditioned lounges of the larger motels toward the main highway. Prettier places.

When his beer was almost finished, Wintone decided he

would drive along the lake road, then up beyond Lynn Cove where woven green vines and saplings grew on dark, moist ground that sloped gradually out into the lake. There the water lay motionless and thick with algae, thick with the pungent, wild scent of dying and growing. And near the lake were steep, wooded bluffs, with bent cedar clinging to their faces, pale juttings of rock like bones forced through flesh. Two days ago a woman had been lost in that area for half a day, and just when everyone was becoming really alarmed she had stumbled onto a road by accident and followed it until she was picked up by a State Patrol car. She was found less than a hundred yards from where she had left her husband in their parked car.

It would be good to keep the patrol car and himself highly visible to the outsiders in the area, Wintone thought, to show some representation of local law.

As Wintone was walking toward the door, Frank Turper entered. His dark eyes, recessed in glistening pads of flesh, glinted dully as if he'd been drinking before his arrival at Mully's. "You seen them outa town papers come in the mayor's mail today?" he asked Wintone.

"Not yet."

"You oughta see some of the drawin's of how Bonegrinder might look. Half-lizard, half-man—that sorta thing. Give you pause to think."

"Pausin' to think ain't a bad idea," Wintone said, and walked past Turper and out the door.

Wintone got into the patrol car, quickly started the engine and turned the air conditioner on high. Absently he pulled the automatic shift lever back and drove slowly toward the beckoning green hills. Heat waves rose in shimmering vapors from the patrol car's flat metal hood.

As he drove, Wintone noticed the surprisingly large number of people on the street despite the heat. Few of them were local. Most carried cameras, fishing equipment or picnic paraphernalia.

It will all fade away soon, Wintone assured himself. When the north shore gets rebuilt and the Bonegrinder thing becomes just another half-interesting bit of Ozark folklore. Eventually things will be as they were.

But a worm of doubt, like a restless silver thread, had begun to burrow into Wintone's mind.

Once changed, did things ever return to the way they were?

ELEVEN

Bill Peterson entered the kitchen through the connecting door to the garage.

He'd been bent over the long wooden bench he'd constructed along one wall, where he often went in the evenings to work out the tensions that had built in him through the day. Thinking too much about the threatened changes that might rend his life suffused him with a curious terror.

Cheryl, domestic-looking in a plain blue housedress, was just finishing wiping the kitchen table with a damp dishcloth. There was something in her domesticity that keenly aroused Peterson at times, though he didn't know why. He liked to approach her from behind at moments like this and kiss the nape of her slender neck, to slide a hand around smoothly and quickly cup one of her breasts. This time he stood still just inside the door and waited until she'd finished wiping the table before speaking.

"It's been four days," he said.

She nodded, held the dishcloth beneath cold running water and wrung it with deft, practiced hands, as if dispassionately wringing the neck of some live thing. Peterson thought she was treating him exactly like the dishcloth. The vulnerability of his love depressed him.

"Has anything changed?" he asked.

"Nothing," she said, draping the dishcloth over the divider between the stainless steel basins of the double sink. She began to place clean glasses two by two in a cabinet.

Peterson watched her for a long time, his breath deep and even. "I have a suggestion," he said.

She interrupted her glass placing and turned to him, as if he'd at last said something positive.

"A fishing trip," Peterson said.

His wife stared at him for a moment, then shook her head in refusal, but not firmly. The kitchen was so quiet that he could hear the inner mechanism of the electric clock on the stove.

"Why not?" he asked. "We haven't been since last year. And it would give you—give us both—a chance to get out into nature and think things over clearly, get a fresh perspective."

"It will look the same to me, Bill."

Damn her, what was she trying to do to him? "What about Melanie? You know how she loves to go fishing with us. If nothing else, it will be one last time for her to remember the three of us together."

Cheryl began putting away the last of the glasses, her lips pursed in consideration. Maybe she did owe him that, owe it to Melanie. It wasn't that she felt guilty. No, there was no guilt involved, only obligation. But she was sure she wouldn't change her mind about leaving with Carl.

She found herself thinking of Carl, strong and impetuous in a lazy, appealing way, longing for new places, new adventures, burning with an eagerness that she wanted to consume her. Carl was to Bill what blowtorch was to candle. But Bill couldn't help it. She had to remember that. And he loved Melanie, even if he only thought he loved Melanie's mother.

Peterson sensed her indecision and pounced on it. "I'll call and make reservations at Lost Pines," he said hurriedly. "All right?" He smiled at her pleadingly. How could she resist that smile?

"All right," she said, and a weight seemed to slip from her, as if to reassure her that she'd made the right decision.

Peterson walked over to his wife and kissed her forehead. Her body tensed to stillness and she stood with her hands at her sides, as if tolerating his kiss rather than endure an argument.

"Things will work out," he said, backing a step and looking intently down into her immobile face. "You'll see; I promise."

"Don't promise that," she said quietly.

Peterson disappeared into the hall where the telephone sat on a small, ornate table they had bought at a rummage sale and he'd refinished.

A few minutes later he walked back into the kitchen, opened the refrigerator and poured himself half a glass of milk. He downed the milk quickly, as if appeasing a great need.

"Lost Pines burned down," he said. "Remember the big forest fire we heard about on the news?"

"I thought it was somewhere else," Cheryl said.

Peterson wiped his lips with the backs of his knuckles and shook his head. "No, it was at Big Water Lake, the whole north shore. I got us reservations farther south, near a place called Colver."

TWELVE

Colver was quiet near midnight. Wintone was sitting at his desk, dressed only in pants and a T-shirt, sipping a glass of ice water and wishing he could feel like sleeping. Only minutes after he'd lain on the cot in the back room, the familiar uneasiness had made him rise, pad barefoot about the office as if seeking something.

Finally he'd decided to forget about going back to bed for the time being, and he tried to do some paperwork at his desk.

That didn't work either. He was too tired to concentrate, yet his eyes refused to close on their dry weariness. So in the shadowed soft light from the desk lamp, he'd paced about the office for a while, tending to small things that needed no tending; then he sat back down at his desk to wish for exhaustion.

Automatically, he had tuned his citizens' band radio to emergency channel nine, and he was seated at his desk with his face buried in his large hands when the call came through.

"Breaker ten seventeen!" the voice said loudly, a surprise from the barely hissing speaker. "This is Molasses. I'm on the lake road an' there's somethin' movin' out in the water!"

An operator named Rag Man asked excitedly what the something looked like. Wintone stretched an arm and adjusted the squelch control for better reception.

"It's dark an' big, movin' some hundred feet out along the bank. I'm followin', but the road curves an' sometimes I lose sight through the trees. Ten twenty-three."

Wintone was sitting at his desk attentively now, leaning forward. He knew who Molasses was: Cal Horton, a sawmill employee who drove an old tan pickup truck equipped with a CB radio. Horton was a reliable sort, a big, redheaded man, practical as he had to be with a wife and five kids.

The speaker crackled. Wintone wished he had a transmitter so he could talk to Horton, but he had only the receiver and no CB unit in the patrol car. All he could do was sit, listen and agonize.

"Breaker," a new voice, a tenor, said. "Give us your ten twenty, Molasses."

"I'm on the lake road a half-mile or so south of Lynn Cove, headed away from the cove."

"Ten four, Molasses. This is Lancelot—we'll try to join you."

"I'm tryin' to stay with this thing, truckin' along on this lovin' bumpy road . . ."

"Breaker, this is Rag Man—"

"Ten six, Rag Man, I'm busy right now tryin' to keep this buckin' truck on the road while I take a hill. I lost sight of the blasted thing . . . if it weren't for the moonlight . . . there it is!"

Wintone stood up from the desk chair, inserted the tips of

his fingers into his hip pockets and began to pace. He was glad Molasses was the type to use good sense. Horton would consider his wife and kids before rushing into anything. At least Wintone hoped he would.

"I wish to Hades I could make out what it looked like," Horton said. "It's too far out, but it's movin' in a line right along the bank. Lost it again! Damn wheel went off the road—back on now."

"Breaker, Lancelot here. What's your exact location now, Molasses? Ten twenty-three."

"I ain't sure now. I been fightin' to keep this heap on the road an' not lose sight—"

"Breaker, this is Rag Man. I'm on the lake road, Molasses—"

"Ten six, Rag Man. Stand by, stand by, I'm busy . . ."

Through the speaker Wintone could hear the roar and rattle of Horton's ancient, laboring pickup truck.

"The road bends away from the lake here," Horton said. "I'm gonna lose sight of the thing behind a rise . . . can't see it now. I'm parkin' where the road starts to curve away an' I'm gonna cut through the trees on foot to get closer. Ten twenty-three."

"Ten four, Molasses. You be careful, hear?"

Don't leave your truck, Wintone almost said aloud. He stood over the radio, rested a hand on it. The speaker was silent but for a soft, staticky hissing, like escaping air. Wintone looked at his watch: twelve twenty-seven.

What had Horton seen? The man was far from a fool, and he'd been raised near Colver, spent his life here. He'd know anything in Big Water Lake. And he must have seen something. Again Wintone heard the words of the veteran reporter McKenna: "Something killed the boy."

Twelve thirty-one.

"Molasses, this is Lancelot. You out there? Ten ten."

"Lancelot, this is Rag Man. He said he was leavin'—"

"I know, I know," Lancelot broke in with his high, tremulous voice, forgetting radio procedure.

The silent speaker hissed.

Twelve thirty-five.

Wintone walked in a circle, away from the glowing dial of the receiver, then back. He thought about getting in the patrol car, racing to the lake road. But it wouldn't be easy to locate Horton's truck immediately, and by the time Wintone could reach the spot he'd be too late one way or the other. Here, at least, he knew what was happening as well as anyone except Horton.

The silence from the speaker seemed to spread, seemed to displace the air in the office. Wintone stepped off another perfect circle on the hardwood floor.

"Breaker, this is Molasses," a breathless voice said at twelve thirty-eight. "I lost sight of it, but I got a closer look. Only thing I could tell about it was that it was big—bigger'n I thought at first—an' it was movin' fast through the water along the bank. I couldn't keep up through the trees an' heavy brush, an' it just disappeared off into the darkness."

Wintone walked back to his desk, sat down.

He was exhausted now, but further than ever from sleep. He reached for the phone, dialed the number of Cal Horton's home, and told a sleepy and wondering Beth Horton that he wanted to talk to her husband when he returned home. Wintone assured her that Cal wasn't in any kind of trouble, and she agreed fuzzily to give him Wintone's message when he returned.

Then the sheriff sat back and listened to the CB enthusiasts chatter harmlessly about Cal Horton's adventure.

Bonegrinder had been seen. Substance was added to speculation.

Not that Cal Horton had seen much, but the press was trying mightily to make much of it.

Horton could only tell the press what he'd told Wintone: that whatever he'd spotted in the lake was very large, but that he hadn't seen it next to anything to really compare size, and of course he'd only seen the part above water. It was black, or at least a very dark color, and it seemed to move smoothly through the water, from what Horton could make out from his bucking pickup truck or while running along the bank to keep it in sight. And he wasn't sure, but he thought it might have made a sound, a low kind of groan like he'd never heard before. Or the sound might have been something else. Or he might have imagined that.

The press continued to hound the man, until at last he took to his house and refused to talk to anyone but friends.

Talk of Bonegrinder was everywhere now, and it was plain that the talk and publicity was the reason most of the tourists and fishermen had come to the Colver area. Mayor Boemer was capitalizing on the situation as best he could, drumming up "items of interest" to give to reporters every two or three days. Everyone said that business couldn't be better, that they'd had to hire part-timers to help out. Every sort of outdoor and fishing equipment was sold, and what wasn't sold was rented. Every motel for miles was filled. Campers and vans were a common sight on the roads.

And still it hadn't rained. Wintone feared another fire, one worse than the fire that had ravaged the dry woods of the northern lake area. The woods were all the drier now, tinder awaiting the spark. And there were plenty of fools streaming into the area capable of striking that spark, plenty of people now to find themselves trapped by a fire whose fierceness they could never imagine.

Chain lightning played in the sky late that Friday, and Saturday morning a light rain fell for about fifteen minutes from scattered, flat-bottomed white clouds that disappeared by midday. Better than no rain, but not enough to be of much help to the parched ground and forest. And the gentle rain left in its wake an almost unbearable humidity coupled with the heat, so that it was almost a pleasure to see the darkened earth lighten again beneath the sun.

The night after the rain, the third death occurred.

Wintone was watching the ten o'clock news on the portable TV in his office when the telephone rang. At first he was glad for the distraction; the news was showing film clips of a three-car accident near Pineyville. Then he heard the voice on the phone and caught the subdued terror in its level tone.

"This is Seth Davis, Sheriff. They asked me to call you. We need you to come to the lake directly."

Seth Davis was a freight hauler Wintone knew slightly. This wasn't his usual voice.

"Whereabouts at the lake, Seth?"

"Near Lynn Cove . . . near where the other one happened."

Wintone felt a coldness move into him. "What's happened, Seth?"

"Bonegrinder again . . . Claude Borne this time."

Claude Borne owned a farm just outside Colver and had a wife and two married daughters. "Is Borne dead?"

"He's gotta be, Sheriff. You best see it . . . I don't wanna tell you. . . ."

"I'll be there."

Wintone hung up the phone, put on his boots, strapped on his revolver. He was outside then, and as he slammed the patrol-car door he realized he'd forgotten to turn off the TV. He didn't go back. Red lights and siren on, he was at the lake within five minutes.

Yellow light up ahead, to the right of the narrow road,

toward the water. Wintone killed the siren and parked on the tilted, grassy road shoulder. He flicked off the flashing red lights atop the patrol car but left its parking lights on, then he got out of the car and jogged down toward the bank where he could see a small crowd gathered in the wavering yellow light of a gas lantern.

Borne was lying on his back on the mud bank, staring up at but not seeing the knot of people gathered around him by the pale light of the Coleman lantern. Night moths circled to add darting shadows to the scene. Wintone shoved through the curiously listless onlookers, and his stomach twisted on itself when he looked down at Borne. The old farmer was still alive, but not for long.

The upper part of Borne's body was laid open in baconlike strips; one arm was bent beneath his back. Even the waist-high, thick rubber wading boots he had on were ripped and shredded as if by razor blades.

Wintone swallowed a metallic taste and bent over him. "What happened, Claude?"

The farmer's sturdy, normally ruddy face was pale and vague in the yellow, flickering light. There was a film over his eyes that would never leave. ". . . Like they said, Sheriff, it come at me from the lake."

"What, Claude? What came after you?"

Horror shaded the vague eyes. "Nothin' like I ever seen, Sheriff . . . big, dark an' shinylike, with somethin' like lumps all over it . . . It stood right up outa the water an' come after me while I was castin' out toward the deep part of the lake. If'n all these people hadn't heard me screamin' an' come runnin' to scare it off I'd be dead . . ." Borne tried to get up, seemed puzzled that he couldn't.

"I'm a doctor," a short, completely bald man who had just arrived said. He wore a flowered shirt that seemed luminous as he moved forward with quick, smooth steps. There was in his attitude something that said he represented both life and death, an authority that transcended Wintone's. "You'd better leave him alone for now, Sheriff."

Wintone nodded and stepped back. "Anybody else see anything?" he asked the circle of silent onlookers.

"Out there," one of the men said, pointing toward the lake. "I saw in the moonlight that the water was sort of swirling."

The man was the only one besides Claude Borne who had actually witnessed anything. Wintone got his name and address. He was a vacationer from Kansas City.

As Wintone slipped his note pad into his shirt pocket, he noticed something dark bobbing in the water just off the bank. He walked a few steps toward the bank, squinted against the night and saw that the bobbing object was a glass jug.

Wintone stepped nearer the bobbing jug, had to put one foot in the cool water, but was able to stretch out and hook one finger about the jug's rounded glass side and propel it toward the bank so he could retrieve it.

It was an ordinary gallon cider jug, capped and about a fourth full. Borne's, most likely. He was reputed to brew and drink the best hard cider in the area. It would be interesting to find out how much cider was in the jug when Borne had left to go fishing.

Then Wintone felt something sticky on his hand, looked more closely at the jug and saw that it was cracked and leaking. Claude Borne might not have touched the jug before the attack, might have been stone sober.

"Doc Amis is on his way, too," somebody said to Wintone. The sheriff put down the jug and wiped his hands on his pants legs.

By the time Doc Amis arrived, Claude Borne was dead.

THIRTEEN

The change in Colver was almost immediate. There was a slowing of pace, a feeling now of diminishment rather than of growth, subtle but undeniable. Wintone could see the change in almost everyone he talked to the day after Borne's death. The silver lining had been ripped away, leaving only the cloud.

First Cal Horton's story, then so soon afterward the horror of Claude Borne's death. Where before they had been merely titillated, people were now frightened deep down. They *believed* in Bonegrinder.

By the middle of the day after Borne's death, half of Luke Higgins's cabins were vacant and business throughout town had dropped off sharply. By the end of the next day, most of the paying customers remaining in the area were the staunchest of fishermen, the hard-core thrill seekers and members of the press or scientific community who were professionally interested in whatever was responsible for the attacks. Colver's optimism had been completely edged out by a gloomy tension that seemed to charge the heated air.

Wintone knew now that Bonegrinder wouldn't go away, that at the very least the area would have to cope with the fear, maybe for years, before a normal confidence returned. And by then the north shore would doubtless be redeveloped.

Wintone wasn't the only one who understood this. He stayed away from Mully's and the running discussion that no doubt raged there.

But through the shimmering heat of the afternoon they came to him, half a dozen of them. As Wintone stood at the office window and watched them angle across the baked street, he was reminded of a lynch mob. Mayor Boemer led them, three paces out in front, jaw thrust out, white hair swept back, leaning forward as if striding into a wind. His followers wore equally aggressive and determined expressions, minds made up and set like concrete. Something, a vague contempt, thinned the line of Wintone's lips as he sat at his desk and waited for them.

Their demeanor was changed as they filed into Wintone's office. Now they wore the expressions of reasonable men set to reason, but ready to anger if anyone was unreasonable enough to disagree with them.

Despite the heat Mayor Boemer wore a tie, but it was knotted loosely and perspiration glistened where his shirt was unbuttoned at the neck. Until a month ago Wintone had never seen Mayor Boemer wear a tie.

"We're here about this Bonegrinder thing, Billy," the mayor said firmly. "We've been talkin' over the situation an' we don't like it."

"That should have been easy enough to agree on," Wintone said, leaning back in his wood swivel chair and crossing his arms.

"Question is what to do about it," Luke Higgins said from where he stood near the wall.

Wintone nodded. "Anybody got the answer?"

"It ain't like we was in a position to do anything about it if we did have an answer," old Bonifield said. His blue eyes, bright and eager, had an unfocused sheen that suggested too many beers. "Ain't our job."

"You got to figure somethin', Sheriff," Frank Turper pleaded across Wintone's desk. "Issue some kinda statement that'll simmer things down. The big-city papers are playin' it up, artists' drawin's of what Bonegrinder might look like an' everything."

"They been doin' that an' you haven't complained before."

"Now it's outa hand! This nonsense is ruinin' the sweetest thing Colver ever had! An' that's what it is—nonsense!"

"Ain't heard you been fishin' in the lake lately," Wintone said.

Mayor Boemer shook his head hopelessly, clearing his throat so that the gesture wouldn't go unnoticed. "The sheriff don't understand the political implications," he said. "An' we can't blame him for that—it ain't his job. I never figured it was when I appointed him."

Wintone knew the mayor was reminding him that his position was an appointed job. But that appointment was for five years and had three years to run. It would be a lot more difficult for Boemer to remove Wintone than it had been to appoint him. Wintone knew he didn't have to point that out to the mayor. He shifted in his chair and stared at Mayor Boemer, and that was all the reminding needed. Boemer seemed to back up a step without moving.

"The sheriff don't accept blame easy," Bonifield said, "which shouldn't come as no surprise."

As Wintone swiveled in his chair toward Bonifield, Mayor Boemer spoke up quickly.

"What the sheriff don't fully grasp is that this is Colver's one chance to become an important town, a town they know about in the state capital an' beyond. We owe it to each other to make sure that chance don't slip away."

"I don't see as how I have much to say about it," Wintone said.

"Tell the reporters Claude Borne was drunk when he died," Luke Higgins urged. "There *was* a near-empty cider jug there—seen it myself. Man'll do or see anything drunk."

Wintone sat looking at his dead wife's framed picture on his desk corner. A fly buzzing nearby was for a moment the loudest sound in the room.

"Weren't none of those big tracks or anything," Turper said. "Nothin' really unusual."

"The attack took place in shallow water," Wintone said, as if talking to Etty's photograph.

"Still an' all, Claude was drinkin'."

"Sheriff oughta understand that," Bonifield said.

"The man is no fool," Mayor Boemer said. "I didn't appoint him 'cause he was a fool." The mayor smiled. "No doubt he has ideas of his own, some possible course of action we haven't considered."

Again the buzzing fly took up the silence. Etty continued to smile from her desk-corner portrait.

Bonifield stood closest to the desk, shifting his chewing tobacco from cheek to cheek as if trying to make up his mind which side of his mouth to leave it in. He leaned forward from the waist up. "What-all you got planned, Sheriff?"

Wintone got up and left the four of them.

The blinds rattled inside as he shut the office door and felt the heat close in on him. As he was getting into the patrol car, he heard the office door open again behind him, then the mayor's voice: "You think things over, Billy."

Wintone pretended he hadn't heard as he started the patrol car, gunned the engine to drown out anything else the mayor might say and headed out of town. He switched the air conditioner onto high and braced himself to wait out the heat until the car's interior would begin to cool.

Wintone drove out to the lake road, past Lynn Cove, and where there was a clearing in the trees between road and lake he parked the patrol car and sat looking out beyond the reeds at the flat surface of water. Usually from this point Wintone would have seen several boats out on the lake, but today the stretch of bluish green water was unbroken. A large dragonfly with a blue-green body the same hue as the lake hovered above the hood of the parked patrol car, as if attracted by the rising heat of the engine. A motion of tall grass caught Wintone's attention off to the driver's side of the car, where the thick woods grew down to within a few feet of the road. A snake, probably. There was a wildness to this end of the huge lake that must have surprised many of the more docile campers who were used to the northern resort areas.

Then, at the edge of the windshield, Wintone did see something on the lake's sunshot surface, perhaps half a mile out, moving against the hazy line of the opposite bank. He got his binoculars from their leather case and trained them on the object. A boat, two men in it. One of the men was wearing a green-striped T-shirt with denim shorts and was smoking a pipe. Wintone didn't know the man's name but recognized him as one of the people from some organization or other that was interested in Bonegrinder. Neither of the men was speaking. They were too busy worrying over some piece of equipment in the stern of the boat. Something trailed on a cable behind the boat, probably some kind of data-gathering instrument. Wintone expected to see more of that sort of thing in the near future.

He scanned the purplish line of trees on the opposite bank, then slipped the binoculars back into their case and started the car engine. He realized where he was going, where he'd unconsciously intended to go when he walked from his office.

Within ten minutes Wintone turned the patrol car onto the rutted gravel drive to the Borne farmhouse.

Helen Borne must have seen him drive up and park in the shade of the lone cottonwood. She was waiting at the screen door of the neat, white frame house when Wintone got out of the car. He felt heat roll against his legs from under the car, and he heard the engine ticking loudly and metallically behind him as he walked toward the house.

"I am sorry, Helen," he said as she opened the door. The door spring made a sound between a crack and a whine. A forlorn sound.

Helen Borne nodded to Wintone. She was a once-pretty, gray-haired woman in her fifties who'd married off her youngest the summer before. Her eyes were red-rimmed now, too, the way Wintone remembered them from the wedding.

"This house is a lonely place now, Sheriff."

"I expect." Wintone stood awkwardly, feeling oversized in the tiny, quiet living room with its dainty furniture and shelves lined with knickknacks. He asked the new widow a few meaningless questions before he got to why he really came.

"A cider jug was found near Claude's body, Helen. Do you know . . . how much he'd been drinkin' before he went fishin'?"

She looked at Wintone, puzzled for a moment, then she gave a sad smile. "It weren't hard cider, Sheriff. Sweet cider was all Claude drank the past year. Doctor's orders. All Claude made or drank was sweet cider that he'd had to have drunk a gallon of to get even feelin' good. That I know for fact."

"Then he couldn't have been . . ."

"Claude left here that night sober as a judge, like he's been for a year."

"Then don't tell anybody otherwise," Wintone said.

"Ain't about to, Sheriff, 'cause there ain't no otherwise."

Wintone thanked Helen Borne and left.

Some of her sadness seemed to cling to him, and he was glad for once to be back out into the heat.

FOURTEEN

Though the narrow road to Colver climbed, dipped and twisted, it seemed to Craig Holt that his Jeep was always headed into the sun. The heat seemed to intensify as it passed through the windshield, causing his eyes to ache behind tinted glasses and his perspiring hands to slip occasionally on the wheel.

While he was aware of his discomfort, it didn't greatly concern him. Some discomfort was to be expected in his job. He often told himself that what was obtained easily usually wasn't worthwhile.

Holt was a tall man, twenty pounds underweight but broad-shouldered, wearing faded corduroy slacks and a white shirt open at the collar. He was in his early forties, and he had one of those regular-featured, handsome faces if bony and a bit bushy-browed. His dark but graying eyebrows matched the color of his hair, which was slightly wavy and beginning to thin drastically at the crown.

He geared down the bouncing Jeep for a sharp turn, tasting for a moment the grit of rising dust. He'd heard this part of the country was experiencing a drought, and the evidence of torrid heat, cracked earth and dry woods confirmed it. A large snake, what was called a blue racer in this part of the country, lay limply coiled and dead in the road ahead. According to local superstition, a snake crossing the road signified rain. Not in this case. Even the snake appeared dehydrated, as void of all moisture as its surroundings. Holt felt nothing as the Jeep's wheels passed over it.

Shifting down and slowing the Jeep abruptly, Holt glanced over to check the crinkled map on the leather seat beside him. The Jeep's fuel gauge was under the quarter mark, and it appeared that Holt had some distance to drive before the winding, hilly road intersected a main highway. He had an emergency gas can strapped to the back of the Jeep, but he didn't want to have to go to the trouble of using it.

There was little sign of habitation along the dusty road, an occasional glimpse of a shingled roof through the trees, now and then a private, partly overgrown road, unmarked and leading off into the woods.

Holt was babying the accelerator pedal, running in a higher gear than he would have normally, to conserve gas, when he saw a crudely lettered sign on the right shoulder of the road: GAS—EATS AHEAD. His foot went from accelerator to brake and he stopped the Jeep next to the sign, leaned so he could see it more clearly out the right side of the windshield.

The hand-painted sign was wood, fashioned from a single cut of cedar, still rounded on the back and covered with bark. It was nailed to a cracked and rotted cedar fence post.

Holt got his camera from the back of the Jeep where he had his luggage and photographed the sign before driving on.

A mile down the road was a scattering of buildings, and

just beyond them a low frame structure with a long wooden porch. There was a faded metal Pepsi-Cola sign nailed to one of the porch posts, and another sign proclaiming the place to be Weller's Restaurant and Service Station. Holt saw no indication of a gas pump.

He was about to park in front of the restaurant when he saw a dull red gas pump down the road about a hundred yards, beneath a Self-Service sign that had obviously been lettered by the same unsteady hand that created the cedar roadside sign. Holt twisted the steering wheel to get the Jeep back onto the road and coasted the distance to the solitary gas pump.

There was no one in sight. Holt got out of the Jeep, raised the hood and checked the oil. It was a quart low. But there seemed to be no oil around, only the ancient red pump. He inserted the nozzle of the gas hose into the Jeep's filler pipe and watched while the pump's meter ran noisily up to ten dollars. The smell of the gasoline seemed especially strong in the hot, humid air.

After replacing the nozzle Holt drove the Jeep back to park in front of Weller's Restaurant. He got out of the Jeep, but before entering Weller's he drew a flat-bowled pipe from his shirt pocket. He packed the pipe bowl with tobacco from a leather pouch, then clamped the stem between his teeth and went through the pipe smoker's puffing ritual of getting the tobacco burning freely.

The inside of Weller's fulfilled the depressing promise of the outside. There were no booths, only a small counter and two tables surrounded by too many chairs. Behind the counter was a grotesquely fat woman wearing a stained yellow waitress's uniform with the name *Billie* stitched over one straining breast. She looked to be in her fifties, and there was no trace of hair around the blue scarf she had wrapped about her head.

"You're the third one in today," she said.

"Am I?" Holt smiled at her and sat at the counter. "Coffee, black."

From a glass pot on a burner she poured him a mug of steaming coffee and carried it over to the counter. Despite an old window fan that kept the air circulating, the inside of Weller's was hot, and Holt immediately regretted ordering the coffee. He sipped at it and regarded the woman, who lowered her bulk onto a stool near the cold grill on the other side of the counter.

"Been at this job long?" he asked.

She nodded, dabbing at her perspiring face with a wrinkled handkerchief. "Some twenty years."

"You've lived in these parts some time, then."

The woman grinned, a grin strangely undersized on her broad face. "All my twenty-one years." She wadded the handkerchief and reached around with surprising ease to pat the back of her neck.

"What do you make of this Bonegrinder?"

"This what?" She raised thin eyebrows in puzzlement, touched her ear to indicate that she hadn't heard plainly.

"Bonegrinder. You know, in the papers . . ."

"Heard tell of it. Ain't read a paper in a while. Killin' folks, is it?"

Holt nodded, took a sip of his coffee, which was very good. "Any idea what it could be?"

"Not a whit."

"In the years you've been here, ever heard of anything like it?"

She squinted at him, perspiration glistening on the folds of her neck. "How come you're so interested?"

"I'm here to investigate, for the government. And I do research on folklore."

"Folk what?"

"Folklore. Stories, beliefs, legends passed on from generation to generation." He smiled at her again and raised his half-empty but still-steaming coffee mug to her. "Craig Holt."

"Billie Weller," she said. "Don't know nothin' about this Bonegrinder. My grampa used to tell me stories when I was young. Can't recollect any of 'em, though. That's my memory—good, but it's short."

Holt finished his coffee and stood. "By the way, I owe you for ten dollars' worth of gas as well as for the coffee."

Billie nodded, raised herself up from the stool and moved down the counter toward him.

"That pump's a long way from here," Holt told her. "Anybody ever take advantage and underpay you?"

Billie accepted his money, and as she gave him his change she crooked a thick finger, then pointed down at the other side of the counter. Holt leaned forward and saw a gas-pump meter mounted on a wood shelf. It read ten dollars.

"I trust most everybody," Billie said with a grin, "but not entirely."

Holt returned her grin and pocketed his change. "Incidentally," he said, "I needed oil, too, but I didn't see any near the pump. Could I buy a quart here?"

"Dale Hollis, 'round in back, will sell you some," Billie said. "Can't miss him. We don't keep oil by the pump 'cause it's had a way of disappearin', what with all the traffic through here of late."

Holt thanked her and went outside. He walked around to the back of the building to find three overall-clad men seated in rusted metal lawn chairs near a corrugated aluminum storage shed. As Holt approached, they stared at him with that blank hostility that often can be shattered with a friendly word.

"Dale Hollis here?" Holt asked.

"Nope," one of the men said, concentrating on the hard ground.

Holt squatted down on his haunches to show that he wasn't going to leave without gaining some information. "Where's he at?"

"Went out to shit an' the hogs et him."

The three men laughed as if they'd never heard that one before, and a stooped old man with a weather-worn face limped around the corner of the shed. He had large, gnarled hands and wrists as thick as Holt's ankles.

"Pay 'em no never mind," the old man said. "Brains like piss ants!"

The three men laughed harder, and one of them kicked at the ground.

"I need some oil," Holt told the old man, "Thirty weight."

"I'm Dale Hollis," the man said. "I'll fetch it for you."

He unlocked the metal storage shed, went inside and returned with a can of thirty-weight Mobil oil.

Holt paid him. "How far to Colver?" he asked.

"'Bout thirteen miles," one of the seated men said. "Blink an' you're past it, though."

"I won't blink," Holt said. He nodded to them and walked away, tossing the oil can from hand to hand.

"Want that can spouted?" the old man asked behind him.

"Thanks," Holt said, "I'll punch a hole in it with a screwdriver."

After pouring the oil into the Jeep's engine, Holt arced the slippery empty can onto an overflowing barrel of trash. As he stood wiping his hands on a grease-stained red rag, he wondered what Colver would be like—a town that wasn't on some of the area's maps.

Then he tossed the wadded rag onto the floor of the Jeep, climbed in behind the steering wheel and drove back out onto the dusty road.

FIFTEEN

From the Borne farm Wintone drove to the lake and walked to where Claude had died.

Wintone remembered setting down the cider jug at the water's edge, but now the jug was gone. Shaking off an uneasy sensation whenever he turned his back to the lapping water, Wintone searched the brush but found nothing.

He stood with his large fists on his hips, looking out at the opaque lake surface. Then he walked back to the patrol car and drove to Hooper's Dock, where he borrowed a fourteen-foot wooden Jon boat with a five-horsepower outboard motor.

Wintone used the sputtering motor to return across the lake surface to the scene of Borne's death, then he closed the throttle and in silence used the oars to maneuver the flat-bottomed boat as close as he could to the bank. He moved the boat parallel to the bank, doing more poling with the oars than actual rowing, scraping bottom occasionally on underwater rises or stumps. With the glistening, empty expanse of lake at his back, Wintone concentrated on the wavering waterline along the bank, peering into the shadows of overhanging brush or decaying tree stumps. The sun glancing off the lake behind him seemed to draw the sweat from him, molding his tan uniform shirt to his broad back.

The overgrown section of bank was a shadowed graveyard of floating debris. Wintone saw a faded brimmed cap adorned with barbed lures, a broken piece of styrofoam picnic cooler caught nearby in the weeds, a splintered oar. And ten minutes later he found Claude Borne's cracked cider jug, half-concealed by an overhanging growth of vines and gently bobbing upside down with the crack above the waterline.

Wintone got the boat in as close as he could and worked the jug over to him with an oar. What liquid was left inside was still thick and golden, mostly undiluted cider. The sheriff uncorked the jug and sniffed at its contents, then he tilted it with the crack away so he could wet a finger to touch to his tongue. Sweet cider, without a trace of alcohol.

Wintone laid the glass jug carefully in the bottom of the boat, then worked with the oars, half-poling, half-rowing for some time until he was in water deep enough to put the motor down and use it. He felt the prop bite into the lake as the bow rose high.

When he got back to Hooper's Dock, he wrapped the jug in an old blanket and propped it at the right angle in the trunk of the patrol car, wedged against the spare tire so it couldn't move. Then he drove back into Colver and went directly to Doc Amis's.

When Wintone entered the otherwise empty waiting room, Sarah was on the telephone arranging an appointment. Though her voice remained professionally serious, her lips shaped a smile around her words as she saw Wintone.

"I guess you're here about Claude Borne," she said when she'd hung up the phone. She looked tired, and the slightly wilted red chrysanthemum pinned to her white uniform did little to add color to her pretty but haggard features.

"Claude's what I'm here about," Wintone confirmed. He felt he should apologize to Sarah for his anger at their last meeting, yet he still resented her intrusion into his most private thoughts. He figured it best to let the matter lie.

"It was like the Larsen boy . . ." Sarah seemed to blanch even paler. The red flower on her dress was like a splash of blood. "The same kind of horrible injuries . . . the lower bone in his right arm was crushed almost flat. Doc Amis said he'd never seen that sort of injury except in industrial accidents."

"Is the doc in?"

Sarah nodded, pressed an intercom button. "Billy Wintone is here."

Doc Amis's voice said over the intercom that he'd be right out.

"Looks like business is slow," Wintone said, glancing at the waiting room's empty vinyl chairs.

"Is slow right now," Sarah said. "In a town this size where you know most everybody, you're glad to see it slow."

Wintone smiled at her. "Same way with my business."

"Maybe things'll slow down even more for you with all those tourists an' such leavin' the area. Leastways you'll only have this Bonegrinder thing to take up your time."

"Way it looks, it's gonna take up a lot of my time. I really figured it'd be over with the Larsen boy . . . one of those unexplainable things that just happens every so many years somewhere or other."

Sarah seemed to look into herself, shook her head in a series of quick little tremors as if cold. "Lord, what could it be?"

"Everybody has a theory," Wintone said, "but what they want is some real live late-night horror-show creature bent on killin'. Or that's what they wanted till a few days ago, when it looked like they got their wish."

"Claude Borne described it, didn't he?"

"As best he could."

Sarah appeared thoughtful. "Nothin's ever been spotted in the lake before, but then this end of the lake's been left pretty much alone. An' the country's wild, frightening."

Wintone was surprised to hear her say that; she'd been raised here.

Doc Amis came into the waiting room, gray, erect and noble. Wintone often thought that many a politician would give up his graft to look like the doctor.

Wintone nodded to him. "Claude Borne," he said.

Doc Amis slipped the fingertips of his right hand into a vest pocket. "He died of massive internal hemorrhaging. He was broken up inside, Billy."

"Outside, too," Wintone said.

"Either way it's loss of blood, loss of life."

"Was Claude one of your patients, Doc?"

Doc Amis nodded, keeping his gray eyes fixed on Wintone. "Most everyone in these parts is, one time or another."

"What was wrong with him?"

Doc Amis seemed to consider answering for a moment. "Cirrhosis of the liver, almost to the serious stage."

"How were you treating him?"

"High-protein, high-carbohydrate diet supplemented by vitamin-B complex and liver extract."

"What about alcohol?"

"I prohibited it."

"How long ago?"

The doctor walked to a file cabinet, pulled open a drawer and checked inside a yellow folder. "Almost a year," he said. "Borne had shown some improvement, too." He replaced the folder and shoved the long drawer shut, shaking his head. "Hell, I should have let him drink and enjoy himself."

"You shoulda told him not to go fishin'."

"Everything's a lot simpler lookin' back on it," Sarah said, fixing her gaze on Wintone, then looking down and rearranging some envelopes on her desk.

"Was there any alcohol content in Claude's blood?" Wintone asked the doctor.

"None whatsoever. He wasn't drunk, Billy."

"Bad as he was hurt, could he have been . . . rational when he told me what happened to him?"

Doc Amis chewed on his lower lip, shrugged. "I wasn't there, so I don't know. If his speech was normal, coherent—in other words, if he seemed rational—he might well have been rational. I don't say that you can assume he was."

"Have you told the newspapers any of this, Doc?"

"Nothing but cause of death. I try to avoid those reporters; they have a way of twisting your meaning. Some of them, mind you, not all."

Wintone thanked him, said good-bye to Sarah and left.

Claude Borne hadn't been drinking; there was plenty of proof on that count. Let Mayor Boemer and the rest of them yammer all they wanted. If they tried to give Wintone trouble or tell the newspapers that Borne was drunk the night of his death, Wintone would release the news of the autopsy report, the jug of sweet cider and Helen Borne's statement.

In a way Wintone wished that Borne had been drinking. But he hadn't been, and he *had* seemed rational just before his death, when he gave his account of what happened to him. That part of it bothered Wintone. About the only thing in the whole business that didn't bother him was the knowledge that people were packing up and leaving the Colver area. The fewer remaining, the fewer he had to worry about.

All the way back to his office, Wintone couldn't help thinking of how rational Claude Borne had seemed.

SIXTEEN

Cheryl Peterson stood looking out the wide window of a room at the Star-vue Motel, looking out past the trees at the edge of the graveled lot to the dual-lane highway. She wished now she hadn't agreed to her husband's idea of a last idyllic Ozark fishing trip.

"I don't care for this place," she said without turning.

"It was the best I could do," her husband explained. His voice was even, without any hint of irritation, as if he didn't want to upset her.

"They got different channels on the TV," Melanie said, her words punctuated by a series of loud clicks as she punished the channel selector.

"The forest fire was bigger than I thought," Peterson said. "All that's left, really, is the south part of the lake, and when I phoned for reservations every place was booked up. This is as close as we could get."

Cheryl stood still at the window, bright light penetrating her professionally fluffed hair. "It looks to me like everybody on the highway's going the other way."

Peterson told Melanie to pick a channel, then leave the TV alone. He sat on the edge of the bed. It was a soft bed, and the room was large, newly carpeted and clean. The lake was only a ten-minute drive away. He didn't know what Cheryl was bitching about. He'd done the best he could, and still she bitched.

"It's getting hot out there," Cheryl said to him. "You can tell just by looking that it's hot."

"While it's still early, let's get out of here and get some breakfast, then we can go explore Colver."

"On the map it doesn't look like there's much to explore."

"How about the motel restaurant for breakfast?" Peterson asked.

Cheryl turned away from the window. "It doesn't matter."

Peterson was getting tired of listening to her say that things didn't matter. Her attitude suggested that she was involved in some sort of minor ordeal that had to be endured.

"Will they have pancakes?" Melanie asked.

"Sure they will," Peterson said.

As they walked across the gravel lot toward the restaurant, he noticed several cars laden with luggage and camping equipment passing on the highway, going north. Only a single car passed headed south. Maybe there would be some vacancies now closer to the lake.

Alan Greer and his wife Kelly found a place to stay very close to the lake. Ten minutes after they'd checked in at Higgin's Motel, Alan pulled his wife down onto the double bed with him. Kelly's resistance softened, was displaced by eagerness. Still drained by the outside heat, they made love with an easy, slow rhythm, his fingers inserted like pitchfork prongs in the mass of her dark hair. Together they worked to make it last a long time.

Alan watched her afterward as she quietly rose to go into the shower, a lithe and beautiful girl with elegant legs and something of the feline to her movements, each step unconsciously precise. Despite serious, dark eyes there was a perpetual good humor about her full lips, as if she couldn't resist enjoying life.

The abrupt thunder of the shower running in its metal stall roared through the tiny cabin. Alan raised himself on one elbow, then effortlessly shifted his weight and stood. He stepped into his jockey shorts, then without knowing why smoothed the worn bedspread. Short, but well-muscled and flat-stomached, he was twenty-six, two years older than Kelly. There was a curved scar near the small of his back from a motorcycle accident three summers ago. After a few more rides to convince himself that he'd exorcised his fear, he no longer rode motorcycles.

Alan walked across the threadbare carpet to where the largest of the suitcases lay near the long dresser. He unlocked and opened the suitcase carefully and examined his photography equipment, working the zippers on the leather cases with practiced ease. He'd forgotten nothing, and everything was in order. With a brief smile he ran a hand through reddish brown, curly hair that grew in bright defiance straight out from his head.

This was an opportunity, to be in on the birth of an Ozark legend, while it was current news. If he could somehow get a photograph of Bonegrinder it would advance his photography career by a long step. He didn't really expect to be that lucky, but even the lush green and hilly wildness of the Ozark country would make a superb subject for a color spread in one of the leading specialty magazines. And the right sort of shot would be in demand by the major newspapers.

Alan picked up the leather case containing his thirty-five millimeter Honeywell Pentax, hefted the expensive camera and case in his hand, then replaced everything in the padded suitcase. After spinning the combination lock on the closed suitcase, it occurred to him that there could only be so much hot water and he joined Kelly in the thundering shower.

When they had toweled dry and were getting dressed, she said, "This is a homey cabin. Everything's a little worn but comfortable."

"Just like home, only everything works," Alan said, buttoning his shirt.

Kelly crossed the room barefoot and began brushing her long, damp hair before the dresser mirror. Alan was glad to see her smile at him. She hadn't wanted to come here, thought the Bonegrinder idea was a bad one and maybe a dangerous one. But he had explained to her the possibilities in the venture, and at least the likely sale of some Ozark shots to the travel magazines to help pay for the trip. And they weren't that far away, so reluctantly she had left Kansas City with him early this morning in their five-year-old Volkswagen, and here they were. Alan was determined that if he did nothing else he would relieve her of her apprehension. He thought he'd made a pretty good start.

Alan slipped his boots on and sat quietly until Kelly finished brushing her hair.

"What now?" she asked. "Dinner?"

"There still good light out there," Alan said, glancing at the window. "Let's walk around awhile and look things over."

Kelly tied a narrow red bandana about her brushed hair, giving her dark features a faintly Indian look knocked out of kilter by her slightly upturned nose. She waited at the door automatically while Alan got his camera.

He was pleased that she was impressed with the beauty of the country, though she said there was more of a wildness to it than farther north, where they had vacationed several years ago. That wildness of sun and deep shadow appealed to Alan's camera eye.

They walked to the lake road, then through a clearing to the lake itself, and there the primitive wildness that Kelly had felt, had almost scented, was stronger. The barely rippling water was brackish and carpeted with patches of darkly luminous green, and the tall reeds stretching out from shore seemed to form patterns of unnaturally deep shadows. The stench of decay was here, subtle movement on the fungus-laden surface of a fallen limb that seemed to be grasping at the water with crooked, leafless branches.

"It's shallow here," Alan said. "Most of the southern part of the lake is shallow near the shore. It's not exactly prime resort area."

Kelly picked up a damp broken branch, tossed it to the side. It landed almost silently in the brush near the bank. They heard a frog leap and hit the water with a solid, plunking splash.

"I wish we hadn't come," Kelly said.

"Don't decide too quickly," Alan told her, unable to restrain the irritation in his voice. "This is a particularly gloomy spot, but so what?"

"So let's leave it."

"A few shots first," Alan said, removing the Pentax from its case.

Kelly craned her neck to look up at the tall trees on either side of them. The trees seemed to arch over her, bending long limbs toward her rather than toward each other. She turned to look with relief at the open, graying sky above the wide lake.

But the lake itself seemed ominous, its flat surface dull and possessive. Glimmers of light on the lazily rising and falling expanses of water seemed to suggest movement below. There was nothing visible on the lake's surface, not a boat or floating debris of any sort, as if everything had somehow been claimed from below, drawn irretrievably down into darkness. Kelly was surprised to find herself wishing she could see a rusty beer can floating out there, anything. Almost anything.

"This is near where the fisherman, Claude Borne, was killed," Alan said, replacing his camera in its case.

"Cheering."

"I want some shots of where the other one was killed, the first one, the boy."

"Does it have to be this evening?"

"No, the light's failing."

They turned away and walked along the barely discernible path through the clearing, back toward the narrow road. Alan knew that Kelly felt the same uneasiness he was feeling with their backs to the lake, the same unreasonable urge to walk faster. He placed a hand on her shoulder, pulled her toward him so that they walked close together. She smiled up at him and he kissed her forehead, which was cool and damp. He realized that he was perspiring heavily himself. The heat hadn't fallen with the sun.

"We haven't seen anyone, Alan. Where are they?"

"Frightened away by the second death, the woman at the motel office said." He knew he wasn't reassuring Kelly, but she deserved the truth. "There's still a lot of superstition down here, but no reason to let it affect you."

"I'm suspicious of anyone who uses 'superstition' and 'reason' in the same sentence," Kelly said.

Alan laughed, welding her body against his side with a spasmodic tension of his arm. The camera swung rhythmically on its strap against his chest. He knew he shouldn't have brought Kelly with him to Borne's death site, but he'd gone there on impulse after leaving the motel cabin. Kelly, more reluctant about this trip than he'd realized, was behaving unlike herself; he would have to be careful.

Ahead of them, above where the thick line of trees broke for the road's passage, a hawk circled high in the darkening sky as if watching the road below. The hawk seemed to luxuriate in the rush of wind, disdaining the heat rising from the earth. Even from this distance Alan could see that since he'd been watching it, the soaring hawk hadn't once beat its outstretched wings. As Alan felt a bead of perspiration roll down his back, he envied the hawk. Alan had always longed for freedom of a sort.

"Let's go into Colver tonight," he said to Kelly, "see if there's a restaurant."

"I don't mind fixing us something in the cabin."

"You don't have to."

"I thought we were counting pennies."

"That doesn't mean we can't spend a few. Anyway, I doubt if we'll wander into the Ritz. We ought to be able to get a hamburger somewhere in town."

After returning to their cabin Alan stood outside and waited while Kelly sat on the bed and picked burrs from her socks and denim pants legs. There was far from enough light now, but as he looked at the cabins he made up his mind to get some shots of the motel before they left. No two cabins were alike in detail, though they were all of the same basic design and obviously had been constructed at the same time. But they were old, and through the years each cabin had acquired a character of its own. A different-colored shingle had been used on one of the peaked roofs here, metal awnings had been added there, this cabin had been covered with asbestos siding, that one simply painted. On the steep roofs of some of the cabins, metal weather vanes turned slowly in the warm air as if seeking direction rather than pointing it out.

And there was a kept-up but ramshackle air about all of the cabins. Native color, Alan thought, real native color.

Kelly came out of the cabin and shut the door firmly behind her, testing it to be sure the lock had caught. They got into their dusty white Volkswagen and headed for town.

Colver was less than they'd expected. The buildings were old, some of them dark red and dusty brick, but many of them frame and in need of paint, and some of the streets were unpaved. Alan dropped the Volkswagen into second and slowed to under twenty. He saw a small grocery store, a liquor store, a tavern . . . There were a few people on the streets. Two middle-aged men in bib overalls crossed in front of Alan with slow, hobbled gaits. He turned a corner, passed a general merchandise store, a sheriff's office. When he'd driven a bit farther he came to a wood-fronted building with wide windows that were decorated with artificial ferns and marked by a wide, half-worn-away border design that looked like a decal. Turper's Grill.

"Good enough for you?" Alan asked, pulling the Volkswagen to the side and braking.

"It looks cheap enough," Kelly said, "and clean as we're likely to find."

Alan turned off the clattering engine. They left the windows down in the car and went inside.

Alan and Kelly took a booth along the wall and were served by a henna-haired waitress with a stiff but sincere smile. The place seemed clean enough, with rough-plastered walls and a scent of fried food that whetted the appetite. They soon found that Turper's Grill served a better than passable hamburger and greasy but good French fries.

One other customer was in the restaurant, a lean old man seated at the counter sipping a cup of coffee. Occasionally he'd glance at them from the corner of his eye, and finally he turned on his stool to face them.

"You folks is new here?" His voice rose in question.

"Just arrived this afternoon," Alan said, sprinkling salt on his French fries.

"Ain't many comin' to these parts now, what with Bonegrinder an' all."

"So I've been told. I find it hard to imagine so many people so scared."

The old man had bright blue eyes that picked up the light. "Oh, you wouldn't find it hard to believe if you was here, if you seen some of the things I seen."

"Do you know a lot about it?" Kelly asked.

Stooped but nimble, the old man slipped from his stool and crossed the scuffed tile floor of the restaurant toward them. "I'm the man what found the body," he said, "the first one was killed. An' I seen the big print in the mud on the bank an' reported it." He pulled up a chair, sat at the end of the booth's table. "Bonifield's my name."

As the old man talked, Alan could tell that Kelly was becoming more apprehensive. But Alan was becoming more interested. He was sure now that the reward would be worth the risk.

When Alan and Kelly left the restaurant, they saw a canvas-topped Jeep parked behind the Volkswagen and they stepped aside to make way for a tall, slender man who smoked a pipe and gave them a friendly smile and nod as he passed.

SEVENTEEN

The tall man standing inside the door to Wintone's office said, "I've talked to Mr. Bonifield."

"That's some unusual," Wintone said. "Mostly folks have to just listen."

The man smiled. He was underweight but broad-shouldered, wearing faded tan slacks, scuffed boots made for hiking and a white shirt unbuttoned at the collar. There were marks on the bridge of his nose from the sunglasses now protruding from his shirt pocket. Wintone guessed him to be in his early forties.

"Mr. Bonifield said it would be all right to speak with you," he said, advancing on Wintone's desk with an easy, long stride. "Craig Holt's my name. I'm from Rothkin University, and I'm with the U.S. Government Phenomena Study Group."

Wintone shook Holt's extended hand, noting a dry, extrafirm grip. "I can guess what phenomenon you're here to study," he said.

Holt smiled his easy smile. "I'm not really a scientist or a reporter, Sheriff Wintone, more an investigator and journalist. Primarily, I'm interested in folklore and its origins and effects."

The swivel chair squealed as Wintone leaned back. "You look on Bonegrinder as folklore?"

"Future folklore. Unless, of course, some very common explanation is found for the killings and mutilations." He gazed over Wintone's head thoughtfully. "But maybe folklore even then. It might well depend on people's needs."

"It might at that," Wintone agreed.

"In any event, right now I regard Bonegrinder as a burgeoning fear-figure of Ozark legend, and I'm interested. In time I think Bonegrinder might surpass Old Wall-eyes as a fearful legend. I suppose you've heard of Old Wall-eyes."

"Most everyone in these parts has," Wintone said. "He ran on the ground like a horse only faster, with teacup-size whirlin' eyes an' a mouth that got bigger the more he ate. An' he could swallow a horse. My old grandfather used to tell me about him, about how once a fella had to keep tossin' meat out of a wagon to slow him down, then finally had to toss out one of his children in order to beat Old Wall-eyes home. There's a hundred different stories, but that don't necessarily mean I believe in Old Wall-eyes. Even as a boy I never believed in him."

"Most of those stories in one form or another appear in almost every culture in almost every corner of the world," Holt said. "Not that they're true, but they must have a common basis rooted deep in the human psyche."

"You're the expert," Wintone said, with only the barest trace of skepticism.

"Tell me about this mysterious track discovered near the Larsen boy's body."

Holt had identified himself with the government. Wintone

knew he had to cooperate with him and might as well do it as pleasantly and painlessly as possible. "I can show you a plaster cast I made," he said, rising from behind his desk. Holt seemed rather surprised at the sheriff's size when Wintone moved toward the filing cabinets. Wintone got out the mud-stained white cast and laid it on the desk corner.

Holt leaned over the plaster form and studied it intently, turning it to survey it from all angles. "Large . . ." he muttered, "very large. . . ." He straightened and looked at Wintone. "Any ideas?"

Wintone chuckled and sat back down behind his desk. "Sure. Either it ain't a real animal track, or it was made by somethin' nobody's ever seen."

Holt jerked his head slightly and appeared startled. "Not a real track? Surely you don't suspect . . ."

"I don't suspect nothin' yet," Wintone said. "I don't know, an' possibly I never will. You get used to acceptin' the fact there are things you don't know about if you live in these parts, Mr. Holt."

"And superstition creeps into the vacuum left by that lack of knowledge."

"That's true everywhere," Wintone said, "even at Rothkin University."

Holt grinned. He pulled a shallow-bowled pipe from a pocket of his corduroy pants and began packing it with tobacco from a leather pouch. Then he began tapping his pockets with his fingertips as if sending some sort of signal code. Wintone tossed him a book of matches from the desk top.

"Is it always so hot in this area?" Holt asked from behind the cloud of smoke he was creating as he sucked noisily on the pipe stem.

"Has been so far this summer," Wintone said. He was surprised to find that the burning tobacco gave off a rather pleasant, sweet scent. "Farmers are worryin' about their crops, what with the heat an' lack of rain."

"The drought was a contributing factor to the forest fire up north," Holt said, tossing the book of matches back onto the desk. "Horrible."

"There's some around here would disagree with you."

"Oh?" Holt removed the pipe from his mouth, pointing it stem first at Wintone as if indicating it was his turn to speak.

"Most of the tourist trade was burned out up there," Wintone said. "Business around here was boomin' for some time like it never has. The Bonegrinder thing seemed to help draw people to the area. Until Claude Borne was killed."

"He was the farmer?"

Wintone nodded.

"How do you explain the sudden departure of tourism, then?"

"People got more scared than curious."

Holt puffed on his pipe and nodded. "Succinct and accurate. Would it be possible, Sheriff, for me to see your files on the Bonegrinder deaths?"

Wintone tapped a boot toe lightly against a leg of his desk. Since Holt represented the federal government, the sheriff knew he probably had no choice but to open his files. Then, too, he didn't see what harm it could do. "You want to look things over now?" he asked.

"A cursory look," Holt said. "If you don't mind, I might have to check for some detail or other at a later date."

Wintone rose and went again to the file cabinets. He pulled out the Larsen and Borne files and set them on the table by the wall. Chair legs scraped on the hardwood floor as Holt pulled a chair over to the table, nodded his thanks and sat down to hunch over the files.

"What about the Jenkins death?" he asked.

Wintone got him that file, too.

"You never can tell where you're going to find pertinent bits of information," Holt said around his pipe stem.

Wintone sat at his desk and busied himself while Holt pored over the files for the next forty-five minutes. Holt barely moved in his chair except to lift his right hand to rearrange the files' contents. The sweet scent of the pipe-tobacco smoke had lost its pleasantness and was beginning to wear on Wintone, to create a vague hint of nausea that came and went.

"The kind of folktale that persists," Holt said absently, still examining the files, "is invariably rooted in our primal fear, our childhood fantasies, perhaps a certain consciousness that we are born with translated into fear."

"You see that possibility in Bonegrinder?"

"Very strongly." Holt turned in his chair to face Wintone. "A thing risen from the water, from whence we came, our primitive selves, our own primal past come to claim us. The elements are there."

"Elements of what?"

"Elements of fear, in all of us. Our instinctive fears are the strongest. Creatures of ancient oral literature are found in various forms in our literature today, both written and oral, in our fears. To greater or lesser degrees, Sheriff, all of us are afraid of the dark."

Holt turned back to the files. Wintone knew that he was right, but he didn't have to be so damned enthusiastic about it.

"I'm surprised the government is interested in something like this," Wintone said.

"They're not."

"You're here," Wintone said to Holt's back.

"The government has much the same attitude toward my work that they have toward investigating UFOs or ESP. They feel an obligation, need someplace to channel crackpot stories and awkward questions so they won't have to deal with them direct. So they created this scantily financed and loosely organized agency. It has a name and an office so people think that something is being accomplished, that someone cares."

"Seems to me you care."

"Oh, I do. The agency cares. But they don't want the agency to find anything; not really. They simply want us to exist, and not rock the boat. We're looking for the truth; they'll settle for anything just barely possible so that the matter can be dismissed."

Holt closed the last file folder, stood up from his chair. "You mind if I come back later and photograph these?" he asked, pointing to the files with his pipe stem. "It would save us both future bother."

Wintone told himself that it didn't matter. Practically everything in the files had found its way into the newspapers at one time or another. "Help yourself," he said.

"Obliged." Holt one-armed his wood chair to its previous position with another loud scraping sound. "I'm kind of curious about the conditions of the bodies. What do you remember about them?"

"They were badly tore up, each of them. The Larsen boy's right leg was almost gone. Most of what I can remember of Claude Borne is blood, deep gashes across his body. You seen the autopsy reports in the files."

"There are details that aren't necessarily mentioned in autopsy reports."

Wintone leaned back and clasped his hands behind his head. "Doc Amis'd be the man to see about that. He's the town doctor and the M. E. for this area."

"I saw his office, low brick building near the edge of town." Holt walked to the door, seemed to brace himself against going out into the heat. "I'm staying at Higgins' Motel, in case you want to get in touch." He smiled and opened the door.

"Obliged," he said again, and was gone.

Wintone sat watching the blinds swing in a shorter and shorter arc until they stopped tapping the window frame. He didn't know exactly what to make of Craig Holt.

He did know later that day that Holt had taken his advice about talking to Doc Amis. And apparently he'd done some talking to Sarah Ledbetter. Wintone saw them entering Turper's Grill from where he was standing on the other side of the street, giving directions to some magazine writers from Saint Louis.

An hour later Wintone walked past Turper's and happened to glance in and see them still sitting over coffee in one of the booths along the wall.

Holt was talking rapidly, tapping a long forefinger on the tabletop, and Sarah was leaning forward attentively with both hands around her coffee cup.

EIGHTEEN

When Holt drove Sarah home from Turper's Grill that night, he drew her to him and kissed her as they sat in the Jeep in her gravel driveway. Sarah was expecting his move and returned the kiss, with definite promise.

Holt grinned at her, ran the backs of his knuckles along the side of her slender, warm neck. "To be continued indoors."

"No," Sarah said, "not on a few-hours-old acquaintanceship." Her eyes shone in the feeble light. She wanted to take him inside the house with her, he could tell.

"Hell, Sarah, this isn't twenty years ago." He laughed to demonstrate that he was amused rather than angered at this quaint eccentricity of hers. And at this point he was amused.

"This is Colver, though," she told him. A cricket began to chirp nearby as if in confirmation of her statement.

"You said you lived for six years in Kansas City. If we were there wouldn't you invite me in?"

"If ducks had fur they wouldn't need feathers."

My God, Holt thought, she means it. Even though she could probably wring out her underpants. "I have a feeling you're being evasive, Sarah," he said mockingly.

"I guess that's about the only feelin' you're gonna get."

Holt shrugged in exaggerated hopelessness. She really was an old-fashioned girl, an anachronism. He was intrigued.

This was back country. Holt would bide his time, observe the ritual, if that was what it took. He kissed her again, feeling the eagerness and warmth of her lean body even as she pulled away from him. After she'd got out of the Jeep and walked up onto the porch of her frame home, he called a good night to her and started the engine.

On the third night, with a charming reluctance, she invited Holt inside. The interior of the small frame home was clean and faultlessly neat, and he realized that she'd probably cleaned house this morning or afternoon, knowing then she would give in this far to his advances.

They sat on a large and comfortable early-American sofa, sipping ready-mixed whiskey sours and watching the late news on television.

"It's got to be a lonely life for you," Holt said, "a small town like this."

"Loneliness is somethin' you get used to."

"I don't think so, Sarah. What made you return here from Kansas City?"

"I got involved with someone . . ."

"And it didn't work out?"

"For him, not for me."

Holt sipped his drink and settled back into the soft cushions. "Painful to talk about?"

Sarah smiled and shook her head. "I wish it was. But it wasn't that deep." She pointed toward the TV screen, where a violently gesticulating man was talking to a newscaster. "It was like that . . . like it was happenin' to someone else an' I was watchin', uninvolved. An' if I didn't like what I saw, there was nothin' I could do about it, no way to turn it off."

"So you came back here . . . for what?"

"Sanctuary."

"There's one big problem with sanctuary," Holt told her. "It becomes a bore."

He moved closer to her, gliding his right hand along her thin shoulders. He would have to go slowly with her, not because she was cold or inexperienced. She simply required a certain courting procedure, a time-ordered sequence. In this country the pendulum seldom swung far in either direction, and it swung with the regularity of life and death. Maybe she knew what she was doing; he wanted her all the more for it.

Yet whatever had happened in Kansas City had changed her, made her frightened of herself. The vulnerability was there, had to be. Holt could always sense it. She was one of those women with a thin protective shell that needed only to be cracked, that would mend slowly if at all. She knew that as well as he did.

He pulled her to him and she leaned against him without resistance. Working his right arm down to the small of her back, he encircled her slender waist, inserted his hand beneath the front of her slacks, down the surprising smoothness of her stomach. He explored with the hand until he found her moisture, her warmth, her trust.

Holt decided his stay in Colver would be at least mildly interesting.

Sarah and Holt were seen together often as the days passed. They went for walks along the lake road, picnicked together, and Sarah introduced Holt to many of the townspeople so he could interview them about native superstition and folklore with his portable recorder.

Holt had a way of ingratiating himself with people, getting what he set out after with a minimum of fuss and bother for everyone concerned. And by telling him about Bonegrinder, the people in the Colver area seemed to talk out some of their fears into the recorder. Not only did they cooperate with Holt, sometimes they sought him out.

It became common to see Holt and Sarah having dinner together at one of the better restaurants on the main highway, and Wintone one sleepless three A.M. noticed Holt's canvas-topped Jeep driving the route from the small, yellow frame house where Sarah lived to Higgins' Motel.

Wintone shouldn't have been concerned with the Sarah-Holt relationship, but he was. He tried to analyze what he felt. Vague stirrings of what? Jealousy?

He was stunned by the idea, then appalled.

NINETEEN

"Now this is positive action," Mayor Boemer said, slapping down a quarter-folded newspaper on Wintone's desk. "Have you seen this issue of the *Call?*"

"Not as yet," Wintone said. He picked up the local newspaper, the *Clarion Call,* and his eyes fixed on the black print that shared the headline space: LOCAL MAN OFFERS $10,000 REWARD FOR BONEGRINDER.

Winton read on to learn that Baily Howe, "described by some as a wealthy eccentric," had put up the reward for the body, dead or alive, of the thing known as Bonegrinder.

Howe was eccentric or crazy, however you happened to view it. His family had made a fortune in lumber, and he'd inherited it all at an early age and misused it as it multiplied. He was a dilettante scientist in several often-unrelated fields. About six years ago he had indulged in what were said to be bizarre ESP experiments at his rambling and luxurious split-log home, some five miles out of Colver atop a tall bluff overlooking a green valley.

After the ESP experiments Howe had suddenly departed on a South African safari which he'd financed to investigate rumors of some living link with primitive man. What he'd returned with was a mild venereal disease and a penchant for expensive firearms. He had bought a huge parcel of land near Hawk Point and opened a gun club, where the regional skeet-shooting tournaments were held, and where it was said that for a fee almost anything could be hunted.

"That goddamn Baily Howe!" Wintone said.

Boemer appeared astounded. "You should thank him for what he's done. We can be confident now that this thing'll be resolved. If nothing's turned up within a few weeks people'll feel it's safe to come here again, an' if by chance some miscreation is destroyed people'll know they're safe."

"The only thing likely to be killed is people," Wintone said. "Do you know how many screwballs an' otherwise are gonna be crawlin' all over an' around this part of the lake? All greedy for ten thousand dollars an' armed wth who knows what? I can tell you it'll be too many, an' it'll be dangerous."

"You're exaggeratin'," Mayor Boemer said, "becomin' overalarmed." But he didn't appear too sure of his words.

That evening there were a few boats in view on the lake from where Wintone stood overlooking the mouth of Lynn Cove. The setting sun distorted the flat plane of water, laying shimmering changes of light and color along its surface. Heat lingered in the calm, humid air, and there was a stillness about the lake that seemed somehow to emanate from below.

Wintone squinted into the angled light to make out the nearest boat, drifting in glimmering hues of red and green. There were two men in the boat, and Wintone saw that they weren't fishing. They were sitting patiently, cradling high-powered rifles.

The sheriff found himself wishing it would rain, or that the heat would break. Anything to change the pattern of madness that seemed to grip the area. As he watched, a large bird, possibly a hawk, passed near the boat but high over the lake. The man in the stern of the boat raised his rifle and a shot cracked like an echoing hammer blow across the flat lake water. The bird changed direction and winged toward the opposite shore.

Wintone was uneasy the rest of the evening, and he barely slept that night.

He had coffee and toast the next morning at Turper's Grill, and instead of the usual emptiness of the past few weeks there were half a dozen customers. Talk was of the reward.

Two of the men, seated at a table near the counter, Wintone recognized as reporters. They ate their ham and eggs slowly and seldom talked except to add a word to keep the conversation going.

"Ain't much I can't do with ten thousand dead presidents," one of the men at the counter said. He was a big man with a sunburned neck and rough, sun-darkened hands. There was a lazy power to the slope of his wide shoulders.

All four men at the counter wore tight, grimly satisfied expressions that somehow linked them in Wintone's mind, though he didn't know if they were together.

The bell above the door jangled flatly. Two men in their early twenties, wearing Levi's and sleeveless shirts, entered and sat in one of the far booths along the wall. One of the men began studying a small black notebook while the other studied a menu.

"Why, all the pussy in the world'd be mine," the big man at the counter continued. "At least for a while. But that's as long as I want it."

In the laughter that followed Wintone saw Velda's henna hairdo pause behind the high serving counter, then continue. She emerged to walk to the rear of the restaurant and take the order from the booth. The big man at the counter, then the three beside him, turned their heads with feigned nonchalance to look at her with varying degrees of appreciation, speculation.

"Do you think you really have a chance for that money?" one of the reporters asked whoever wanted to answer.

A man at the counter wearing an amazingly shapeless gray fishing hat over long hair swiveled slowly on his stool to face him. "Good a chance as any, better than some."

The reporter twisted his lips and nodded as if forced to agree. "What about the element of danger?"

"That'll make the reward all the sweeter," the big sunburned man said. "How 'bout a warm-up on the coffee, sugar?" he called to Velda. "Or any kinda warm-up." He grinned. Velda poured the coffee and looked at him as if he were junk at an auction. The big man cleared his throat uncomfortably.

"I'm curious," the other reporter said. "How do you intend to go about finding Bonegrinder, then dealing with him when you do find him?"

The man in the shapeless hat grinned secretively. "I got my methods, all thought out."

"A thirty-aught-six rifle is how I intend to earn my money," the big man said. "Special bullets."

"You gotta find somethin' to shoot at first," Shapeless Hat said.

"First you should determine if your bullets will have the desired effect," one of the younger men in the back booth said. He was the one who'd been studying the notebook. "We're dealing with an unknown quantity, as it were, and the first step should be to acquire some knowledge of what we're seeking."

"And how do you intend to do that?" one of the reporters asked.

The young man in the back booth took a sip of his coffee before answering. "Instrumentation and analysis."

The reporter stood and walked back to introduce himself to the man.

Wintone finished his buttered toast, exchanged glances with Velda and left.

He returned to the lake to find that the surface was now dotted with boats.

Wintone stood and watched from the same high spot where he'd stood the evening before, and though he'd expected something of this sort he was surprised at the number of boats. Mostly they were flat-prowed Jon boats, though out in the deeper areas of the lake there were a few larger boats, a metal pontoon boat glinting in the sun, even a few cabin cruisers. A small speedboat snarled as if trying to escape its rooster-comb wake as it passed to the left of Wintone, a man with a rifle slung on his back standing to peer over the windscreen. Because of the shallowness, the reeds and the underwater tangles of growth and jagged stumps, none of the boats could get close to shore.

But along the shore where it curved away to Wintone's right, he saw a few signs of activity at the edge of the woods, heard distant, shouting voices. He lifted his binoculars and focused them in time to see two men with backpacks disappear into the woods toward a rise of land. Sweeping the binoculars across the lake, he saw that most of the boats contained more than one man, there were even a few women, and most of the men were armed in one way or another, with weapons ranging from high-powered hunting rifles to sidearms. Mounted on the prow of one of the boats was a device that resembled a harpoon gun.

Wintone heard a vehicle grind to a stop on the gravel road beneath him and turned to see Craig Holt's canvas-topped Jeep through the trees. A few minutes later Holt approached him, long arms swinging in disjointed rhythm.

"It would be ludicrous," Holt said, sweeping an arm to cover the distant lake surface, "if it weren't so tragic." He was standing loosely and casually, wearing patched white denims and a faded blue shirt. His shallow-bowled pipe, unlit, was clamped in his teeth.

"It's liable to get more tragic," Wintone said.

"They'll be out in increased numbers tomorrow, you know."

"I expect it'll get worse."

Holt shook his head. "It makes serious investigation damn near impossible, all those fools out there and swarming all over the bank."

"What I'm bothered with," Wintone said, "is the idea that one of those fools is gonna get killed before this is over."

Holt removed the pipe from his mouth, glanced down at it as if considering lighting it. "I'd be surprised if somebody didn't get accidentally killed. There's no way you can stop them—no law, I suppose?"

"Nothin' to keep a man from makin' an ass of himself." Wintone handed Holt the binoculars and watched him focus them expertly with one hand and scan the lake. Holt hadn't shaved, appeared as if he'd had a rough night.

"Unbelievable," Holt said. He handed back the binoculars by their rawhide strap.

"There might be one thing I can do about it," Wintone said, "an' that's talk to Baily Howe an' see if I can get him to withdraw the reward. Everybody swarmin' around this end of the lake's got ten thousand reasons to be here, but I doubt if many of 'em's got ten thousand an' one."

"Who exactly is this Baily Howe?"

"He's a man with money who mostly does what he wants, an' what he wants usually only makes sense to him."

"He's opened up the prospect of real trouble here," Holt said, pointing with his pipe stem toward the lake. "No doubt you should talk to him."

"Want to come along?" Wintone asked. "Kinda throw the government at him, if you follow my meanin'."

Holt's features slipped into his easy smile. "I don't know if my employers would like that. Besides, I'm tied up for the day. I'm supposed to conduct some interviews up on Yellow Ridge."

"With Sarah?"

"Matter of fact, yes." Holt's eyes met Wintone's gaze quizzically. "I'm not poaching, am I, Sheriff?"

"Not on me, you're not. How come you'd ask?"

"I know you two were close once. Sarah talks about you a lot."

"Don't mean nothin'," Wintone said. "You go ahead an' do what you want." He smiled and jerked his head toward the lake. "Like them fellas out there." He wound the rawhide strap around the binoculars and turned.

"Let me know how it comes out then," Holt said, "your talk with this Baily Howe."

"Surely will."

Wintone could feel Holt watching him as he walked bent-legged down the uneven, grassy slope toward the parked patrol car.

As if there weren't enough to worry about.

TWENTY

"I'm beginning to worry," Kelly said, sitting on the wooden glider outside their motel cabin. "You have a camera, they have guns."

Alan took a drink from the beer can he'd set aside in the freezer of the cabin's hard-working old refrigerator. The can was still so cold that the rounded metal stuck to the flesh of his palm. He'd found that exactly twenty minutes in the freezer brought the beer to perfect drinking temperature. "You talk like they're out there hunting me."

"They're hunting ten thousand dollars. They'll look at what they've shot after they've shot it."

He smacked his lips in exaggerated appreciation and took another sip of beer. "I'm too little to be Bonegrinder."

"I wish you'd be serious."

"I am serious about my work. That's why I'm here. You want me to put a beer in the freezer for you? I'm going to have another."

Kelly tucked her bare legs under her and shook her head. "Save me some of that one." She wanted to leave, but not without Alan. She wanted him to leave. Now that so many of the tourists had left it seemed that there were few women in the area, at least few young women. When Kelly had gone into Colver this morning in shorts she'd felt exposed, the object of attention of every man on the street. It had never occurred to her that few of the local women ever wore shorts, even in this unending heat.

That was her imagination, she told herself. There were other women around, right here in the motel, and they occasionally wore shorts. Maybe she'd wanted to be the object of attention this morning.

Alan walked over and sat next to her on the gently rocking glider, handed her the half-empty can of beer. She was surprised at how cold the beer was, and how good it tasted.

"I used a wide-angle lens this morning," Alan said. "Found a high spot on the bank with a terrific view. I got some really unique shots of the lake. And some good mood shots."

He wasn't going to leave; she knew that.

"I wonder what this Baily Howe would pay for a photograph of Bonegrinder," he said. "Or what the wire services would pay."

"Do you really believe there's . . . something out there to photograph?"

"I don't know, Kel. A lot of people do believe it. It's a strange world. Consider the abominable snowman."

"God, no. Not here. Not now."

Alan laughed. "It's just another job. Don't let your fertile imagination get you going."

"You're right. I know you're right. But all those reward seekers out there aren't imaginary, with their guns and walkie-talkies and phony bravado. I heard shots fired today, three times so far."

"Sound carries over the lake."

"And there's nothing to stop a bullet from carrying."

He kissed her on the ear. "You're too damned sensible, you know that?"

"Maybe it's the heat."

"That's better. Be your normal, cheerful self—that's the self I love." He grinned at her. "Not that I don't love all your selves."

She had to smile, and that was what he wanted.

"I've got to do some work," he said, pushing himself up from the glider. "I came back to eat lunch and I've been here over an hour. Want to come with me? I'm going to drive north a few miles and see if there's anything interesting."

"I don't think so," Kelly said. The glider was almost out of the shade now, the cracks and minute imperfections of one wooden arm glaring in harsh sunlight. "I'll go back inside and bask in the air conditioning." She thought of telling him to be careful, but that would be pointless, harping.

Kelly had never underestimated the importance of Alan's work to him. Even before their marriage she'd made up her mind to defer to that importance. It was a sacrifice she'd been willing to make, telling herself it was better to be jealous of a camera than another woman. But sometimes, lately, she wondered.

"I'll have one more beer while I'm checking my equipment," Alan said, starting for the cabin door. "Absolutely sure you don't want one?"

"I'm sure," Kelly said.

While Alan was inside she watched a hawk high against a sky deep blue and void of clouds, soaring in unpredictable arcs on unpredictable currents of air, until the pattern of its graceful flight took it out of sight beyond the towering limbs of an oak tree near the cabin.

Later she watched Alan wave to her and saw the dusty white Volkswagen disappear beyond the trees at the road's bend, the whining beat of its engine seeming to hang in the air, then settle with the dust.

TWENTY-ONE

Wintone played the accelerator pedal skillfully as the powerful patrol car climbed the steep and narrow graveled road to Baily Howe's bluff-top home. The road was straight for long sections, then it would right-angle twice to climb in the opposite direction, like a turn in a staircase landing. Far below him Wintone could make out the almost dry bed of Mopey Creek, a dark, indistinct ribbon winding its way among the trees.

The patrol car's engine was laboring as if it might overheat, and Wintone sat uncomfortably behind the wheel in the air-conditioned interior, feeling a stiffening, steady warmth on the left side of his face as the sun's glare worked its way through the rolled-up window. Then the road leveled out, curved, and he could see the cedar-shake roof of Howe's home through a stand of tall pine trees. The unpredictable Howe had agreed without hesitation to see Wintone when the sheriff had phoned earlier. That, at least, was encouraging.

Wintone braked the car before a low oaken gate topped high with barbed wire. An eight-foot cyclone fence stretched away through the woods on either side of the gate, and there was a red-lettered No Trespassing sign, freshly painted, nailed to the gate's top rail.

The sheriff got out of the car and opened the gate, aware of the heat and the odor of cooked oil from the idling engine. He drove through, shut and latched the gate behind him, then drove the rest of the way to the house.

Though Baily Howe's house was of split-log construction, there was nothing crude about it. Long, low wings stretched on either side of a peaked-roof center with its tall, ornately carved door beneath a huge entranceway light. A line of evergreen shrubs huddled against the front of the house, and off to one side were some recently planted maples with taut, staked supporting ropes to guide them to a straight start of growth. Wintone turned off the ignition and began to get out of the car when a large, black Doberman pinscher trotted around a corner of the house and froze staring at him.

The tall front door opened, and Baily Howe stepped out. He was of average height, a man in his late forties, muscular but thickening around the middle, wearing a blue-trimmed white sport shirt, dark blue slacks and white shoes. His hair was thinning but still dark, cut short and parted with precision, and he had one of those heart-shaped, broad-featured faces that but for their eyes project a boyish image well into middle age. Glancing at the poised Doberman, Howe gave a palm-out, downward-pushing motion with his right hand, and the dog sat and seemed to lose interest in Wintone. Then Howe motioned for Wintone to come inside and stood by the open door.

It had been almost a year since Wintone had seen Baily Howe in Colver. The man looked much older, possibly slightly heavier. After shaking hands with Howe the sheriff followed him into a huge room with rough-sawn beams crisscrossing the ceiling and a wall that was a single sheet of thick but clear glass overlooking the valley of green treetops and winding road. There was a bulky stone fireplace along another wall, flanked by ceiling-to-floor bookcases crammed with books in haphazard arrangement, some on edge, some in stacks, a few lying open atop other books. Howe motioned for Wintone to sit on a long, brown-leather sofa. It was a quiet room as well as large, as if all sound sank heavily to be absorbed by the thick beige carpet.

"Something to drink, Sheriff?" Howe asked, facing Wintone with his arms crossed.

"A beer would feel good goin' down."

Howe walked around a paneled corner and returned in a minute with a frosted mug of beer for Wintone and what looked like a glass of watered-down Scotch for himself. Wintone accepted the beer and sampled it.

"Is the criminal element in Colver being controlled?" Howe asked, sitting down in a leather chair that matched the sofa. He stirred his drink with his finger.

"Crime's not my main worry right now, Mr. Howe."

"Bonegrinder?" Howe's blue eyes were quizzical over the clear rim of his glass.

"Yes an' no," Wintone said. "What I came to see you about is that reward you put up. It's causin' me some concern."

"Oh? Has it created much interest?"

"Too much interest. There's people out there by the hundreds maybe, an' some of 'em too eager for your money."

"Surely you want Bonegrinder found," Howe said. "I should think you'd be grateful for the help."

Wintone sipped his beer. He had the feeling he was being

led, didn't like it. "I'm doin' my job, Mr. Howe, but why are you so interested in Bonegrinder?"

"Curiosity, of course. The acquisition of knowledge, scientific development. You must understand that."

"Do you really think there's somethin' out there that'll add to scientific development?"

Howe swirled his drink in his glass and smiled at Wintone. "Perhaps that's the difference between myself and you, Sheriff. I believe there's something out there worth finding because of its uniqueness."

"Good an' well," Wintone said, "but all these people swarmin' over the area are like as not creatin' a situation where nothin' is gonna be found."

"Since we're dealing with the unknown, I have to conclude that the more people searching, the more likely it is that the object will be discovered. You're concerned with possibilities, Sheriff, while I'm concerned with facts. Facts are my life. I live in a world of facts, and my object is to expand that world."

Wintone was beginning to sense that the conversation was rudderless and that he had no way to guide it. "My concern is that somebody's gonna get killed."

Howe sat quietly for a long moment, the sky and valley like a sweeping three-dimensional mural behind him. "Are you asking me to withdraw the reward, Sheriff?"

"I'd appreciate it, Mr. Howe."

Howe seemed to squint at something in the distance beyond Wintone. "Do you know anything about trajectory?"

"Like a bullet's trajectory?"

"Not just a bullet's, Sheriff . . . Life is a series of trajectories, some of them intersecting, either fortunately or unfortunately. Either way, perhaps it is no accident that Bonegrinder should make his appearance at this time, in this place, where I am. Perhaps you're asking me to refute my destiny, Sheriff."

"That's a mite strong, Mr. Howe. One man's already died by accident, an' that was before this end of the lake was crawlin' with people with guns."

"You're interested in people, Sheriff. I'm interested in facts."

"But don't you care if somebody gets killed?"

"Good Christ, yes! But should the Panama Canal not have been built because of yellow fever? Should the legions of Japanese not have been turned back because the task demanded blood? Stop looking through that microscope of yours, Sheriff. Try to take the larger view."

Wintone shifted his weight on the soft leather sofa. "I can't," he said, "maybe 'cause I'm under that microscope myself. Maybe all of us are."

Something changed in Howe's wide-set blue eyes, a hard, deep, flipped-object kind of turning. "In any case," he said, "I can't do as you request."

"All right," Wintone said. "Leastways you been asked." The unnatural silence of the big room was beginning to annoy Wintone, as if the real world were being held at bay outside the thick glass of the window behind Howe's chair.

"Consider," Baily Howe said, "that you also are eligible for the reward."

Wintone shook his head. "County don't allow us to accept reward money, Mr. Howe."

"There are possible arrangements . . ."

"'Fraid not."

Howe set his glass on a table, sat back cross-armed in his chair. "What are your intentions now, Sheriff? Regarding Bonegrinder?"

"Why would you ask?"

"I'm interested. I know the man who appointed you quite well. Mayor Boemer."

Wintone felt his face flush with a tingling of anger. "I've heard you do. You threatenin' me, Mr. Howe?"

Howe raised his eyebrows in middle-aged boyish innocence. "I thought you were threatening me, Sheriff."

"I only came up here to head off trouble."

Howe stretched out his legs, crossing them at the ankles to reveal blue silk socks, threw back his head. "In a sense that's my militia down there, my mercenary militia, doing my bidding to accomplish the first step of discovery. In Africa . . . but never mind. You'll thank me when this is over, Sheriff—as will they all."

"Could be you're right," Wintone said, placing his damp beer mug on the carpet and standing. "I just don't want none of your militia to get killed."

Howe stood to escort the sheriff to the door. Despite his elegantly casual attire, there was something disturbingly military in his bearing.

"Is there anything I can do to make you change your mind about that reward?" Wintone asked, stepping out onto the cement porch.

"Not so that I wouldn't change it back," Howe said seriously.

Wintone nodded. "I thank you for the time." He walked to his car, past the intent gaze of the Doberman that was still sitting where it had been when Wintone entered.

"Come back again, Sheriff," Howe called as Wintone was getting into the patrol car.

"I expect I might."

As Wintone drove away from the house, he looked in the rear-view mirror and saw the Doberman lie down in sections, as large dogs do, still watching him.

Wintone breathed easier on the other side of the gate with the No Trespassing sign. There was no point in trying to reason with Baily Howe, he realized. But at that Howe was saner than some of the people he'd lit a fire under with his reward money.

To a degree the situation took care of itself, but only to a degree.

Within a few days it became obvious to many of the hunters on and around the lake that they were bucking odds greater than they'd imagined. Monotony took its toll, as did the sun. Gradually the ranks of the reward-seekers thinned, and each day that he checked Wintone saw the lake dotted with fewer boats.

Wintone was standing outside Mully's, watching an overloaded old station wagon, its roof luggage-rack stacked high with tied-down cartons, pulling a trailer as it headed toward the main highway, when he heard someone walk up behind him.

"They're running out of money," Holt said, "and patience."

Wintone watched the trailer sway as the station wagon slowed, then took a corner. "Still plenty of 'em left, though."

Holt gave his ready smile. "More than enough—the fanatical ones who'll do whatever's necessary for the reward. Still, your task should be easier. Mine, too. I'm thinking about going out on the lake tomorrow to take some soundings."

"Wear something bulletproof." Wintone didn't say that he couldn't see that much difference between Holt and the rest of them out on the lake. Maybe Holt was just as fanatical as they were, but wanted a different kind of reward.

"Have you turned up anything new on Bonegrinder, Sheriff?"

"I talked to Baily Howe. He refused to withdraw the reward offer."

"Did you explain to him that someone was liable to get killed?"

Wintone nodded. "That don't seem to be one of Mr. Howe's concerns."

"If his serious concern is in finding Bonegrinder, you should convince him that what he's doing is self-defeating. Whatever Bonegrinder is, it's not likely to show itself with an army of ignoramuses in the area."

"Nobody convinces Mr. Howe but Mr. Howe."

"Then he's as eccentric as they say?"

Wintone traced a zigzag pattern in the dust with his boot toe. "Them callin' him eccentric would be his friends."

The late morning sun was beginning to bear down, foretelling another hot, dry day. Wintone excused himself from Holt and turned to go into Mully's. He noticed that Holt walked away in the direction of Doc Amis's.

Half an hour later, seated at the bar in Mully's, Wintone heard a dull explosion, like someone smacking the meaty part of a fist on a thick door. His empty beer mug inched sideways across the smooth bar.

Mully tilted his head to one side, tucked a corner of his ragged white bar towel into his belt. "What the hell was that?"

Wintone couldn't answer at first, and then he placed the sound.

"They ain't got the God-given sense of a horsefly," he said, getting down off the bar stool. He walked quickly outside, then jogged to where the patrol car was parked in front of his office.

As he opened the car door, another dull explosion told him which direction to drive in and gave him a hint of distance. He started the patrol car and steered it in a tight U-turn through its own dust.

Near Lynn Cove half a dozen parked cars and pickup trucks caught Wintone's attention, and he pulled to the road shoulder behind a truck with a metal camper mounted on its bed.

Even as he got out of the car and looked around, Wintone could feel the heat draining him. Instead of jogging, he walked at a fast pace down the hard dirt path toward the bank.

There were several people standing on the bank, looking out at the wide lake. Every head turned, without surprise, at Wintone's approach, as if they'd been expecting him. Then they turned their faces back toward the lake, as if indicating to him where to look.

The object of everyone's attention was a small Jon boat well out on the lake. Wintone squinted and held a cupped hand to his forehead to ease the glare of sunlight reflecting off the sparkling blue-green water.

There were two men in the boat, seated facing each other. As Wintone watched, the man in the bow suddenly straightened and threw something off to the side away from the bank with a straight-armed, slinglike motion. He sat back down, and Wintone noticed that the man in the bow was cradling a rifle.

A geyser of water rose on the other side of the boat and a moment later another dull *whump!* like the two earlier explosions, only louder, reached the bank.

Without speaking Wintone reached over and borrowed the binoculars from a man standing nearby.

"Dynamitin' in fishin' water's illegal, ain't it?" someone asked.

"It is that," Wintone said, pressing the binoculars to his eyes. Around the distant boat he could see the glinting silver bodies of concussion-killed fish, bobbing on water still in turmoil from the last explosion.

Wintone drew his revolver from its holster and fired a shot into the air to attract the attention of the two men in the boat. As they both turned toward him, he holstered the revolver and waved them in to shore.

The two men looked at each other and seemed to be talking, as if debating whether to bring the boat in. Wintone felt a surge of anger, placed his fists on his hips.

Then the man in the stern twisted his body. Wintone saw the out-and-backward motion of his elbow, and the sputtering drone of an outboard motor came faintly across the water. The boat moved in a large circle, dead fish bobbing in its spreading wake, until its flat prow was aimed at the bank.

The water was extremely shallow off the bank where Wintone was standing, so he moved down to where he knew it was deeper, and the half-dozen people who'd been watching the dynamiting walked with him.

Even here the lake was shallow near the bank, and fifty yards out the man in the boat's stern killed the outboard motor and tilted it up to free its propeller from bottom weed. Both men worked to get the boat in closer to the bank, poling with the oars. Then the man in the bow, who was wearing dark green wading boots, jumped into the water and pulled the boat in close enough to tie the rope he was gripping around the trunk of a crooked sapling. The man in the boat's stern wasn't wearing boots, but he lowered himself into the hip-high water and, with a great deal of unnecessary splashing, waded toward Wintone. He was a slender, long-haired man wearing a rumpled gray hat with a blue, flowered band. Wintone remembered seeing him in Turper's Grill.

"Bring what's left of the dynamite," Wintone ordered.

The other man was already standing on the bank, working the thick suspenders of his wading boots from around his shoulders. "We was only tryin' to bring Bonegrinder to the surface so as to get a shot at him," the man said angrily.

Wintone didn't answer, watched the man in the rumpled hat wade back to the boat and lift out a small, metal tackle box. The man waded back to the bank with the box up on one shoulder, held there with both hands. When he reached the bank, he laid the box in the mud, then moved away from it and stamped some of the water from his shoes and pants legs.

Wintone stooped and opened the tackle box, found a waterproof oilcloth packet containing three long-fused orange sticks of dynamite.

"You two know dynamitin' in fishin' waters is against the law?" Wintone asked, standing.

"We wasn't doin' it for the fish," the man with the wading boots said.

"There's sure a hell of a lot of dead ones on the surface," Wintone said flatly.

The man in the rumpled hat shook his head as if finding it incredible that Wintone should question their actions. "Two people's been killed. These ain't exactly usual circumstances, Sheriff."

"If you can convince the State Police of that you got no worries," Wintone said. He jabbed his thumb backward over his shoulder. "Your car parked up there?"

The man nodded, looking disgusted. He removed his rumpled hat to reveal a sunburned half-dollar-size bald spot on the crown of his head.

Wintone carried the dynamite in the tackle box and followed the two men up to where the cars were parked on the grassy road shoulder. He was annoyed to realize that the scene was being photographed by a short man with a detached yet intent expression beneath a head of unruly reddish hair. With the man was a young girl, more a woman really, who drew so much of Wintone's attention that he slowed his pace, then had to walk fast to catch up with the two dynamiters.

At first Wintone didn't know what there was about the girl that had so caught his eye, then with a pang of emotion he realized that there was something of Etty in the girl, in the calm, dark eyes and the smile sketched with light about the wide, full lips.

The man in the rumpled hat stopped, and Wintone almost walked into him. They had reached an old, rusted Pontiac. The larger man opened the car's trunk, cursed and threw his wading boots in on top of a bald spare tire.

Wintone took their driver's licenses, then instructed them to drive ahead of the patrol car into Colver. As the sheriff slid behind the sun-heated steering wheel, he tried to ignore the young man with the thirty-five millimeter camera, now down on one knee to photograph at an upward angle. The girl was standing directly behind the man, seeing what the camera saw but with seeming disinterest. Wintone started the patrol car and followed close to the rear bumper of the rust-scarred Pontiac.

When they reached Colver, Wintone locked the two men in the back room holdover cells and phoned the State Police.

Wintone thought that the arrests, along with the passage of time, would calm things in the Colver area. But apparently Holt was right; those searchers left were too fanatical or oblivious to danger to be discouraged. If anything, the fervor of the search picked up.

Until the day of the shooting.

TWENTY-TWO

"You better come down here to the doctor's, Billy," Sarah said to Wintone on the phone. There was an irritated concern to her voice.

The sheriff felt no surprise, only an unreasonable anger at himself for being unable to prevent what he suspected had happened. "Who and how bad?" he asked.

"Man named Flynn. It's more painful than serious; the bullet passed through his arm."

"I'll be there directly, Sarah."

Wintone tucked in his tan uniform shirt and walked from his office. The afternoon taunted with the possibility of rain. Lead-colored, bloated clouds hung in the sky above a hot, humid stillness. The thick air was charged as if presaging a thunderstorm, but it had been that way most of the morning and no rain had fallen. As he walked, Wintone looked at sun-parched brown grass, at fine zigzag cracks in the earth like cracks in brittle china, and at the implacable gray-mottled sky. Maybe it would never rain again, only hint at it.

In Doc Amis's waiting room sat three men wearing dusty outdoors clothing, guardedly anxious expressions on sunburned faces—probably friends of the wounded Flynn. They interrupted their subdued conversation to look at Wintone with distrust.

Sarah glanced up from where she was working at her desk. She looked cool and clean in her white uniform, younger, as if she'd just taken a shower and somehow washed away worry and years. Standing, she smiled at Wintone, walked to the door behind her desk and held it open for him.

"In here, Billy," she said, and when he walked through the doorway she followed, closing the door behind her with a soft click.

Doc Amis was standing at a small washbasin rinsing his hands with a doctor's smooth dexterity. He turned only his head and nodded at Wintone. "Sheriff Wintone," he said, "this is Ed Flynn. A large-caliber bullet passed through his upper left arm this morning, missing the humerus bone by a quarter of an inch."

Flynn was a stocky man in his forties, with a paunch and work-worn brown hands. He was wearing boots and bloodstained gray pants, sitting bent forward on a vinyl-covered padded table. His upper left arm was thickly bandaged in white gauze and held against his bare chest in a high sling. There was a stubborn, anticipative jut to his heavy jaw when he looked up at Wintone, but pain had taken something from his eyes.

"How'd it happen, Mr. Flynn?" Wintone asked.

Flynn gingerly touched his injured arm with his free hand. "We were out in the boat, barely moving with the trolling motor on the down leg of our pattern, when some asshole in another boat opened up with a rifle and shot me."

"Down leg of what pattern?" Wintone asked.

"What we did is take a map of the south end of the lake

and break it into sections." Flynn swallowed loudly and his eyes narrowed, and Wintone realized that the man was in great pain. "Each day we run the boat in a pattern over one or two sections, dropping weighted lines with deep-sea hooks baited with beef. We were almost finished with our first section today when I heard six or seven shots and my arm felt like it was hit with a hammer. They tell me it was some clown in another boat blasting away with a rifle into the water. One of the bullets must have ricocheted off the surface and hit me."

"They'll do that," Wintone said. "They can skip on the water like stones. What about the man in the other boat? What did he say?"

"When we started yelling that I'd been hit, the boat came over by ours. The fella who'd done the shooting said he thought he'd seen something just under the surface of the lake, moving deeper, and he wanted to hit it while he could still see it."

Wintone angrily let out his breath. "What was the man's name? Where is he now?"

Flynn clenched his teeth and shook his head. "Can't answer either of those questions, Sheriff. When the men in the other boat saw I wasn't hurt bad, they revved up their outboard and went off toward the big part of the lake."

"How many men were in the boat?"

"Three."

"What did they look like? Especially the one that did the shootin'?"

"The guy with the rifle is the only one I really paid any attention to, a bald man with a mustache, wearing a red shirt. That's all I remember about him."

Doc Amis dried his hands thoroughly with a few quick motions of a white paper towel. "Flynn here won't be the last casualty if something's not done," he said to Wintone.

Sarah took the wet towel from Doc Amis and dropped it in a lined waste can on her side of the room. "I hear they were even usin' dynamite to try bringin' somethin' up," she said.

"Heard true," Wintone said. "The only thing comin' up is their court date. But the damn fools are probably out there again on the lake right now tryin' somethin' else while they're waitin'."

"One thing for sure," Flynn said with painful resolution, "I don't intend to give up."

Wintone looked at him, at his tense, stocky body and his Hollywood expression of determination. If the bullet had been a quarter of an inch over and had smashed bone, Wintone knew Flynn would be less brave and more sensible.

"Where you from, Mr. Flynn?" Wintone asked.

"Wood River, Illinois. I work in a refinery there but I'm on leave of absence."

"What you best do is go back to Wood River, back to what family you got."

"Where he should go is to a hospital," Doc Amis said. "He should get that wound looked at by a specialist."

"It's not that serious," Flynn said. He got down off the padded table and winced in pain. Sarah picked up a bloody checked shirt, draping it over his shoulders like a shawl.

"There's no way I can make him go,' Doc Amis said to Wintone.

"No there's not," Flynn said. "I got something personal against Bonegrinder now."

"You got somethin' personal against some idiot in a boat who blasts away at lake water without thinkin'!" Wintone said angrily.

Flynn shook his head. "It was an accident."

Wintone felt the anger heat up and spread through him. "A goddamned predictable accident!"

Flynn's jaw jutted farther and his ruddy face set with renewed stubbornness.

"Billy. . . ." Sarah said in a soft warning voice, placing her fingertips on Wintone's shoulder.

Wintone realized he was holding his breath, exhaled in a long sigh that eased tension, not just in himself but in the tiny, green-walled room. "I need you to come down to my office," he said to Flynn, "to sign a written statement. Your friends have to come, too. I need their account of what happened." Wintone held the door open for Flynn.

In the waiting room the three anxious men stood up, looked at Flynn and Doc Amis questioningly.

"Nothing serious," Flynn said.

One of the three men, a bearded giant with small, sleepy eyes, whooshed out an exaggerated sigh of relief. They walked over near Flynn, looking at the bandaged arm. Despite his pain, Flynn seemed to be enjoying the attention.

"Bullet went right on through," Flynn said, sucking in his paunch. "We're not going to let this stop us."

"Damned right we're not!" the bearded man said in a bass voice. "We shoulda shot back at the bastard!" The four of them laughed at what was right now a joke. One of the men took off his glasses, as if he no longer needed them now that everything was all right.

"You got state fishin' licenses?" Wintone asked suddenly.

Laughter stopped. "I do," the smallest of the four said.

"We weren't fishing," the man with the glasses said.

"You was out on the lake in a fishin' boat, an' accordin' to Flynn there was fishin' equipment in that boat."

"*Was*," the bearded man repeated, his eyes less sleepy.

"And not for catching fish," Flynn said. "You don't catch lake fish with our equipment."

Wintone's voice was soft but meaningful. "Next time

you're out in that boat with so much as a hook you all better have your state licenses; if you got a handgun you better have a permit for that; you better be at or under your limit if there's fish in the boat; you better not have nothin' out of season or nothin' in the boat or car or on your person that constitutes a dangerous weapon."

The bearded man drew up to impressive full height. "You goin' to harass honest citizens, Sheriff?"

Wintone walked to the outside door, opened it and stood waiting for the honest citizens. "I'm gonna uphold the law like I never done before."

In Wintone's office the four men gave their statements. Flynn's story was corroborated. Nobody was able to describe in any detail the men in the other boat — only the scant description of the bald, mustached man wearing a red shirt.

After the four men had left, Wintone sat at his desk thinking of Baily Howe and his reward money. Word would soon reach Howe that Wintone was applying the law to the letter, discouraging the hard-case searchers who were left—the militia. Probably Mayor Boemer would be on the phone to Howe by morning.

Let them try for his job, if that was their decision. Wintone wouldn't make it easy for them. Howe might be rich, but he still had his limitations. And Mayor Boemer was afraid of Wintone, for what he might know, and for what he might do. Boemer's reelection for term after term had been almost automatic, unopposed. It didn't have to be that way.

The office seemed to have gotten smaller around Wintone. He got up, filed the statements on the Flynn shooting, then went out and got in the patrol car.

Wintone drove to several points on the lake shore, scanning the water and the bank with binoculars, looking for a bald man, or a man with a hat, wearing a red shirt. He had what luck he expected: none.

But as the sheriff was driving back to Colver, near Higgins' Motel, he rounded a dusty bend in the road and saw the young photographer and the girl.

They were standing alongside a dented, white Volkswagen that was jacked up on one side and tilting away from the road. The left rear wheel had been removed and was lying flat near the elevated side of the car, and the photographer suddenly squatted over it, his elbows on his knees and his head bowed. The girl was standing near the front of the car. She appeared worried and was gnawing her lower lip.

Wintone braked and pulled the patrol car to the side of the road, twisted to look over his shoulder, then backed the car to park in front of the crippled Volkswagen. He got out of the car and walked back.

The photographer, his bushy, reddish hair matted and glistening with sweat, was standing now over the detached wheel. "Flat tire," he said simply.

Wintone smiled. "Got a spare?"

The young man mustered what feeble laughter he could and shook his head. "This is the spare. When I got it out I found it had gone flat. Looks like a leaky valve stem."

Wintone looked at the girl close up then for the first time. He felt a wave of emotion break through him. She didn't really look like Etty, and she was much taller, but still there was something . . . the eyes, maybe . . . the lips definitely . . . and something in the way she held herself, the tight arch to her back. But she was very young, in her early twenties at most, a very young girl.

"We're almost within walking distance of the motel," she said, seemingly to both men.

"Hot day," Wintone said. "No point in walkin'. I'm Sheriff Billy Wintone."

"Alan and Kelly Greer," the photographer said. There was something about him Wintone liked, and envied. He wished Alan and Kelly Greer more luck than had been his and Etty's.

"We're from Kansas City," Kelly said, as if that explained what they were doing standing next to a broken-down old car at the side of an Ozark road. "We saw you earlier this week. The dynamiters. Remember?"

Wintone smiled again and nodded. "I remember." He looked down at the tire at Alan Greer's feet. "Why don't I drive you into Colver, get that valve stem replaced an' the tire aired up? We can drop your wife at the motel on the way."

Alan grinned. "All right. Listen, Sheriff, I appreciate it."

Wintone waved the thanks away, walked to the rear of the patrol car and opened the trunk so Alan Greer could put the Volkswagen tire inside. With very little effort Alan lifted the flat spare tire and walked back to lay it sideways in the trunk. Then he brushed his hands and took a few half-running steps back to the white Volkswagen. He reached inside through the rolled-down window and pulled out his camera in its leather carrying case.

"Nothing else in there of value," he said, as he slung the case's strap around his neck and returned to the patrol car.

Alan Greer got into the front on the passenger's side while Wintone held open a rear door for Kelly. She edged onto the seat with a flash of tan inner thigh.

"I've read a few things about you in the papers, Sheriff," Alan Greer said as the car accelerated and rocks pinged off the fenders. "I'm a free-lance photographer, here to put together something on Bonegrinder. I'd be interested in any of your opinions or suggestions."

"Only so much you can photograph around here," Wintone said. "Shouldn't take you long."

Alan Greer shook his head. "To a photographer's ey

there's a world of variety in this area, Sheriff. What do you think Bonegrinder is?"

Wintone stared straight ahead through the dust-streaked windshield. "I don't expect we'll ever know. Like you said, there's a world of variety in this area, and strange things have a way of happenin'."

"It's beautiful around here," Kelly said from the backseat, "but it scares me. As if in an Eden like this there must be a serpent."

"Snakes a'plenty," Wintone said. "More likely the biggest danger's from all the armed fools still roamin' around here. Man was accidentally shot out on the lake earlier today. Only in the arm, but he's too dumb to know it coulda been otherwise. Tell you the truth, I'd advise you to leave. I aim to put a stop to some of what's goin' on, but it can't all be stopped."

"What do you think's going to happen, Sheriff?" Kelly asked.

"I think somebody else is goin' to get hurt or killed, and I'd as soon it wasn't either of you two."

They had reached Higgins' Motel, and Alan Greer pointed to their cabin. Wintone braked the patrol car close to the front door and waited while Kelly got out. Alan handed her the cabin key through the car window, telling her he'd be back soon. She bent low for a better view of Wintone through the open window and told him thanks again and it was nice to have met him. He glanced at her graceful figure as she walked toward the cabin, and sensed that her husband had anticipated his look. Wintone quickly turned away and tapped the accelerator.

"I meant what I said," he told Alan Greer, when they were back on the road and dust was finding its way in through the still-rolled-down window. "Both of you should leave, but you should at least get your wife outa here. Let her wait for you in Kansas City."

Alan hastily rolled up the window and wiped dust and perspiration from his eyes with his soiled sleeve. "Kelly won't leave while I'm here, Sheriff, and I have to stay until I finish my work."

"She leave if you ask her?"

"I doubt it." He folded his hands over the camera case in his lap.

"What if you tell her?"

Alan Greer laughed. "Kelly's nothing if not stubborn, Sheriff, and in her own way she considers herself as capable as I am. She'd say if it's too dangerous here for her, it's too dangerous for me—we both go or we both stay."

"That's a shame," Wintone said.

Alan Greer shrugged. "I don't think I'd want her any different."

Wintone smiled. "Guess not." He took a curve in the road with his gentle touch on the wheel. "She reminds me of my wife."

"Oh? I'd like to meet her."

"She's dead," Wintone said. "A fool's victim."

Wintone could see that he'd surprised Alan Greer, and the young man chose to keep his silence the rest of the way into Colver.

Just as well. Wintone felt like being silent himself.

TWENTY-THREE

Bill Peterson sat on the edge of the motel bed and watched his wife browse through some travel brochures they'd picked up at a souvenir shop. She was seated at the small writing desk near the window, and her lean face appeared tranquil in the light diffused by the closed blue drapes. Peterson had been able to talk to her lately, and as long as they could communicate, he knew there was some hope for their marriage.

He studied her elegant, lean figure, the curve of her hip on the chair. Melanie was at the lake fishing. The desire to make love to Cheryl here in the quiet motel room while they had the opportunity awakened in Peterson's loins, but he was sure she'd reject him. And an unsuccessful attempt at seduction might undo whatever rapport they'd achieved in the last few days.

The opportunity for reconciliation was eluding him. They would be starting for home soon, probably tomorrow evening. A quiet panic moved through Peterson.

Footsteps sounded on the pavement outside. Peterson thought it might be Melanie returning from the lake, but it wasn't. "Glad we came here?" he asked his wife.

"Melanie seems to be enjoying herself. You were right about that."

"Only that?"

"I think so, Bill." Cheryl put the stack of color brochures aside on the small desk. She had hesitated.

Peterson reached to the table by the bed for his pack of cigarettes and lighter. As he touched flame to tobacco, he watched Cheryl's thin shoulders, the line of her cheek against the sun-bright drapes. "Carl isn't for you," he said.

Cheryl turned in the small wooden chair to face him squarely, the light at her back. "I haven't changed my mind, Bill."

"But you've thought about it."

"I've never really reconsidered . . ."

Peterson shook his head. "You must have. The very fact that you've thought about the matter means you're not sure."

"It means I've thought about it," Cheryl said simply, "as I promised you I would."

"If you've thought about it objectively," Peterson said, "you know Carl isn't for you—not on a permanent basis."

Peterson felt a dark frustration as he saw Cheryl's face assume its now-familiar dispassionate mask, this time the smiling variation that revealed nothing.

"Not much in this world is on a permanent basis, Bill." She sat very still against the light, as if solidified by the truth of her statement.

"But some things are certain," Peterson said firmly, "and one certain thing is that Melanie will be harmed by what you're proposing."

"Maybe not in the long run—maybe it will be just the opposite. I'm as concerned as you are with Melanie's welfare, but she wouldn't be the first child of divorced parents."

"But damn it, I'm her father! Me!" Peterson stood up from the bed. He was getting excited, and he didn't want that. "You just don't seem to realize the seriousness of what you're considering," he said in a softer but vibrant voice. "I don't want Melanie to suffer."

"I don't want anyone to suffer," Cheryl said, "either her or you. This isn't easy for me."

"And it isn't right for you."

"That's for me to decide."

"But you can't decide, can you? Not for sure."

Uncertainty shattered the mask of her set features. "What you're doing to me . . ." she began, but the doorknob rattled and she broke off.

Melanie rushed through the opened door, dropping her fiberglass fishing rod outside with a clatter. Her chest was heaving and her thick glasses magnified the fright in her eyes.

"Did you run here all the way from the lake?" Cheryl asked.

Melanie nodded, more frightened than breathless from running. "I was fishing and I heard something. . . ."

"Heard what?" Peterson asked, moving next to her and resting his hand on her shoulder. He didn't know if the heartbeat he felt was Melanie's or his own pulse.

Melanie looked up at him. "I heard some splashing, real near me, then a—" She made a low, gravelly, moaning sound from deep in her throat.

Cheryl's face was older now, creased with concern. "The stories in the papers, Bill . . ."

"That's ridiculous!" Peterson snapped. He bent and patted Melanie's back, pressed her to him for a second. "You probably heard a fish or frog jumping," he said gently, "or some quirk of the wind."

"But I did hear something!"

"Nature is never quiet, Melanie. There are always things to hear if you'll listen."

"Maybe you ought to listen to Melanie," Cheryl said.

"I'm telling her there isn't any reason to be afraid," Peterson said, "and there isn't. But if it'll make you feel better," he said, stooping to talk to his daughter, "we'll go to some other part of the lake. I know a place where they're supposed to be biting on any kind of bait."

"Is it close?"

"No, pretty far."

"Good." Melanie had calmed down now. She raised the tail of her cotton shirt to wipe the perspiration from her forehead and eyes while Peterson held her glasses. He kissed her on the cheek and she smiled. It made him feel proud and useful to be able to erase her fears with his reassurances.

"Why don't we go out and get some breakfast first," Peterson said, glancing up at Cheryl.

"Pancakes?" Melanie asked.

"Pancakes it is," Peterson said. "But definitely fish for supper!"

He was glad to hear Melanie laugh, gladder still to receive the hint of a smile from Cheryl.

When they'd finished breakfast the Petersons returned to the motel to change clothes and get their fishing equipment. Then they drove down a rutted, tree-lined road to the boat dock where their flat-bottomed aluminum rental boat was tied.

After loading the boat Peterson cautioned Melanie to stay seated, unknotted the docking rope and pushed away from the worn-out automobile tires lashed as buffers to the wooden dock. He started the outboard motor, adjusted the throttle and steered the boat out into the lake, then headed south parallel to the increasingly rugged shoreline. The lake was relatively calm today, a blue-green reflective plane of wavering, distorted images. Formless clouds drifted overhead casting vast indistinct shadows.

The motor wasn't very powerful, but the flat-prowed boat managed surprising speed, the small waves spanking the aluminum bottom with metallic slapping sounds.

Melanie was in the bow, slumped forward so she could drag her hand through the cool water. Cheryl sat in the middle of the boat, facing backward, toward Peterson. She was smiling. The breeze carried cool flecks of water against Peterson's face as the flat bow struck the low waves, and everything seemed fine.

When they had traveled south for about twenty minutes, Peterson cut back on the throttle and steered in closer to the bank. The trees grew down to the water here, some of their trunks partly submerged and moss-coated. Thick growths of tall reeds covered much of the lake in near the bank, and green algae lay thick on the calm surface. The forest had a dense, almost tropical look, deeply shadowed, as if the darkest of nights lay just inside the line of trees.

Peterson steered out farther onto the lake, cutting the motor. The boat drifted in abrupt silence as he opened his large and many-compartmented tackle box and sorted through his array of equipment. He baited both Cheryl's and Melanie's hooks, then his own, and he cautioned against dropping anything or striking any part of the metal boat body, thereby drawing attention to their presence as the vibrations traveled down and out through the lake water.

They sat quietly then and fished. Peterson reached into the portable cooler, drew out a cold can of beer and sat sipping it as he felt the rising heat of the sun reflect off the metal boat. Occasionally he passed the cold can to Cheryl, who didn't divert her eyes from the water as she sipped. She'd always been patient in her fishing.

An hour passed. Cheryl and Melanie had gotten a few nibbles, but only Peterson had caught anything, a small rainbow-hued sunfish worthy only of being tossed back into the lake. Melanie was beginning to squirm on the metal bench seat as she became bored. Just when she suggested finding another spot, her bright red-and-white cork bobbed violently—but she didn't notice.

Peterson and Cheryl agreed to Melanie's idea, and the three of them drew in their lines. Their movements caused the boat to rock and the sun-heated aluminum to creak.

After handing his half-full beer can to Cheryl, Peterson adjusted the throttle and yanked the starter cord on the outboard motor.

The motor coughed twice, didn't start.

Peterson tried again, yanking the cord harder, with the same result. He unscrewed the gas cap, saw that the tank was almost full. Bracing his left foot against the boat's stern, he yanked with all his strength on the starter cord and the motor sputtered its way to life.

The stern dropped as he steered in a semicircle to head farther south, keeping roughly the same distance from the bank. Peterson accepted the cold beer can from Cheryl and sipped on it, spilling some of the beer down his shirt front as the boat dipped and bucked on the lake surface. The cool liquid and the breeze of motion made Peterson realize how warm the sun had become; soon it would be too hot to fish from the metal boat.

Then he saw what he'd been looking for. A thick finger of land, overgrown with trees, extended about a hundred yards out from the bank. He pointed the raised bow of the boat toward the jutting land and yelled to Melanie over the snarl of the motor.

"We'll let you out there for about an hour—see if you can show us up and catch more fish."

She blinked behind her thick glasses and grinned acceptance of the challenge.

Peterson worked the boat in close to the bank, then tested the depth of the water with an oar. Carrying her fishing rod and the can of bait, Melanie waded to shore, glancing back as she leaned into water well above her knees.

"Be careful," Cheryl called to her. "Fish right here and don't stray!"

Melanie nodded and waved to them with the bait can as Peterson turned the bow back out toward the lake.

Peterson knew this might be his last opportunity to talk calmly and rationally with Cheryl, without interruption. When he got well off the bank he cut the motor, letting the boat bob in the warm silence. Cheryl knew what he wanted, didn't bother to put her line in the water.

As they talked the boat drifted, beyond the point of ground jutting into the lake, out of sight beyond the deep-shadowed line of trees that seemed to lean into each other as if whispering green secrets. Peterson and Cheryl were heedless of where they were as they leaned like the trees toward one another.

Above the line of trees a large, solitary crow rose in the thick air, flapping its black wings awkwardly as if sending dark signals.

TWENTY-FOUR

"Another'n!" old Bonifield shouted to Wintone.

Bonifield was trailing Frank Turper as they crossed the street to intercept Wintone, Turper with his head bowed and a sad, thoughtful cast to his small, dark eyes. Wintone stood with his arms crossed, waiting for the two men and feeling the dread settle into him, hoping he'd misunderstood what Bonifield had shouted.

They were both out of breath when they reached Wintone. Turper had been almost running ahead of Bonifield. There was dark spittle on Bonifield's unshaven chin.

"You wasn't in your office," Turper said, breathing deeply and standing hands-on-hips. "Got a phone call sayin' to find you, tell you there's been another Bonegrinder killin' . . ."

"Out past Lynn Cove," Bonifield added. Muscles danced along his lean jaw as he worked his tobacco. "You best hurry."

"Who did the phoning?" Wintone asked Turper.

"Somebody from the boat dock, didn't leave no name. Just said nobody answered the phone in the sheriff's office an' to find you an' send you. Said Bonegrinder had killed another."

Across the street stood two men watching the obviously excited conversation. Wintone recognized the paunchy form and lumpy features of McKenna, the reporter from the *Globe Dispatch*. It came as no surprise to Wintone when he saw McKenna and the other man step into the street and walk toward them.

"That all the man on the phone said?" Wintone asked. "Nothin' else?"

Turper shook his head quickly. "Nothin' else."

Bonifield spat. "You best hurry."

"Hurry is what I'll do," Wintone said, starting to jog back to where the patrol car was parked. When he'd gone a few steps he stopped and turned. "See if you can keep this quiet for a while . . ."

But old Bonifield was already running with his quick-limping gait toward McKenna and the other man, who was wearing a brown business suit and carrying a camera.

As he drove over the lake road, Wintone kept a close watch on his rear-view mirror. Occasionally, through the plume of dust behind the patrol car, he glimpsed the grill and hood of a big light blue or gray car following him closely. The car followed him beyond Lynn Cove. Then Wintone ignored it, concentrating completely on the road ahead.

A sun-darkened man in a sleeveless white T-shirt was waiting for him on the road shoulder, waving his arms and moving out toward the center of the road. Wintone braked the patrol car beside him, rolling down the window while the car was still rocking in the dust that drifted to catch up with it.

"'Round that bend, Sheriff," the man said, "then you'll have to walk."

Wintone drove forward a hundred feet and took the bend

in the road slowly, stopping among several parked cars. He noticed the Greers' white Volkswagen, one of its doors hanging open like a mouth gaped in surprise. As Wintone got out of the patrol car, he saw the big blue-gray car, a late-model Oldsmobile, parked behind him. McKenna was behind the steering wheel, and beside him in the front seat were the brown-suited man and Bonifield.

"I'm the one that phoned," the man in the sleeveless T-shirt said. "Down this way, Sheriff." Without looking back he moved off through high weeds toward the lake.

There were over a dozen people gathered on the bank, most of them wearing that expression common to scenes of violent death, a combination of pity, revulsion and fear. But Wintone saw no body. A green metal Jon boat was grounded at an angle in the shallows off the bank, a rope dangling from its flat bow.

Then Wintone saw the man standing off to the side. The others stole quick glances at him, as if they were embarrassed by his presence. He was leaning against a thick tree trunk, his arms thrown about his head to hide his face. There was mud on his shoes and pants legs, and he was wet but for splotches of dryness from the sun. The disheveled, dark hair that showed on the back of his head was wet, individual droplets glistening with jewel brightness.

"He's the one you want to talk to, Sheriff." Alan Greer had spoken. He was standing to Wintone's left with his camera in his hand, the empty leather case slung about his neck.

Wintone nodded and walked over to the man beneath the tree, placed a hand on his shoulder and felt spasms of weeping play beneath his fingertips. The man's back expanded as he breathed in to gain control of himself and stood up straight with his arms limp at his sides.

"Melanie?" he said, his eyes darting.

Wintone withdrew his hand and stepped back.

"She's okay," someone said from the group of people that had moved with Wintone toward the man. "She's over here."

Turning, Wintone saw an older woman comforting a girl of about ten who appeared to be in shock.

"Best if you went and phoned Doc Amis," Wintone said to the man in the sleeveless white T-shirt. Then he turned to the man who'd been supporting himself against the tree, a medium-height, regular-featured man in his late thirties, eyes red-swollen and moist in his fleshed-out but still handsome face. "Melanie your daughter?" Wintone asked.

The man nodded.

"She'll be taken care of," Wintone said. "What's your name?"

"Peterson . . . Bill Peterson."

"What happened, Mr. Peterson?"

The man's eyes widened but seemed to focus on nothing. "My wife . . . it killed Cheryl . . ."

"What killed her, Mr. Peterson?"

"Bonegrinder, is what." Old Bonifield spoke out from where he was standing next to McKenna.

"Work hard at bein' quiet," Wintone advised him.

"We were out there, in the boat," Peterson said, pointing toward a distant part of the lake.

"The three of you?"

Peterson shook his head. "Just Cheryl and I; thank God we'd let Melanie out on the bank to fish. We were just drifting, talking, when we heard a sound, like someone swishing their arm through the water . . . Then something surfaced next to the boat, on Cheryl's side . . ."

"Somethin' like what?"

Pressing his right fist into his thigh, Peterson seemed to seek adequate words, find none. He spoke anyway, haltingly, in a hoarse whisper. "It was dark-colored . . . with a long neck, but thick . . . more like a lizard than a man . . . but somehow like a man only bigger. Cheryl screamed and hit at it with an oar, and something like a clawed flipper came up out of the water and slashed her arm and shoulder. Then she was gone . . . just gone without another sound over the side of the boat . . . and the lake was quiet again . . ."

"What did you do then?" Wintone asked.

"I called for her, waited for her to surface. But she never did. I started the boat's motor and got out of there. I should have dived in after her . . . I should have done that."

"No, Mr. Peterson, not many would've."

The older woman was slowly walking the young girl up the rise away from the bank, to wait for Doc Amis by the road. Wintone watched them till they disappeared among the trees, then he turned and looked out at the lake, at the fraction of it that was its surface. Almost touchable silver ripples of sunlight glimmered there as if projected from below. These things couldn't happen, didn't happen. Yet people were dead and an explanation of sorts was demanded.

"It shouldn't have happened," a sobbing Peterson said helplessly. "We hadn't been getting along . . . we were going to separate. Then this morning we decided to try to make things work out. It's as if certain things aren't meant to be . . ." He began to beat at the unyielding tree trunk with the flat of his hand, his eyes clenched shut. Wintone caught his right arm on the backswing, held it near the shoulder. Another man stepped forward and gently took Peterson's other arm and they moved him away from the tree, held him until his body stopped quaking and he was breathing evenly. His strength had left him.

"C'mon away from here an' we'll talk," Wintone told him.

"Mr. Peterson," McKenna said, "who saw Bonegrinder first, you or your wife?"

Peterson appeared surprised, a man roused from a dream. "Why, both of us at the same time, I guess . . ."

The man in the brown suit had been taking photographs;

he was turning a knob on his camera while staring at Peterson. The camera made a soft, ratchety sound.

"Did either of you say anything when you saw it?" McKenna asked.

"She screamed," Peterson said. "Cheryl screamed. But it made noise when it broke the water and we both saw it."

"Enough now," Wintone said. He gripped Peterson's elbow and guided him away from the bank.

"Mr. Peterson!" McKenna said again, but Peterson didn't answer.

Wintone had Doc Amis drive Melanie into Colver, so Peterson could be questioned in the patrol car without the girl being present. As Wintone pulled out onto the road and accelerated, he passed Holt's canvas-topped Jeep going the other way, saw Sarah sitting in the passenger's seat. No doubt Holt would fall in behind the other cars trailing the patrol car back to town.

Wintone didn't press Peterson during the drive into Colver; there was little point. Peterson repeated exactly the short and incredible horror story he'd told at the lake. Then he sat with his head bowed, his body limp, and seemed to lapse into a sad withdrawal where he could be alone with his grief. His damp and muddy clothes gave off the sharp scent of the lake.

After parking the patrol car behind Doc Amis's, Wintone led Peterson in through a rear door. A minute later Sarah came in the front way, looked at Wintone briefly, then went to tend to the girl. The sheriff left Peterson with Doc Amis, after making sure the grieving widower knew Wintone wanted to talk with him later.

"What now, Sheriff?" old Bonifield asked, as Wintone was trudging back to the patrol car.

Wintone didn't answer, but caught himself wondering if there was some way he could arrest Bonifield.

"Mr. Bonifield asked a fair enough question," McKenna

said, leaning against the sun-warmed dusty fender of the patrol car.

Wintone knew the reporter was right. He stood and backhanded the perspiration from his forehead and eyebrows. "Now we search for the body," he said. "And I examine the boat."

There was no shortage of body-searchers, but Wintone was left alone with the metal Jon boat. He worked his legs into his black rubber wading boots, then moved slowly through the still water to where he could grasp the half-inch rope that lay snaked from the boat's bow.

Empty, the light, flat-bottomed boat drew very little water, and Wintone towed it up onto the sloping bank easily, feeling the metal bottom skim soft submerged mud. Stenciled in black on the side of the boat was the name of a rental dock located farther north on the lake.

The boat's metal was almost too hot to touch from time spent in the sun. There was a large, light gray tackle box beneath the middle bench seat, one oar lying in the inch or so of water that sloshed in the bottom, two fishing poles and a fiberglass rod and reel, its line baited with a yellow-feathered lure. In the stern of the boat was a Styrofoam cooler containing a few unopened cans of beer resting in the still-cool water of melted ice.

Wintone examined the painted surface of the boat. There were the usual nicks and scratches, but none of them appeared fresh. The inside of the large tackle box revealed only the wide assortment of lures and fishing equipment that might be the property of any avid fisherman.

After carrying the contents of the boat to the patrol car, Wintone loaded them into the trunk to be returned to Bill Peterson. Then he walked back down to the lake, stood away from the bank so he could be in the shade, and looked across the blue-green water to where Peterson had said the thing had surfaced and attacked.

There were three boats out there now, moving in slow circles and dragging the depths with grappling hooks. They weren't being too methodical, but Wintone didn't know if the men in the boats were afraid or overeager. Even from this distance he could see the rifles in their arms, the tenseness of their bodies. As if to mock their search for Cheryl Peterson's remains, a light, directionless breeze played over the lake, momentarily rippling the bright water as if to reveal the darkness below.

Winton turned away from the lake and walked through ankle-clutching weeds to the patrol car. After returning to Colver and phoning the rental dock to tell them where they could recover their boat, Wintone joined the search for Cheryl Peterson's body.

She hadn't been found when darkness fell, nor had she when darkness fell the next night. Wintone suspected then that the body wouldn't turn up for some time, if at all. Either it was still on the dark lake bottom or had drifted to some reed-grown or brush-secluded spot near the bank. The less responsible newspapers were discussing the obvious, more gruesome possibilities. Wintone wondered if Mayor Boemer and some of the others regretted now all the publicity they'd sought for Colver.

Peterson had become the focal point of the press. He was cooperative at first, repeating his brief story so they could embellish it and speculate on it. But as the endless stream of questions became more personal and probing, the strain on Peterson began to show. Wintone heard that there had been arguments and antagonism, and that now Peterson was trying to avoid the press.

At the end of the week, when he came out of the afternoon heat into Wintone's office, tne strain of his predicament seemed to have drawn Peterson's face thinner, etching deep lines about the corners of his mouth. He tried a smile as he nodded to hello to Wintone, then moved halfway between the door and the sheriff's desk. His hands were unsteady and he slipped them into his pants pockets with exaggerated casualness.

"Do you think she'll ever be found, Sheriff?" he asked.

Wintone sat rolling a pencil nimbly between his thick fingers. "If she's not, Mr. Peterson, it won't be due to a scarcity of people lookin'."

Peterson nodded, as if to demonstrate that he had no complaint about how the search was being conducted. "She has to be found, Sheriff. I couldn't bear to know . . . to keep thinking about her . . . still out there. If you're not a married man, maybe you can't understand . . ."

"I understand, Mr. Peterson."

"This has become an ordeal." Peterson moved to the side with a puppetlike gracelessness, as if suddenly weary of standing, and sat in one of the cushioned hickory chairs. "I sent Melanie back to Saint Louis, to stay with her grandparents for a while."

"Seems best."

"It was the press," Peterson said. "They even badgered *her*. You wouldn't believe the questions they asked her, a ten-year-old girl who'd just lost her mother."

"I know how they can be," Wintone said.

"There's one named McKenna, from Saint Louis. I think because we're from the same city he feels he has some kind of claim on me. He's relentless."

"That seems to be the biggest part of bein' a newspaperman. I know Mr. McKenna."

"Then maybe you could suggest to him that he be a little less persistent. It doesn't matter so much for myself, and I know that in his mind he's only doing his job. But some of the questions he put to Melanie upset her. She's been having nightmares as it is, crying half the night. Doctor Amis said it would be a good idea to get her away from here; that's why I sent her back to Saint Louis."

"I'll talk to McKenna, but I can tell you it'll help no more'n water on a grease fire. He's of a breed."

"I'd leave here myself but for Cheryl," Peterson said. "I can't go until she's found."

Wintone nodded, understanding.

"I've rented a cabin at Higgins' Motel, and I intend staying here as long as I have to. I plan to isolate myself from the press as much as I can, so you'll be able to find me at the cabin almost anytime, in case there are any developments." Peterson stood up from the chair, supporting himself on the high wood back.

"Mr. Peterson," Wintone said, leaning back in his swivel chair, "I don't want to make noises like the press, but are you sure about what you saw on the lake that day?"

Peterson smiled a humorless, tired smile.

"Not now," he said, "but I was sure when I saw it."

TWENTY-FIVE

The next day brought a cooling wind carrying flecks of rain. Low gray clouds scudded in reaching forms across an even grayer sky that was lighted from time to time by silent lightning.

Returning from a late breakfast, Wintone glanced up at a sky pregnant with dark promise as he faced into the wind to cross the street. It seemed a cleansing wind, though it raised high clouds of dust which he hoped would be drummed back to earth by the rain. The material of Wintone's tan uniform pressed cool and pleasant against the front of his body, and he was sure that today, any second, it would rain the hard, proper rain that was needed.

"Gonna come a'shower!" Rufe Davis shouted from where he was hurrying to move his outside display of merchandise into his store.

Wintone waved to him and smiled agreement. It was good to think of the rain falling in a steady tattoo on the thirsted crops, pattering and working its way down into the dark, rich earth, striking the top green leaves of the trees thick on the hills, and eventually trickling down through the drought-parched woods. The lake's wide surface would shimmer innocently in windblown patterns of falling rain. Wintone hoped that some senseless passions would be cooled—perhaps Colver's drab dustiness would be washed away, taking with it the ominous mood that pervaded the area.

The blare of a horn startled Wintone as Craig Holt's Jeep passed him, then pulled to the curb in front of him. As Wintone moved toward the Jeep he could see the rhythmic vibrations of the idling engine run through the taut canvas top.

"We'll get rain if it doesn't blow over," Holt said when Wintone was beside the driver's side of the Jeep. "Anything new on the Peterson woman?"

"Somebody found a torn blue blouse half a mile south of Lynn Cove. Peterson said his wife was wearin' a blue blouse an' white slacks when she was pulled from the boat."

Holt leaned forward, interested, and peered harder at Wintone. "Has Peterson identified the blouse?"

"Hasn't seen it. I was gonna drive out an' show it to him this mornin'."

"Get in if you want—I'll be glad to drive you."

Wintone saw no reason not to accept the offer. He walked around to the other side of the Jeep and climbed in. Holt worked the gears, let out the clutch and the Jeep shot forward.

Holt drove fast, with seeming expertise. They stopped by the sheriff's office to get the tattered blue blouse, then rattled out of Colver, bouncing over the lake road toward Higgins' Motel. Wintone kept waiting for raindrops to speck the windshield, but the glass remained clear. The woods seemed very dark and still in the close morning air. To his right Wintone occasionally glimpsed the green-gray expanse of the lake, motionless and leadlike, through the trees.

"Sarah still talks highly of you," Holt said suddenly.

Wintone didn't know what to say to that, said nothing.

"Highly and often," Holt got his pipe from his pocket and clenched it in his teeth, made no attempt to light it.

"No doin' of mine," Wintone said.

"Oh, I suppose not."

Wintone was beginning to feel an unreasonable dislike for Holt, which he tried to ignore. He reached around to the rear of the Jeep and got the torn blue blouse, still damp with lake water. Two of the white oval buttons were missing, there was a rip from just below the rear of the collar to the hemmed blouse tail, and one of the short sleeves was half-torn from the shoulder seam. The label was simply lettered STYLE SHOPPE, and there were no other markings. The blouse showed no signs of blood, but after all this time the lake water might have taken care of that. If Peterson identified the blouse, there would be lab tests.

"You'll have to admit it now, Sheriff," Holt said, glancing for a moment from road to blouse.

Wintone turned to look at him. "Admit what?"

"That there's something out there in the lake, something unique and deadly."

"I wouldn't state that as fact without hard evidence," Wintone said. "I'm surprised that you would."

"Hard evidence? . . . . I'll have to say there's an absence of that, but circumstantial evidence, the three deaths, the unidentified track, the eyewitness accounts—circumstantial evidence couldn't be stronger. And this is a region where such a thing is possible, maybe one of only a few such regions in the country. We are surrounded by a deceptively beautiful primal wilderness, something you might take for granted. Superstition is a way of life here. These people forecast the weather by interpreting the chirping of crickets or the lay of an animal's coat. They watch for a death when a hen flies in the house through an open window. They witch for water with dousing rods made from cherry boughs."

"Superstitious, maybe," Wintone said, "but we're practical folk as well. If a man believes he can witch for water it's 'cause he's seen it done. I'll believe in Bonegrinder when I see him."

"You've seen what he's done," Holt said around his pipe stem.

"I've seen what somethin's done."

Holt chuckled and shook his head, as if amused and exasperated by Wintone's inability to grasp the truth.

"The most superstitious man I ever met," Wintone said, "was a stock market speculator from New York City. He never bought a stock when the barometer was falling, but he'd probably laugh at the idea of witchin' for water."

"Point taken," Holt said, bouncing in his seat and gripping the wheel with both hands for a particularly rough stretch of road. "Whether he has substance or not, Bonegrinder is real in the minds of a lot of people. For my purpose, in a sense it doesn't actually matter if he doesn't exist."

"In a sense."

"I've been out in a boat with my depth sounder," Holt said. "The lake bottom around here is unusual, irregular and pitted with narrow, deep holes."

"This is cave country," Wintone said. "There's caves here that's never been discovered. It don't surprise me that the lake bottom's like you say."

"Tell me, Sheriff, why would it surprise you if something alive and unusual existed in the lake?"

The directness of the question threw Wintone. "I suppose 'cause nothin' existed there before."

Holt chuckled and shook his head again, removed his pipe from his mouth and held it by the stem against the steering wheel. "Four hundred years ago people thought they knew all there was to know. Then somebody discovered that the earth revolved around the sun. It took a long time for people to believe him, but all that time the earth kept revolving around the sun."

The Jeep took a banked curve and began to climb, the road stretching narrow and dusty ahead like a tenuous intrusion into brooding green density. Wintone thought about the shadowed depths of the lake, and the depths beyond.

"Meanin' somethin' might have been in this part of the lake for years."

"And years and years. This is wild, almost virgin country, Sheriff."

"To outsiders," Wintone said. "I was raised here an' my father an' his before him, an' on back farther'n I know. I don't say there is or isn't somethin' in the lake; I will say a lot goes on in these parts nobody's ever understood, an' maybe never will."

Holt again clamped his pipe stem between his teeth and drove silently, as if considering Wintone's words.

When they reached Higgins' Motel, Holt made a sharp turn onto the gravel parking area and braked the Jeep in front of Peterson's cabin. Wintone folded the blouse in some semblance of neatness, got out of the Jeep and walked to the door with Holt.

They didn't have to knock; Peterson had seen them drive up. He swung back the door as they approached, invited them inside.

Peterson looked tired, anxious. He was in his stockinged feet, wearing dark slacks and a striped green shirt that were as wrinkled as the blouse Wintone held. The cabin's window air conditioner was off and the one screened window was open to the breeze, making the inside of the cabin naturally airy and comfortable.

Wintone introduced Holt to Peterson, but Holt smiled and said they'd already met when he'd interviewed Peterson jus after the tragedy. Peterson kept his eyes trained on Wintone.

"You've found something?" he asked.

"Only this," Wintone said, holding out the tattered blouse. "It was found on the bank not far from where you'd been fishin'. Can you identify it as your wife's?"

Peterson shook his head. "The color's too light . . . unless the sun faded it." He held the blouse up, shook his head no again, more firmly. "It's not Cheryl's. It's too small, and the collar's not the same." He wadded the blouse in his hand and hefted the damp mass casually before handing it back to Wintone, as if the blouse had suddenly lost some power it had held over him.

Wintone wasn't greatly disappointed. The blouse might have drifted for some distance before reaching the bank. He glanced around the cabin. "The press bothered you much here?"

"Not lately," Peterson said. "They've wrung me dry and they know it." He looked with a trace of embarrassment at Holt. "Mr. Holt here was one of the few exceptions who was considerate."

"I'm not exactly press," Holt said smoothly but too quickly. He seemed to have been miffed. "I hope my academic and government affiliations place me at a loftier level."

"Speakin' of press," Wintone said to Peterson, "I never got a chance to talk to McKenna for you."

Peterson waved a hand limply. "No difference. McKenna really was no worse than the rest of them. . . . I was just more upset than usual that day."

"Understandable," Holt said, as if realizing his previous pettiness and trying to temper it with simple concern.

Wintone moved to the door, and Holt followed as if reluctant to leave.

"Is there anything at all I can do to help in the search?" Peterson asked Wintone.

" 'Fraid not, Mr. Peterson, unless you remember somethin'

else that might be useful. One more searcher more or less out there wouldn't make much difference."

"And the press would descend on you again," Holt said sympathetically.

Peterson pressed his palms to his face and slid them downward in a slow wiping motion, as if seeking to change his identity. "You're right," he said, breathing out loudly. "I just wish something would happen."

"Some advice," Wintone said to him softly. "Somethin' might never happen . . . you best allow for that."

Peterson started to answer, swallowed and nodded instead as he let Wintone and Holt out. He shut the door after them quickly, as if the visit had been an ordeal to end with the click of the latch.

As he walked across the gravel back to Holt's Jeep, Wintone was dismayed to notice that the sun was out bright and hot, and the clouds that had promised rain were broken and blown from the area.

Holt squinted up at the marbled blue sky. "Not today," he said philosophically. "But without any rain, I'll be able to get some work done."

He reached into his pocket for his key ring, then pulled himself up into the Jeep for the drive back to Colver.

Another week passed, and still Cheryl Peterson's body hadn't been recovered. The search continued but on a much reduced scale. And those doing the searching were seeking Bonegrinder for Howe's reward as much as they were searching for Cheryl Peterson.

But for a brief late-night shower, the drought held, and the Colver area was caught in a lethargy of fear and dust. If no rain fell, profits did.

"There's talk goin' around," old Bonifield said to Wintone one night in Mully's, "that somethin's gotta be done about Bonegrinder."

Wintone regarded his beer. "The talk say what?"

"It says who," Bonifield snapped back. "Looks to most folks around here like you're the one to figure out the what an' how of it."

"Maybe," Wintone told him. "I'm open for suggestions—you got any?"

"Ain't my job," Bonifield said, wiping beer from his gray-grizzled chin. "I just thought you oughta know there's talk goin' around."

"I can figure the roots of that talk."

Frank Turper leaned over the bar so he could see around Bonifield. "The roots of the thing is you're sheriff an' have a responsibility to do somethin'."

"I ain't one fer repeatin' it," Bonifield said, "but there's some sayin' you're afraid."

"Some ain't sayin' it to me."

"Myself," Bonifield said, "I figure you just don't know which way to step."

"I know where I'd like to step."

Mully moved down the other side of the bar toward Wintone. "Don't get het up, Billy."

"It ain't like we don't know you got your own problems," Turper said. "Maybe that's what's makin' you indecisive."

"What's makin' me indecisive," Wintone said, "is I don't know what to decide. An' I can't think of anybody who does know."

"You're missin' the point," Frank Turper said. "Somebody's gotta decide, Billy! You're sheriff. That somebody's you."

"Another point," old Bonifield said, "is if you don't do nothin' as sheriff, Mayor Boemer is forced to act."

"He's been actin' for years," Wintone said, taking a long pull of his beer. "An' what you just said is surely the official line of bullshit."

"Could be," Bonifield said. "Ain't none of my business."

Wintone finished his beer in a hurry and left Mully's. As he walked the dark street toward his office, he looked up at the star-scattered sky, losing some of his anger in the vastness.

He knew that Baily Howe and Mayor Boemer were behind the talk of fear and indecision, trying to lay the groundwork for his dismissal. Boemer would have feared to take any such action alone. With Wintone out of office the frenzied and dangerous search for Bonegrinder could resume, and the newspaper and TV people could be told anything.

"Makin' your evenin' rounds, Billy?"

Sarah's voice.

He turned and she was at the corner behind him, walking toward him. She was wearing denim slacks and a short-sleeved pullover blouse, dark blue or black; Wintone couldn't tell which in the dimness.

"Late to be walkin', Sarah. How come you're not with Craig Holt?"

She smiled. "Didn't know there was a law said I had to be."

"If there was, I wouldn't enforce it." He was unaccountably self-conscious, embarrassed by their clumsy fencing, as if they were teen-agers again. They were bound by time, special to each other despite themselves.

"Where were you headed?" Sarah asked.

"Back to the office to bed down." The night brought the lightly perfumed scent of her to Wintone like an offering. He wondered how long it had been since he'd been near her when she was wearing anything but her white nurse's uniform. "Got a few reports to write up," he said. "Ain't no nine-to-five to this job." He stood watching her in the darkness. Her eyes picked up the starlight, gave off a pale and gentle luminosity. He couldn't make out the expression on her face, though, and he couldn't read her eyes. Maybe, he figured, that was just as well.

"Why don't you ask me, Billy?"

"Ask you what, Sarah?" Immediately he wished he hadn't spoken the words, forcing her to tell him, as if to bolster his manhood.

Her voice was guileless, without urgency. "To spend the night with you . . . to heal you where you hurt . . . where you won't heal yourself . . ."

Wintone's big hands were clenched into fists, whitened at the knuckles.

"Etty wouldn't have wanted you an' her both to die . . ."

Wintone spun and struck wildly at the wood wall at his left, retaining enough sense to open his fist an instant before it struck. Pain bit like a thousand teeth into his palm as the shock traveled down his arm.

He hoped the pain wouldn't stop as he walked toward the office, toward the desk-corner portrait of Etty, Sarah at his side.

TWENTY-SIX

Baily Howe stood at his wide window overlooking the valley, watching the sunrise as if it were occurring for his personal inspection. A low-lying incandescent haze was visible now on the horizon, but Howe knew it would soon be burned off by the sun, devoured by scorching rays to leave an unblemished sky like the inside of a finely glazed blue bowl to reflect the heat.

Howe lowered his gaze to the valley. He stood with his hands clasped behind him, peering down at the sloping carpet of distant green treetops. To his extreme right he could see a narrow blue cove of Big Water Lake.

Despite Sheriff Wintone there still were searchers down there, Howe was sure. He narrowed his eyes as if he could see them below, teeming like social insects obeying a directive of instinct. They were that, really, and the instinct was greed. He had pressed the correct button, and they had responded. If only there were more of them . . .

Howe took a last look at the brightening sky, turned away from the window and walked to the brown leather sofa. He sat down, stretched out his legs and methodically lighted a slender, greenish brown cigar.

It was simply a matter of receiving credit. This time Howe had been clever enough to arrange it so that he alone would come out on top. No matter who found Bonegrinder, it would be at Howe's direction—he would possess the monster. Unless whoever it was might be fool enough to refuse a quick, sure ten thousand dollars.

Howe drew on his cigar and frowned. In a fashion, Sheriff Wintone had refused the reward. At least he said he would refuse if the money were offered under the table. The sheriff was that most dangerous of men: a simple, idealistic fool. Men like that were constantly getting in the way.

A movement outside the window caught Howe's attention, and he turned his head to see several large, black crows flapping past outside almost at eye level. He had often sat out on the balcony and brought such crows down with a shotgun. But there was really little sport in it. The crow, that wiliest and most gun-wise of birds at lower altitudes, was simple to kill at this level, where it presumed itself safe.

As with crows, so with men.

Howe got up, carried ashtray and smoldering cigar to the small telephone table. He dialed and stood patiently with the receiver at his ear. After several rings Sheriff Wintone answered.

Howe noticed that the sheriff's voice was rather thick and slow, the voice of a man recently awakened and still tired. All to the better, Howe thought. "Sheriff, this is Baily Howe."

A pause. "Mornin', Mr. Howe."

"I'm calling in regard to the Bonegrinder matter."

"I figured."

"I was hoping you'd had time to think things through, perhaps see the magnitude of what you're hindering. When you left here, I was sure that you'd eventually have the insight to realize that the solution to the Bonegrinder mystery might be the most important thing that has ever touched our lives."

"What are you askin', Mr. Howe?"

"That you stop intimidating the people who want to find Bonegrinder. You're making the entire operation extremely difficult."

"I'm not intimidatin' anyone, Mr. Howe. I'm only doin' my job an' upholdin' the law."

"There's such a thing as being too inflexible, Sheriff."

"That holds true for everyone."

"Is there any possibility of you changing your mind about the way you're dealing with this situation?"

"None, Mr. Howe. We've already had a man accidentally shot out on the lake."

"I suspected that was what prompted your program of strict, unreasonable enforcement. I don't understand how you can let a single unfortunate accident impede an endeavor of this . . . this possible scientific import."

"I want to keep it to a single accident, Mr. Howe."

"But don't you see—"

"No, Mr. Howe, I don't." Impatience had put an edge on the sheriff's voice.

Howe sighed loudly into the receiver. "All right, Sheriff, I tried. I thought I should try one last time. Since you can't see it from the reasonable perspective, I want you to know I respect your integrity and persistence, however misguided you may be."

"I thank you for that, Mr. Howe."

Was there irony in the sheriff's voice? Howe realized Wintone didn't believe him. The sheriff was a cynical man; Howe had to give him that.

"Have you heard anything on the Peterson woman?" Howe asked.

"Not a sign of her, but we're still looking."

"A tragic thing, that."

"I'm glad you feel that way, Mr. Howe."

"Oh, you needn't think I don't have compassion, Sheriff—it's just that I also recognize priorities."

There was silence on the other end of the line, the sheriff's way of telling Howe that he chose not to argue.

"The law is explicit and that's that," Howe said. "Given the narrow point of view, you're only performing your duty. I can't fault you for that. Good luck, Sheriff."

"Thanks, Mr. Howe."

Again the irony in Wintone's voice. It lingered in Howe's ear as he replaced the receiver.

Howe went into the gun room and got his custom-made Browning twelve-gauge shotgun from the polished cherry-wood cabinet. He fed shells into the magazine, then carried the loaded gun outside to his private shooting range. Humming tonelessly, he loaded the English-made target thrower that automatically flung clay pigeons at irregular intervals and in varying arcs.

Howe took a few shots to reorient himself to the feel of the gun before he began shooting in earnest.

When he had shattered six clay pigeons in a row, he walked back inside and made another phone call.

At noon that day Mayor Boemer phoned Wintone and asked him to walk down to his office above the new souvenir and antique emporium. Wintone wasn't surprised. He knew where he stood, and it wasn't where the mayor could catch him unawares.

Mayor Boemer had Wintone wait while he went through his act of pretending to read something at his desk. Wintone took a chair, noticing that the pale green office had been freshly painted. An American flag had been mounted alongside the state flag on one wall. Wintone sat quietly.

When the mayor became impatient, he set the paper he'd been holding aside, rested his elbows on his desk top with his hands clasped and looked at Wintone. The mayor's white hair was swept straight back and still damp, as if he'd just combed it. "There's been talk," he said.

"That's how things get around," Wintone replied.

"Well, things have been gettin' around that are causin' us a a problem. An' don't pretend you don't understand what I'm sayin'. Folks are demandin' action on this Bonegrinder thing."

"I keep hearin' that," Wintone said, "but when I ask just what action folks are demandin', nobody seems to have any inklin'."

Mayor Boemer dropped his hands out of sight below his desk, leaned back in his chair. "That's 'cause you're supposed to have the answers, Billy. Unreasonable or not, that's the way it is, an' I got no choice but to demand you come up with some answers, take the proper action."

Outside the office window the leaves of a hickory tree broke the pattern of sunlight that shadowed the closed drapes. Silence seemed to fill the room while Wintone sat and waited.

"Understand," the mayor continued in an unsteady voice, "I'm under pressure myself, Billy."

"From Baily Howe?"

"From my constituents. I'm the mayor, an' I got responsibilities . . . just like you got as sheriff. Comes a time a man has to be unbendable."

"A man with Howe as a backer could play politics in this state," Wintone said, "maybe go fairly high."

Boemer's ruddy face clouded over, looking more like rain than the sky had looked for a while. "I won't deny Howe's talked to me, but he's a citizen with a right to demand action. And it's my obligation to demand action from you."

"Strong word, 'demand.'"

"Then let's say I got a suggestion to make to you, one that'll maybe solve both our problems."

Boemer did show promise, Wintone mused. Already he was nimble at passing the buck. The mayor's problem, really, was Wintone.

Boemer struck a firm attitude. "I know you're acquainted with Craig Holt," he said. 'He's not only an expert on folklore, but he's authorized by the government to investigate these goin's on. I think it might be a good idea if you teamed up with him to find Bonegrinder."

"Holt's a writer an' researcher," Wintone said. "What he ain't is any kind of stalker.'

"But he knows his subject; he'd have ideas."

"I've heard some of his ideas."

"Don't you understand, Billy? This way, if you don't find Bonegrinder it's not just you failin', it's the U.S. government."

"The U.S. government is failin' without me. All I've seen Holt do is run around these parts with that portable recorder an' those instruments he takes out on the lake."

"He ain't no fool," Boemer said. "An' he seems to know how to go about gettin' what he wants. He was in town no time an' he had everybody talkin' to him an' was puttin' it to Sarah Ledbetter."

Wintone stood up and paced through the dappled pattern of sunlight on the carpet. "The whole thing sounds like a bad idea. You tell Baily Howe that was my reaction."

Boemer stared at Wintone, his face knotted in frustration. Wintone stopped pacing and looked at him, and the mayor looked away.

"Not long ago it was a pacifyin' statement you wanted from me," Wintone said, "not action."

"We had a different cat to skin then."

"Well, you made your suggestion," Wintone said, and stood to leave the office.

"You think hard on it, Billy," Mayor Boemer said, as the sheriff closed the door.

What Wintone thought about on the walk back to his office was Sarah. He was still trying to sort out the effects of last night. It all clashed in his mind: the guilt, the agony, the pleasure collided and changed things like the accident. Or had it changed anything at all?

His mind caressed the soft memory of Sarah, her body so smooth and pale yet surprising in its warmth. Etty, ghostly but real, had been with them last night, they both knew, and she would always be with them unless Wintone let her go.

When Wintone got back to the office, he pulled the blinds closed and sat heavily in the squeaking swivel chair behind his desk. He didn't regret his words to Mayor Boemer, but he wondered what he would do if he actually did lose his job. Law enforcement was all he'd learned much about in his lifetime. He'd have to stay in the field somewhere.

He might have to leave the area, if Baily Howe and Mayor Boemer got their way. If they weren't thrown some and slowed by Wintone's unwillingness to give ground. Boemer was leery of Wintone's capacity for vengeance and might influence Baily Howe. Howe could help Boemer politically, and help him a lot, but Wintone had the ear of the press and could hurt the mayor by taking a strong stand against him. Any smart man feared an enemy with nothing to lose. And Boemer was smart enough to know that.

Wintone drummed his fingertips almost silently on the smooth, familiar desk top. He wondered what action he could take against Bonegrinder. Spending his days on the lake cradling a high-powered rifle was hardly a solution. An organized search party was out of the question, with Howe's reward-seeking maniacs still prowling the area. And none of the deaths offered any avenue of investigation.

The situation would be simpler, Wintone thought, without people like McKenna and Holt getting in his way. And people like Alan and Kelly Greer for him to worry about.

TWENTY-SEVEN

Kelly Greer padded barefoot across the sun-faded linoleum to the window of the motel cabin. She was wearing nothing but a robe and despite the heat she held it clutched around her body as if the terry cloth were some kind of armor. The green, sun-washed view outside had taken on an ominous aura lately, like a killer's bright smile.

She turned to Alan, who was seated on the bed worrying over an assortment of photography equipment spread out on the white sheet. The sheet was still wrinkled from their lovemaking of the night before, and it seemed almost an insult to Kelly that he should now be using it as an impromptu work table.

"Haven't we been here long enough?" she asked. "You've taken hundreds of pictures."

Alan held up a color filter and examined it, one of his eyes screwed shut. "You frightened?"

"It isn't only that. Probably nothing's going to happen. At

least nothing that anybody understands or can do anything about. Bonegrinder isn't going to be found, and you're not going to be able to photograph whatever it is."

Both eyes open now, Alan smiled at her. "If I were as sure of that as you are, I'd start packing."

Kelly walked over to him, stepped playfully on his bare foot with her own. "I'm spooked, I'll admit it. I don't like to be threatened by what I can't understand."

He put down the filter and looked up at her. He was wearing only a pair of threadbare walking shorts, and insect bites among the coarse red hair on his chest glistened with the thick ointment he'd used to treat them. "Why don't you go back, Kelly, wait for me? I can find somebody driving to Kansas City; you could go with them."

"It's you I'm worried about, and I'd worry more at a distance."

Alan shrugged; he'd known it was useless to ask.

Kelly put her hands in the robe's baggy pockets and stood with her feet apart, as if enjoying the cool smoothness of the linoleum. The cabin was still shaded and fairly cool. The color TV at the foot of the bed was on, silent and unwatched, its picture rolling.

"That poor Peterson woman," Kelly said. "How do you explain it?"

"I can't," Alan said. "That's one reason I'm staying." He swiveled his body and lay down on the clear side of the bed, clasping his hands behind his head on a wadded pillow. "That one got to me a little, especially after I talked to Peterson. You're not the only one who's slightly spooked, but I have to stay and see this out. Especially now."

"Why especially now?"

"Craig Holt," he said. "We've agreed to collaborate on a book. I can't run out on that commitment. Anyway, Holt is no small-fry, and since he's connected with the government it should help sell the project to a publisher. It could be a major break for us."

Kelly dug her hands deeper into the robe's big pockets and shook her head. "Holt is just like you, only he has his tape recorder and instruments."

"He has a curiosity," Alan said, "and a trained mind. His knowledgeable text and my photographs should be the most comprehensive coverage of what's happened here."

"And of what might happen," Kelly said uneasily.

Alan's angled glance found her from half-closed eyes. "I'll tell you what," he said. "We can make this whole thing more tolerable for you. We'll spend more time together, maybe hike out and go on a picnic. You might even wind up having fun."

Kelly sat next to him on the edge of the bed. "I don't want to interfere with your work or be a stone around your neck, Alan."

He grinned, settled his head and knitted hands farther into the pillow. "You said yourself I've got plenty of good shots. I can let up some now, see what happens next. It was what I'd planned to do anyway."

"I'll bet."

"I wouldn't lie."

She bent and kissed his sunburned forehead. "I guess you wouldn't."

He watched her as she rose from the bed. She seemed to notice for the first time that the TV was on and turned it off on her way past. Then she walked again to the window, her figure lending grace to the long robe.

"Maybe we could do something tonight," she said, "drive someplace."

"Sorry, can't tonight. I have to meet with Holt to work out a format."

Kelly nodded but continued to stare out the window.

Alan drew a chest-heaving breath and sighed, as if trying

to throw off a weight. "Don't worry," he said, "it'll work out."

He sat up again, careful not to disturb the equipment on the bed, selected a lens and held it to the light. Kelly appeared in the lens, small and far away. Alan had the feeling that if he shouted loudly at her image, it would slowly turn its head, barely hearing him.

"Why don't we get out of here now?" Alan said, putting down the lens. "Go for a drive."

Kelly smiled at him and said that was a good idea.

Alan laced his dust-streaked white deck shoes and watched her get dressed. She put on a yellow halter and a pair of cutoff jeans, tilted back her head and shook her hair so that it whipped in slow motion against her graceful back. She brushed her long hair hurriedly, and they were ready to leave.

"Don't forget your camera," she said when they were at the door. But he already had it.

The dust-coated white Volkswagen labored up steep and winding hills, gained speed almost joyously on the downgrades. The woods grew close to each side of the dirt road, shading it for long stretches, sometimes joining leafy branches above as if to conceal the road from the sun's eye. The unremitting hammer of the Volkswagen's engine was loud among the crowded trees, changing tone and volume now and then when the road broke from the woods to overlook green valleys or cleared hillsides.

"There is a certain beauty here," Alan said, gearing down the car to take a steep grade. "I can see how if you were born and raised here you wouldn't want to leave."

"Or couldn't leave," Kelly said beside him. "It might be difficult to adapt."

Alan glanced sideways at her and grinned. "I guess that works both ways, city girl."

"Better slow down, Alan."

His grin widened. "Christ, a backseat driver now! This is no Cadillac—I need the speed to take the next hill."

Kelly didn't answer, knew Alan was right—she was too edgy. Opening her vent window and guiding a cooling stream of air onto herself, she scooted down in her seat, rested her head on the backrest, and tried to relax. There was a soothing quality to the greenness rushing past her, enveloping her.

Alan slowed the car as they passed a house near the road, small and covered with faded asphalt sheet-siding poorly disguised as brick. A woman was standing on the wood front porch, striking a broom handle against a post to dislodge feathery-looking dust from the straw bristles. She was wearing a flower-print dress and her blond hair was pulled back and tied with a ribbon. Without changing expression she lifted a hand to wave to them as they drove past. A large gray hound got up from the shade of the porch and trotted after the car for a short distance, then lost interest and turned back.

Kelly turned her head to look at her husband. "Do you know they believe here that if a dog howls clearly three times in the night it's an omen of death?"

"Didn't know," Alan said, concentrating on the road.

"Or if you carry a small potato in your pocket, it's a cure for rheumatism?"

"Might work," Alan said. "I've never seen a rheumatic potato. You've been reading up."

"I've been talking to Craig Holt. He's really a storehouse of information about this region."

"It's his job," Alan said.

"And his passion. Like photography's your passion."

"Is that bad?"

"Not in your case. But in Holt there's something more, something I'm glad I don't see in you. He seems to be driven by the need to stay secure in his superiority. There's a calm relentlessness about him."

"He can feel as superior as he wants," Alan said, "as long as I get my third of the book's advance and royalties for my photographs."

"Did you say a third?"

"I did. And Holt thinks he can get a three-thousand-dollar advance against royalties." Alan averted his eyes from the narrow road for a quick sideways look at his wife. "What's the matter? You look strange."

"I was just thinking, they're very superstitious about the number three around here, especially concerning death."

Alan reached over and patted her bare knee. "You're too sexy to be spooky."

They'd turned a sharp bend and the tires thundered over the uneven planks of a covered bridge. The car broke into sunlight and silence. Below the bridge was a wide, dry creek bed. A gray squirrel ran up the barren slope of the shallow creek, scampering madly among last fall's crisp dead leaves.

"Bonegrinder's claimed three victims," Alan said. "Maybe that means the Peterson woman will be the last. Another victim would be contrary to local superstition."

Kelly's lips parted, but she didn't know how to answer him, didn't know if he was being serious.

"Why don't you ask Craig Holt?" he said, downshifting for a sudden, dipping curve.

Kelly looked away from Alan, out the side window, into the dank and shadowed woods. "I will," she said.

But she knew she wouldn't. She'd keep her concern to herself.

Kelly sensed that Holt was the sort before whom it was unwise to reveal any weakness.

TWENTY-EIGHT

Wintone had never seen Holt in Mully's. If he hadn't happened to glance toward the dim back booths he wouldn't have seen him this time, but there Holt was, seated facing the door and sipping a mug of beer. His pipe and a book of matches lay on the table before him next to a glass ashtray. Wintone nodded to him and took his customary stool midway down the bar.

Old Bonifield was sitting farther along, and beyond him sat a man named Whelan Eberly, a sawmill worker.

Mully set up a beer for Wintone. "Look like rain out there, Billy?"

"I wish. Sun ain't quite down an' you can already see the stars."

Wintone took a first long pull of the cold beer that tingled the back of his throat and slaked the thirst in him. The mug was half-empty when he put it down.

"Talk ain't died down none, Sheriff," Bonifield said from down the bar.

"Wouldn't know," Wintone said, not looking at him.

"Thought you oughta."

Frank Turper came in, waved a hand in greeting and sat on the other side of Wintone. Sweat shone on his padded cheeks, and the back of his collar was damp. "Hell's got nothin' on the weather out there," he said. "Gettin' bad when a man wakes up in the mornin' an' looks forward to evenin' when it'll cool off."

"Mr. Holt here's a educated man," Bonifield said, swiveling on his stool. "Maybe he can tell us when we're gonna get some rain."

"You'd do better to go out and see if there's a halo around the moon," Holt said.

"I checked an' there ain't," Frank Turper said. He turned to Wintone. "What you got figured, Billy?"

"On the weather?"

"On Bonegrinder."

"Stands as it was."

Turper looked at the sheriff with surprised dark eyes, incredulous tiny pits of exasperation in the expanse of his fleshy face. "You best do somethin' soon, Sheriff! By the time the fear lets up around here the business'll be gone for good. From what I been told, there's already hammerin' and sawin' on the north bank. I ain't listenin' to none of this talk about you, but I need results."

"The way to stop loose talk is to deny it," Holt said.

Wintone didn't answer him. He'd wondered what game Holt would choose.

"Folks is sayin' you gone downhill last six, seven months," Bonifield said to Wintone. "I ain't agreein', mind you. But who am I to deny it if'n you don't?"

Wintone snorted. "Nobody's askin' you to deny anything."

"No need to get tight in the jaw. It ain't like you don't need somebody stickin' up for you."

"Not your kinda stickin' up." Wintone finished his beer, ordered another.

"The stories I hear are about your wife's death," Holt said.

Bonifield, who had started to speak, lapsed silent, and Turper bent over his beer. Wintone stared straight ahead as if he hadn't heard, but an almost lifeless stillness settled over him.

"They say it should have been looked into more closely," Holt went on. "They say it was an accident that shouldn't have happened."

"No accident should happen," Mully said, moving down the bar toward Holt. "If you're done with your beer I'll take the bottle."

"But I'm not done. They say if anyone but a law officer had caused the accident he'd have stood trial for manslaughter. At least that's the story I get. And who am I to deny it if the sheriff doesn't?"

"Don't mind him, Billy," Mully said quickly. "He's had four beers an' it's this heat. Time he left."

Wintone barely heard Mully. His throat was dry and his stomach tight. He told himself he didn't care what Holt thought or said, repeating that to himself over and over, and believing it less each time.

"No, I'll be leavin' now," Wintone said, looking down at his somehow remote clenched fist on the bar.

He pushed himself away from the bar with the fist, swiveling on the stool to step down and begin walking toward the door, past Frank Turper still bent over his beer as if he were sitting alone at his own kitchen table. Wintone heard the footsteps behind him on the plank floor.

"They say the accident could have been avoided," Holt said in a slightly slurred voice.

Wintone broke stride. Then, to his own surprise, he almost laughed as he walked on toward the door. Holt was cutting a ridiculous figure, a man trying to work a scene from an old Western movie. The hell of it was that it was effective; the anger was smoldering in Wintone's gut, threatening to ignite.

The footsteps dogged Wintone out into the street, and Holt was suddenly in front of him, facing him. Holt was holding his empty pipe lightly by the bowl, smiling his easy smile, and his eyes were clear. Wintone knew then that Holt wasn't drunk at all; he had perfect control of himself.

"They say you killed her," Holt said softly.

It was the smile Wintone swung at. His fist grazed Holt's cheek and the smile disappeared as the smaller man sprawled in the street, twisted to rise immediately and rush at Wintone. Wintone chopped with his left fist, connecting with hard bone just behind Holt's ear.

"Billy!" Mully's voice called. A door slammed.

Holt was up again, bleeding from where the first blow had struck. He charged Wintone again, but the anger had gone out of the sheriff. He was consciously trying not to hurt Holt now. Wintone stepped aside and was going to grab Holt's wrist, but Holt pivoted and landed a numbing blow to Wintone's shoulder. Wintone raised a forearm defensively that caught Holt across the face, pushed him away. Holt charged again, was pushed away again to fall in the street. His nose was bleeding now, and his pale shirt front was spotted.

He lay there without trying to rise this time, propped on his elbows and looking at Wintone through a mask of congealing blood. Wintone could tell by the expression on Holt's face that Holt had won, that he'd accomplished what he intended. In Sarah's eyes, Wintone would look like a brutal redneck.

Holt contorted his long legs and struggled to get to his feet; someone helped him. He stood staring at Wintone, rocking lightly back onto his heels and cautiously touching his bleeding face as if assessing damage. "I won't press charges, sheriff," he said thickly. "You needn't worry . . ."

Wintone spun, pushed past several of the people gathered at the scene and walked fast toward his office.

He was enraged at himself, and not a little ashamed.

TWENTY-NINE

"He had no excuse to hit the man," Alan said, fastening the zipper on his canvas backpack.

Kelly was sitting on the bed, lacing shoes over thick socks to protect her ankles from burrs and insects. "You can't be sure," she said.

Alan looked at her in surprise. "Come on, Kel, Wintone's a representative of the law. He lost his temper, sure, but that's more serious for him than for someone else."

Kelly stood, adjusted the thermostat on the motel window air conditioner so the cabin would be cool when they returned from their hike and picnic. "You're right," she told her husband, "only when Craig Holt told us about it this morning, I couldn't help getting the impression he was almost glad the whole thing had happened."

Alan laughed. " Why would he pick on a man like Wintone, a county sheriff who outweighs him by fifty pounds?"

"He admitted he might have had too much to drink."

"Well, maybe that explains it." Alan slipped the aluminum-framed canvas backpack onto his shoulders and adjusted the straps for comfort. "Still, Sheriff Wintone's supposed to be able to handle aggressive drunks half his size."

Standing by the door, Alan looked at his wife with appreciative suppressed longing. Her baggy T-shirt and slacks couldn't conceal the grace of her body. Her long hair was tied back with a green ribbon, in the same fashion as the hair of the woman on the porch of the ramshackle house they had passed during their drive yesterday.

"About ready?" he asked.

"Almost."

"Anything else you want to put in the backpack?"

"No, but what about that?" She pointed to a goat-bladder wine container lying on the dresser, the sort of container seen emitting a thin stream of wine while held above the eager, open mouths of perspiring Spaniards in postcard photographs. Alan had bought it in a souvenir shop in Chicago.

He picked up the bladder, made sure the cork was tight. The leather strap was too short to sling over his shoulder, so he turned and had Kelly fit the bladder into one of the backpack's zippered canvas pockets. "That's a quart of sweet strawberry wine," he said, "poured in there carefully without benefit of a funnel, so be careful."

Precious as the wine was to him, she noticed that his camera was more precious, slung separately by its leather strap about his neck. There was actually a callus along the back of Alan's neck from the strap.

"Did you pack the sandwiches?" Kelly asked.

"First thing," Alan told her. "Local-butchered ham I bought in Colver. Let's stop playing Did You Forget or we'll forget to go."

They left the cabin, locking the door behind them. Alan was slightly surprised by the intensity of the heat, but they would be in the woods from time to time, shaded and cool.

Kelly trailed him as they followed the lake road for about half a mile. Then they cut onto a faint grassy path into the woods where the ground was flat. A rabbit broke from its camouflage of brown stillness in front of them and made the cover of high brush in three long bounds. The trilling chatter of birds sounded from every direction. Among the trees it was shaded enough for Kelly to be grateful for the sun's warmth when they passed through areas of light.

In a small clearing they sat at the base of a huge elm for a while, talking and joking while Alan prodded the hard ground with a gnarled stick he'd picked up and proclaimed to be walnut. When they rose to walk on, he took some photographs of the clover-dotted green clearing, which was almost too pastoral to be real.

Soon there was no semblance of a trail, and the woods grew thicker and more shadowed. Kelly didn't worry about being lost. Alan was an experienced hiker, and always carried a compass in the backpack. He walked loosely with his hiker's stride in front of Kelly, casually easing the way by swishing at the brush with the gnarled walnut. Around them was constant, subtle movement, birds flitting, the scurrying of unseen animals. But the day was too clear and warm to be menacing. There really was nothing frightening here, within the shadows that had seemed so foreboding to Kelly from outside the woods.

Alan stopped suddenly and pointed with the gnarled stick. Through the trees they could see the flat blue-green plane of lake water.

"I thought you knew where we were," Kelly chided him.

"I do. I just didn't know where the lake was. I know where we're at in relation to the motel."

They changed direction to angle away from the lake. Alan tried to remember the contour of the shoreline in their vicinity, but the map he'd seen had shown a line too irregular to recall in detail. For that matter, the lake was so large and undefined that he was sure there'd be coves and bends to the shore not shown on the map.

They walked on for another twenty minutes, through woods that suddenly had become almost too thick to allow passage. The sun was only occasionally visible through the intertwined, leafy branches above. And the ground had become uneven, a series of rocky washboard hills that made passage difficult.

Then they were out of the woods into brilliant sunshine, standing in another clover-strewn clearing, this one larger than the last. And beyond the clearing, on the other side of a sparse growth of wind-sculpted trees, the lake again, its flat surface almost unnaturally tranquil in the still air.

"The shoreline must curve south to west here," Alan said. He looked at his wristwatch. "It's almost noon, and I can't think of a prettier place to have lunch."

"Don't try," Kelly said. She skip-ran to a spot near the edge of the clearing, where the ground was perfectly level in the shade of the tallest of the nearby trees.

Alan walked over to join her, squared his shoulders and wriggled out of the canvas straps so he could lower the aluminum-framed backpack gently to the ground.

While Kelly got the sandwiches and cheese from one of the backpack's canvas pockets, Alan walked toward the lake, gazed through his camera viewfinder, checked the angle of the sun over his shoulder. He turned then, and though the light and range weren't right, he took a shot of Kelly spreading a large red-and-white checked cloth napkin on the bent grass.

Kelly sensed too late that she was being photographed, and she gave him a mock-angry grimace and then smiled, motioned with her arm that it was time to eat lunch.

The ham sandwiches were as good as Alan had predicted. He and Kelly ate slowly and deliberately, savoring the surroundings as well as the food.

When they were finished with lunch, Alan lay on his back with the canvas backpack for a pillow, experimenting with the wine bladder to see how high he could hold it above his open mouth and still be accurate with the steady stream of sweet strawberry wine. Kelly sat back, supporting herself with stiff arms in an oddly little-girl posture, watching him with amusement tempered by the knowledge that she would have to wash his shirt. Both the shirt and the backpack were already soaked with wine.

"I hope you drown, if it's possible," she said.

He started to laugh, choked and sat up, swallowed. "It's possible!" He lay back down and resumed his game. "We can't stay at the motel forever, you know" Kelly said, "even though the rates have come down."

"It's deductible."

"As long as there's something to deduct it from."

"There will be," he assured her, holding the wine bladder again at arm's length. This time he was accurate. "Enough talk of room rates and taxes," he said, placing the cork in the wine bladder while he was ahead. "Why don't I photograph my favorate model?"

"Does this come under the category of work?"

"More pleasure than work, in this case. But if enough comes of it to make the deductions worthwhile . . ."

"You've made your point," she said with a laugh. She stood and brushed her slacks with both hands, building up a rhythm.

"Not here," Alan said, stuffing the remains of the picnic lunch into the backpack. "We'll walk to where there's better light and background." He got to his feet with the effort of a man well fed and hoisted the backpack onto his shoulders, working his arms through the straps.

Alan and Kelly walked past the opposite edge of the clearing, beyond the wind-bent trees.

Kelly quickly removed her clothes. Alan had taught her something about modeling, and she obeyed his instructions smoothly and efficiently, striking practiced poses, accentuating the smooth, tanned lines of her body for the camera.

"Down by the water," Alan said, "just barely into the water."

Kelly walked down the bank until her feet were submerged to her ankles. The water was pleasantly cool, moving with a gentle tugging motion not discernible on the surface.

"Good," Alan said. He squinted at her through the camera's viewfinder, then walked down to her. He stooped and applied handfuls of water at strategic spots on her body to bring out the highlights, rubbing clinically so there would be no droplets. Kelly stood very still. Back up on the bank, he checked again through the viewfinder.

"How about 'September Morn'?" she asked half jokingly, assuming the classic nude pose.

He waited until she broke the pose before triggering the shutter, freezing her graceful natural movements. The trick was in the surprise. He tripped the shutter several times, rapidly.

Sidestepping a few feet to his right, he studied Kelly again through the camera. "Use any pose—"

A low, rasping sound came from the thick woods near the bank on Alan's left.

"Alan!" Kelly moved up onto the bank. Alan lifted an open hand for silence.

Kelly felt suddenly cold, exposed and vulnerable. On her

arms she noticed the most exaggerated gooseflesh she had ever seen. She had never felt more nude.

The woods near the bank were silent; perhaps nothing—

Again the sound came, softer this time, but just as unidentifiable.

Kelly moved closer to Alan. He was examining his camera. "Three more frames. . ." she heard him mutter.

"Alan, let's—'

"Be quiet!" His voice was a sharp whisper, alive with fear and hope. He looked hard into her eyes, his own reflecting the blue-green glare of the lake. "Stay here where you're safe, Kel! Promise me you ll stay right here!"

"For God's sake, Alan—"

But he was walking softly away from her, toward the woods, toward whatever they both had heard. Kelly watched his back, the camera strap dark against the red tan of his neck. She wanted to scream his name, knew that if she did he would never completely forgive her. Her body was bent with cold trembling, and she knew what people meant when they talked about flesh crawling.

Without turning his head Alan disappeared into the woods.

Her back to the calm lake, Kelly stumbled to where her clothes were folded on the grass. For the first time in her life she began to put on her shoes before anything else. And the shoes were suddenly too small, unyielding to her frantic efforts. She'd managed to get the left one on, unlaced, when Alan screamed.

Kelly stood erect, paralyzed. A loud thrashing sound came from the woods near the bank, where Alan had disappeared. Kelly took a step toward the sound, another—she had to help him some way.

The thrashing grew louder. Kelly stopped and felt an icy

explosion of horror in her heart. Through the trees she could see a huge, dark form in violent motion. Alan screamed again, in an old woman's voice, a mindless, trailing shriek.

Backing away, Kelly stepped on something sharp with her bare right foot. She hardly noticed the pain. Behind her there was a sound like a large branch snapping.

Her breath shrieking in soft mimicry of Alan's final scream, she ran.

Web Hooper saw her running down the lake road toward his red pickup truck. In his surprise he stepped down so hard on the brake that he rose partway out of his seat as the truck stopped. He watched Kelly with intrigued amusement until she drew nearer, then he was stunned by the terror in her eyes.

Wintone got the story out of her with difficulty. Kelly's lips were so rigid and distorted with fear that she could hardly talk, and when she did manage to pronounce words, they burst in almost incoherent disorder from her. She sat on the bed in her motel cabin, wrapped in the dirty wool blanket that Web Hooper had thrown over her.

Luke Higgins was there. With Wintone's permission he gave Kelly a glass containing a good measure of apricot brandy and coaxed her to drink. The scent of the brandy mingled with the scent of grease from the blanket.

The brandy seemed to help, and the shivering lessened.

Craig Holt stood at the foot of the bed, puffing on his pipe and calmly watching Kelly through the smoke. He had been in the cabin with Luke Higgins when Wintone arrived. "Do you remember where it happened?" he asked around the pipe stem.

Kelly didn't answer, stared at Wintone. She was fighting

going into shock, trying to comprehend what had happened.
"It might help if you took us there," Wintone said.
"I don't . . . know if I can."
"Would it be easier if we drove back to where Web picked you up?"
She started to speak, then nodded.
Wintone helped her to her feet, watched her get some clothes from one of the dresser drawers and make her way into the tiny bathroom. A full five minutes minutes passed before she emerged dressed in brown slacks and a faded striped blouse. Wintone reminded her that she was wearing only one shoe, and she nodded, walked to the closet and put on a pair of light tan sandals.
"If you want," Web Hooper said, "follow my truck an' I'll show you where I found her."
Holt rode in the truck with Hooper, Wintone and Luke Higgins following in the patrol car with Kelly. Wintone stayed well back, away from the dust raised by Hooper's old red pickup, as they turned onto the lake road and drove for about a mile and a half. Kelly sat quietly, her hands clasped between her thighs just behind her knees.
Then Hooper's truck pulled to the side of the road, and Wintone parked the patrol car behind it.
"I came out of the woods farther up that way," Kelly said, pointing through the dust-smeared windshield. Wintone honked the car's horn, motioning to Hooper to drive farther along the road. When Kelly pointed a second time, Wintone tapped the horn ring again and braked behind Hooper's parked truck.
As they got out of the car, Wintone looked at the woods where Kelly had pointed. This was a particularly wild area, not half a mile from where the Larsen boy had been killed.
Kelly led the way, pausing from time to time to get her bearings. The walking, the mental game of backtracking her

panicky flight, seemed to help her regain her composure. Wintone knew she was steeling herself for the fear that would grow in her as she approached the spot where she'd last seen her husband.

It took them over an hour to find the clearing on the lake bank. Kelly stood in the center of the grassy clearing, in bright sunshine, and pointed toward thick woods at the edge of the bank.

Wintone told Web Hooper to stay with her, then walked forward with Holt and Higgins on either side of him. The only sound was that of the tall grass whipping at their boots.

When they entered the woods, Wintone felt the chill of the sudden shade. Immediately he saw what looked like trash strewn about the ground among the trees just ahead. As they approached slowly, he made out some bits of brown paper, a torn red-and-white checked strip of material, shredded pieces of canvas. In the center of the scattered debris was a large, shapeless mound of what looked like more rubble, tattered canvas and twisted pieces of aluminum. Extended almost straight upward from the midst of this was something mottled red and slightly crooked. Wintone stopped without being conscious of it, stood staring as he realized he was looking at an arm minus the hand.

"Merciful God . . ." Luke Higgins said in a strangled whisper.

"Best not let that girl see this," Wintone said. A tangy, coppery taste was coating the sides of his tongue, creating saliva. Alone, he walked forward to examine the body more closely.

He saw that the bent aluminum had been the framework of a large canvas backpack, which was shredded now with its contents spread about the ground. Alan Greer's badly crushed and torn body lay on its side in an awkward death posture, his ruined face frozen in a grotesque expression of horror.

Higgins and Holt walked over slowly to stand by Wintone. Higgins's face wore nearly the same expression as the dead man's. Holt appeared almost bored, but the flesh near the left corner of his compressed lips was ticking rapidly.

"What do you suppose? . . ." Luke Higgins said.

"I can't suppose anything," Wintone told him. "Don't move around here, neither of you. Back off the same way you walked to the body."

Holt was bent over, picking up something.

"Leave it!" Wintone snapped.

But Holt had already straightened, looking guiltily at Wintone.

"What are you holding?" Wintone asked him.

From out of sight at his side, Holt held out a thirty-five millimeter camera. "Greer and I were working together on a book," he explained. His cheek was still marked by a square of adhesive tape and one eye was faintly ringed with purple.

"It's evidence," Wintone told him. "I best take it."

"I'm under the auspices of the U.S. government! . . ."

Wintone held out his big hand palm up. "Investigation of a death by violence takes precedence. You know it." Wintone wasn't sure of his words, but then neither was Holt.

Holt bit off whatever else he wanted to say, handed Wintone the camera and backed away. The camera appeared undamaged and contained a roll of film that had been used but for two frames.

"Go back and tell Web Hooper to take the girl to the motel," Wintone said to the two men who were now standing some ten feet from him. "Then either phone or have Hooper drive into Colver an tell 'em to send someone out for the body."

"You stayin' here alone?" Higgins asked.

"I'm gonna be lookin' things over careful," Wintone told him. "Do me a favor an' see that the girl's treated right. Get in touch with Doc Amis an' Sarah."

Higgins nodded, his round face still distorted in a look of disbelief. "Should I . . . tell the girl what we found?"

"When she sees you," Wintone told him, "she'll know for sure."

When he was alone, Wintone examined the area around the body, walking head down in slow circles. The ground was disturbed, but there were no clear prints. Lake water lapped only a few feet from where Wintone stood, and he examined the bank, thinking that the mud might have been worked up. There were marks in the ooze, but nothing distinct.

Wintone took another careful look around the death scene, then he moved as close as he could to the sunlight and sat with his back against the cool hardness of a tree trunk, waiting for the sound of human footsteps. He was still holding Alan Greer's undamaged camera. While Wintone was curious about what the undeveloped film might contain, he was too experienced to be hopeful.

Over an hour passed before a sudden crashing in the woods made Wintone practically leap to his feet. He stood leaning away from the sound, surprised by the watery weakness in his limbs. Then low, leafy branches parted and Frank Turper stepped into view red-faced and perspiring, followed by two men carrying a portable stretcher. Wintone showed them the body.

The next afternoon Wintone sat at his desk staring at Kelly's detailed account of the events surrounding Alan Greer's death. The printed words before Wintone told him little that might be of help, but he hoped that by linking them with the package of developed photographs that had just arrived by messenger from the State Police lab, he might be able to learn something.

He peeled back the thick nylon-reinforced tape that sealed the brown package and spread the photographs on the scarred, dark wood of his desk top.

The prints were developed and packaged according to the order in which they'd been taken. The top photos were of the lake, some detailed studies of old buildings. Wintone recognized Seth Perkins's silo.

The nude photographs of Kelly Greer were examples of her husband's art—tasteful and sympathetic. Wintone gazed at them with an aching heart and a loneliness for Etty. Despite a gulf of years, there was a similarity between Etty and Kelly that transcended physical resemblance . . . or maybe the similarity was in Wintone's mind.

He gently arranged the photographs in a stack, all but the last one, the final costly shot taken with Alan Greer's camera. Wintone picked up that photo, had to hold it at various angles to determine top from bottom.

The last print revealed blue sky and the blurred high limbs of overarching trees, as if the photographer had been falling when the shutter was triggered. In the lower right corner of the photo was something dark, something with an almost glazed luminosity to it and textured like smooth, wet stone.

That was all.

No clue as to what the rest of the object might look like; it was simply as if one corner of the photograph had been blacked out.

Wintone studied the photograph, trying to imagine what it was that the lens had caught in the corner. Due to the camera's movement and the awkward upward angle of the photograph, it was impossible to judge height or width.

The sheriff put the photo aside, sat back and again reviewed Kelly's account of everything that had happened from the time she and Alan left Higgins' Motel. He could glean nothing from any of it.

Without looking directly at them, he picked up the artistically posed and photographed pictures of Kelly and slid them back into the package. Then he set out to return them to her.

During the drive to Higgins' Motel, Wintone wondered what he should do with Alan Greer's last photograph. Holt would be pestering soon to find out what the camera's film had contained. Wintone could simply lie to him, tell him the last frame had shown only a view of the lake, but then when the photograph was made public—as it would have to be eventually—Wintone would be open to criticism for withholding the facts.

He decided to stall Holt for a while, keep the newspapers out of it as long as possible. Wintone could imagine what some irresponsible members of the news media could construct out of that final photograph. And he dreaded Baily Howe's and Mayor Boemer's reactions.

Wintone parked the patrol car in the shade in Higgins' Motel's lot and walked with crunching footsteps across gravel to Kelly Greer's cabin. As he approached, he saw that the curtains were drawn closed, but the side-window air conditioner was laboring with a high-pitched, faintly gurgling hum. Wintone had only to knock once and the door opened.

Kelly was wearing the same brown slacks and faded striped shirt she'd had on before, but her dark hair was smoothly brushed now, and there was no sign of grief on her face except for the redness about her eyes. She stepped aside for Wintone to enter.

The cabin's interior was dim and almost cold. Wintone thought Kelly probably hadn't opened the door or looked out a window all day. She parted the curtains now in the front window to admit harsh light that seemed to set her on edge. Her left hand clutching her right wrist as if to restrain that arm, she stood looking expectantly at Wintone.

"I brought these," he said, holding out the package of photographs. "Thought you might want 'em."

She opened the package and examined the contents without any expression of embarrassment or self-consciousness.

"Thank you," she said to Wintone. She smiled at him, for him.

"Are you . . . all right?" he asked.

"Better." She said it as if it meant nothing.

"Time'll help," Wintone told her.

She nodded with skeptical politeness. Another smile survived for a while, but her eyes were misted. "My father's driving here from Memphis to take me home."

Wintone was glad to hear that she had family to take care of her. "Before you leave," he said, "if there's anything else you can tell me . . ."

She shook her head. "Craig Holt asked me the same thing."

"He been botherin' you?"

"Not really. He might if I'd let him." She walked over and looked out between the parted curtains, as if to reassure herself that existence was possible outside the cabin. The reassurance seemed to leave her unmoved. "Alan had been drinking strawberry wine that afternoon," she said almost dreamily. "He had one of those goat-bladder containers, and it amused him to try to drink like a Spaniard . . ."

Wintone remembered this from her original statement, but didn't interrupt her.

"I'm the one who wanted him to relax, forget about his work for a while. I tell myself he might not have gone into the woods to investigate that sound if he hadn't been drinking, but I don't know . . ."

"He'd have gone, Mrs. Greer," Wintone said firmly. "I don't think you should have any doubts about that." But he knew she'd doubt; some part of her would doubt forever.

A car crossed the parking lot outside the cabin. Wintone stared at Kelly and listened to the slowly revolving tires crunch loosely packed gravel. It was like his soul breaking up inside him. "You're young . . ." he said to her.

She faced him and nodded. "I guess I'll hear that a lot over the next few days."

"'Cause it's true."

"You lost your wife in an accident not long ago, didn't you, Sheriff?"

"I figured you'd heard. Most everybody has."

Kelly tilted her head, the light from the window softening her long hair. "What you said," she told him, "it means something to me. And it means something to me that you brought me these photographs."

Wintone was struck awkward by her gaze. He gave her a quick smile, a good-bye nod, and walked to the door, his business finished.

She followed, stood squinting in the bright sunlight of the open door as if she might any second turn back inside to escape the glare.

"Thank you, Sheriff," she said. "You've been . . . more than thoughtful."

Wintone couldn't work his words past the tightness in his throat. He walked to the patrol car, listening to the gravel beneath his feet.

He didn't have to look back to know she was still standing hesitantly in the cabin doorway, watching him, as he drove from the lot.

Back at his office in Colver, Wintone sat at his desk, sipping a cup of strong coffee and pondering. Something was hanging fire in the back of his mind, some realization he knew he should have grasped but hadn't.

He decided to spend the next hour or so reviewing the file on each Bonegrinder death, hoping to strike the key that would clarify the thing that was hazy and undefined on the edge of his consciousness, and to forget his conversation with Kelly.

Wintone was just pushing himself up out of his swivel

chair with a downthrust of his powerful arms when the office door opened and old Bonifield came in. He stood for a while framed in the open doorway, chewing his tobacco with a stern-jawed intensity that matched the excitement in his blue eyes.

"Shut that damned door!" Wintone told him, standing all the way erect.

"Ain't no need to get het up," Bonifield said, closing the door with deliberate, slow care.

"Ain't no need to stoke this place up like a furnace, either," Wintone said.

Bonifield walked slowly, casually about the office, studying individual objects as if they were pricetagged. He had some bit of information so precious that he hated to let it go.

But he would let it go; that was why he had come here. Wintone was patient. Nothing ever entered Bonifield's mind that didn't eventually find its way out through his mouth.

"Thought you might oughta know they found Cheryl Peterson floatin' in the lake," Bonifield said.

Wintone walked out from behind the desk.

"Who found her?"

"Couple'a fellas from Branson," Bonifield said, shifting his egg-sized wad of tobacco to his left cheek. "Body's down at the doc's now." He grinned at Wintone, walking to the door and opening it to spit tobacco into the street. He took his time about closing the door.

The telephone rang and Wintone answered it, still looking at Bonifield.

"Doc Amis here, Billy. The Peterson woman's been found."

"I know," Wintone said. "I'm on my way."

Bonifield held the door open for him.

THIRTY

Wintone stood with Doc Amis over Cheryl Peterson's body. The time in the lake water had taken its toll, and Wintone swallowed back the hollow revulsion that climbed his throat.

"She died when the back of her head was crushed," Doc Amis said, motioning with a forefinger toward the now bloodless injury amidst the tangle of drying hair. The forefinger moved with Doc Amis's words. "She's also got these deep slash-marks on her face, neck and shoulders. The rest of what you see is the result of her being so long in the lake."

Wintone turned away from the body, knowing he'd have no difficulty recalling details. "You sure it's her?"

Doc Amis nodded. "Reasonably so. What you see here would have fit her description." He pulled a white sheet up over the pale form on the table. "You'll have to get the husband to make a positive identification."

"I know," Wintone said. "He heard yet she's been found?"

"Not to my knowledge. You better tell him before somebody else does."

Wintone walked from the small, cold room, Doc Amis behind him. The reception room was empty, Sarah's desk bare.

"Where's Sarah?" Wintone asked the doctor.

"She's off today. Some personal business to tend to." His arms straight, hands gripping the desk edge, Doc Amis sat on the end of Sarah's desk. "She gave me her notice earlier this week."

Wintone felt the coolness again that he'd felt in the room with Cheryl Peterson. Something dead. "Didn't know that."

Doc Amis nodded. "Going to Chicago with that Craig Holt. Can't blame her for giving up on things here, this little town . . . She's not going to be easy to replace."

"I suppose not."

"You driving out to pick up Peterson now?"

"Sure."

"You okay, Billy?"

"Heat," Wintone said. "Just the damn heat."

"It wouldn't hurt you to rest awhile," Doc Amis said, standing up straight. "Nobody I know of ever got used to looking at what's in the next room."

"You ain't met the exception in me," Wintone said. He pulled a red print handkerchief from his pocket and wiped his face, saw Doc Amis staring at him with concern. "Just the heat," he assured the doctor again. He folded the damp handkerchief and returned it to his pocket. "I'll be back in a short while with Peterson."

"I'll be waiting for you," Doc Amis said, "but I won't be looking forward to it."

"Seems like there ain't no easy jobs," Wintone said as he went out. He tried to ignore the sensation of loss that was gaining its grip on him.

Peterson hadn't struck Wintone as the sort who would

break down and sob; he was more the type who either angered or kept his deepest emotions inside himself. But he had sobbed. Of course, who could predict how anyone, even oneself, would react to what Peterson was put through?

After the identification Wintone drove the silent man back to his motel cabin and left him there with the final reality of his wife's death, left him there to live with the persistent image of what he'd seen.

On the drive back to Colver, something stalked again at the edge of Wintone's mind. It was like a rustle of movement in the deep shadows of a barn, probably just a field mouse or barn owl, but maybe not.

When the sheriff got back to his office, old Bonifield was lounging outside as if disinterested. Wintone walked past without acknowledging him and went inside.

For over an hour Wintone sat at his desk, painstakingly reviewing the file on each Bonegrinder death. He was staring at the photographs of the site of the Larsen boy's death, hunched forward in his chair, when he sat up straighter and rubbed his chin.

There was one thing all the deaths had in common—at least, one thing they *might* have in common.

Cautioning himself not to put too much stock in his theory, Wintone returned the photographs to their file folder. Chickens didn't necessarily mean eggs.

Wintone left the office and locked the door behind him, flipping a fifty-cent piece into the air as he stepped down into the street.

"You, Bonifield, buy yourself a beer!"

The old man caught the glinting coin with a look of amazement. Wintone got into the patrol car and drove out of town. He had to talk once more to Bill Peterson.

Peterson seemed to have recovered from the initial shock of viewing his wife's corpse. He'd known all along she was dead, after all, and perhaps now his grief was tempered by the relief of having found the body so that the episode of her death itself could be ended. He agreed readily to go with Wintone to the point on the bank where he had grounded the rental boat after the attack.

He stood with Wintone on the bank, a man visibly weighted by circumstance. They were in the shade, and a slight breeze came off the lake and rippled the pearl gray, silky material of the pullover sport shirt Peterson was wearing. Wintone unfastened the top buttons on his uniform shirt, hoping the breeze would bring rain.

"What I'd like, Mr. Peterson," Wintone said, "is for you to try to point out the exact spot on the lake where the attack took place."

Peterson put his hands on his hips, squinting out at the lake's sun-touched surface. His shoulders as well as his chest rose and fell regularly with his breathing.

"Imagine a line from this point to the center of that rise on the opposite bank," he said. "It happened on that line, about . . . three hundred yards this side of where that piece of land juts out."

"That far off the bank? Are you sure?"

"Positive. It's not something I'd forget." There was an unsteadiness to Peterson's voice. His regular, squared features appeared haggard in the late afternoon light.

"Can you remember exactly what you had with you in the boat?" Wintone asked.

"What we had with us? . . . You mean, besides fishing gear?"

"Including fishing gear. Anything might be important."

Peterson continued to stare out at the lake, as if projecting himself back in time and out onto the water, in the gently bobbing Jon boat again with his wife.

"There was my tackle box," he said, "a cooler with some beer in it, our two fishing rods . . ."

"What was in your tackle box?"

Peterson shrugged. "Everything you'd expect to find in a tackle box. Fishing lures, line, lead sinkers, pliers, a knife with a fish scaler . . ."

"Any bait?"

"Only artificial lures. Cheryl wouldn't use worms, so we left the worm can with Melanie on the bank."

"Any food in the boat?"

"No, we'd just eaten breakfast when we started to fish."

"What was in your pockets?" Wintone asked him.

"Oh, I can tell you that exactly," Peterson said. "Not that I see how it can help. I had my key case, my wallet, some loose change and a pair of sunglasses."

"How about your wife's pockets"

"Cheryl's? . . . Well, nothing. Do women usually carry anything in their pockets?"

Wintone had to concede that they didn t.

"She'd left her purse in the car," Peterson explained.

"Can you think of anything else that was in the boat?" Wintone asked. "Anything at all, small or large."

Peterson sucked in his lips, narrowed his eyes in thought. "There were the two oars, of course, in case the motor went out on us, a couple of life jackets we probably should have been wearing . . . that's all. I'm positive."

Wintone's face creased in a picture of disappointment, puzzlement. He thanked Peterson for his cooperation, then drove him back to the motel.

The sheriff was still in low spirits when he returned to Colver. He felt like a man trying to piece together something in the dark without any assurance that it was possible.

That night Wintone carried his beer to a booth in Mully's, which wasn't his usual fashion, and sat sliding the mug back and forth to make damp patterns on the tabletop. It was the Peterson death that puzzled him, everything about the Peterson death.

Mully brought Wintone another beer, set it smoothly on the table and scooped up the empty bottle.

"They say it rained some up north," he said.

Wintone nodded, looking ahead. "That don't help us none here."

Seeing that the sheriff wasn't conversational, Mully carried the empty bottle back behind the bar.

Wintone settled farther into the booth, resting a shoulder against the wall.

By the time his second beer was half drunk, he found himself thinking of Etty, thinking of Kelly Greer and of Sarah. They were all together in his mind, their faces, voices and bodies merging into meaningless words and gestures. He took another pull of beer and considered Sarah and Holt together, wondered if Holt had promised marriage. Doc Amis hadn't mentioned marriage in Sarah's plans, so probably neither had Sarah when she gave notice. Sarah and Holt . . . together in Chicago. . . . Wintone told himself it didn't matter; it was no business of his. Not now. A sadness almost akin to desperation engulfed him. He had another beer for a nightcap and stood up from the booth to leave.

When he was halfway to the door, old Bonifield entered. He grinned his tobacco-misshapen grin when he saw Wintone.

"I did mean to thank you fer the price of a drink," the old man said, " 'cept you run off the way you did."

The beer wasn't setting right on Wintone's stomach, and the appropriate blast of hot air that had followed old Bonifield in sent a lightness and dizziness through him. He held onto the bar for a moment, then waved a good night to Mully, told Bonifield he was welcome and walked on to the door.

"I will say the sheriff seems a mite jug-bit," old Bonifield said behind him in a mock whisper. "I will say, maybe we're seein' a trueness now that ain't exactly a revelation."

When he reached the office, Wintone stepped in out of the

heat, breathed deeply of the cool air and felt his stomach settle to the point where he knew he'd soon feel better.

He sat on the cot in the back room, removed his boots, then stretched out on his back, closing his eyes to invite sleep. But his mind was a silent tumbling of unpleasantness. The cot groaned as Wintone rolled onto his side. He lay there recalling word for word his conversation with Bill Peterson.

An hour passed without sleep. Somewhere in the dark and quiet room a mosquito droned in a lilting, monotonous rhythm. The rhythm seemed to feed on itself, to grow until the whole room pulsated. A cricket began to trill nearby outside.

Wintone sat up on the cot, raked thick fingers through his hair. He turned his wrist to look at the luminous hands of his watch, green cat's eyes in the darkness. Then, despite the lateness of the hour, he went into the office and sat before the telephone.

He called an old friend of his who lived in Springfield and owned a sporting goods store. After a brief conversation Wintone went back to bed and slept soundly.

THIRTY-ONE

When Wintone returned from Springfield late the next afternoon, he saw Sarah from the patrol car, walking in the direction he was driving. As she heard the car approach her, she turned, and something in her face made Wintone press his foot to the brake, stopping a hundred feet in front of her.
He sat, his heart beating time with the idling engine, and she opened the right-hand door and got in beside him. There was a scent of jasmine about her. Unfamiliar.
"I was on my way to see you," she said.
"I figured." He reached forward and twisted the ignition key. They sat in the silent aftermath of the turned-off engine. The heat began to move in.
"Doc says he told you I was leavin'," Sarah said.
"Mentioned it." Wintone toyed with the key ring dangling from the steering column.
"I'm going to Chicago, with Craig Holt."
Wintone nodded thoughtfully. "Can't blame you. Not much here for you, Sarah."

She rubbed a taut hand across the top of her thigh, as if she'd just burned her palm. "I have to go, Billy. I feel that."

He breathed out hard. "About the fight I had with Holt . . ."

"It's nothin' like that makin' up my mind, Billy." Her voice was tighter now, forcing its way from her. But it was a sure voice.

Wintone flicked at the dangling keys.

"It's the waitin', is what it is. I can't wait forever, not even knowin' for what. Sometimes I hear time goin' by me, Billy, roarin' in my ears. I'm on the downhill, an' I need a handhold." She turned her head to look squarely at him. "You don't understand that, do you?"

"I do an' I don't."

She laughed a sad laugh that forced its way from her throat like her words. "That's the way I feel."

"I knew you was pulled two ways." Wintone rested both hands on the steering wheel that seemed now to be coated with a light, oily film. "He gonna marry you, Sarah?"

"I don't know, Billy. Don't care."

"Time to take your chances then, is it?"

"Past time."

"You need luck then, Sarah, and I wish it for you."

She thanked him. But it wasn't as if the air had been cleared between them, or ever would be. Her right hand, long-fingered and pale, somehow restful, went to the chrome door handle, pulled it but didn't open the door.

"What are you gonna do, Billy?"

"If I'm not sheriff any longer?"

"Or if you are."

He shrugged. "What I been doin', I guess. What comes my way."

She tried a smile. It caught and held, but barely. "Like as not, things'll work out for you, for both of us."

"Like as not."

She opened the car door now. She was leaving. Wintone didn't know whether to kiss her or shake her hand, decided shaking her hand would be absurd and kissed her lips lightly, a cool, parting kiss.

Sarah got out of the car, closed the door softly behind her and walked away not looking back. Wintone caught sight of her for a second in the rear-view mirror, then looked quickly away, as if he'd caught himself spying on her.

He wouldn't think about Sarah. Not for a while. He made up his mind to that. There was no reason he should think about her.

Quickly he started the engine.

Instead of parking in front of the office, Wintone drove to the rear of the building and parked the car by the wooden storage shed, its rear bumper near the padlocked double doors.

Standing next to the car, he breathed in and arched his back, stretched his legs. He was stiff from his time behind the steering wheel, road-weary, but he still had a lot to get done. He walked to the storage shed and unlocked the steel padlock, swung out the squeaking double doors. A large wasp droned angrily out of the heated dimness, circled a few times, then disappeared behind the shed.

Wintone's Jon boat was inside the shed on its boat trailer. There were several cardboard cartons stored in the boat, and after removing them and stacking them in a corner, Wintone wheeled boat and trailer outside into the sunlight. He checked the five-horsepower outboard motor, then went into the shed and got a dented red gasoline can and set it in the boat.

After hitching the boat trailer to the bumper hitch on the patrol car, Wintone closed and relocked the storage shed. Then he drove toward the lake.

The afternoon was clear and hot, with a humidity that could almost be seen. Leaves on the trees along the road seemed to droop from their branches as if burdened by the weight of the atmosphere. Insects flitted about clumsily above the road's dusty surface, seemingly hindered by the thick air, striking the patrol car's windshield with regularity. The boat trailer swayed slightly behind the car and bounced more than was good for it. The rest of the way to the lake Wintone kept an eye on the flat wooden bow of the boat in the rear-view mirror.

Before putting the boat in the water, Wintone opened the patrol car's trunk and got out the scuba-diving equipment he'd brought back from Springfield. He checked the equipment and loaded it into the boat.

Then it occurred to him that he'd need an anchor. There was plenty of rope in the car, and he searched around and came up with a good-sized heavy rock that could be held firmly by a knot.

Within ten minutes he was out on the lake, the boat's motor smoothly chugging, pushing him before a gentle wake toward the spot where Cheryl Peterson had died.

The lake was calm today, murky and green beneath the late afternoon sky. Water slapped lightly at the upraised, flat bow of the boat as Wintone sat in the stern and held his course by his distance from the shoreline. He had changed to swimming trunks and a white T-shirt, and the sun felt warm on his bare legs, glanced off the water to pain his eyes.

When Wintone reached the spot on the lake that Peterson had pointed out the day before, he cut the motor and dropped his makeshift anchor. He noted by the length of played-out rope that the lake's depth here was a good twenty feet. That would make his task all the harder, but still worth a try.

Wintone double-checked the diving equipment as he'd

been instructed, then strapped the twin oxygen tanks onto his back. He fitted the rubber flippers to his feet, clipped the battery-operated waterproof lamp to his belt and clamped the air-hose mouthpiece between his teeth. When he was ready he turned his body and clumsily tipped himself backward over the side of the small boat, fearing for a moment that it might capsize as he sank into the cool, sun-shot water.

Surfacing, he held onto the side of the boat with one hand, sloshed a bit of water on the inside of his face mask, and put it on more firmly. Then he released his grip on the boat.

Beneath the surface it was dimmer than Wintone had imagined, and he moved through layers of coolness as he propelled himself downward with the flippers. He unclipped the underwater lamp from his belt and turned it on, aiming its beam downward, and found that he was almost on the lake bottom. He saw smooth mud, gently waving weeds, and on the fringes of the lamp's beam an occasional gliding form. Wintone was surprised at the ease with which he could control his angled body with the flippers. His legs moving in a gentle, almost subconscious rhythm, he began to probe the cool and silent lake bottom with the beam of light. He swam surrounded by gloom, trying not to think of anything beyond the small area of illumination before him.

Wintone located his stone anchor with its almost vertical rope, and he used that as a reference point so he wouldn't be circling to search the same area. A rusted tin can lay half-submerged in the mud within the beam of light. When Wintone picked it up, it decomposed in his hand to drift in bits back to the bottom. He continued to search, for what he wasn't exactly sure.

He searched until darkness above him turned the surrounding water to black ink, then he surfaced. Feeling oddly out of his element in the air, he hauled himself awkwardly back into the boat.

That night Wintone rested poorly, shifting his weight constantly on the narrow cot. He never quite woke nor slept, and his mind wavered in that twilight, indefinable world between the two states. Around him towered darkness, and half-dreams—half-recollections of shadowy, gliding forms, some of them poignantly familiar, grotesquely human-shaped, impossible to see clearly. Occasionally he'd imagine he was drowning, and his breathing would take on a wheezing, almost panicky note, his chest heaving as if straining for air.

The next day he returned to the same spot on the lake and resumed his search, dropping from the building heat of morning into the coolness of dark water. The angle of the sun, Wintone discovered, had something to do with the amount of light in deep water, and his search was conducted in a gloom not so thick as the evening before. He was aware of more movement around him, at the edges of his vision, and this gave him even more of an uneasy feeling than he'd experienced yesterday. He tried to concentrate on his search, eyes fixed on the lake bottom as he swam in slow, deliberate patterns.

Something to his left, barely outside the beam of light, caught his attention, and he twisted his body and worked the flippers to propel himself toward the spot. Amid thick growth, slimy to the touch, was something that didn't belong. Wintone reached into the depths of the gently waving growth and pressed his fingertips to a firm smoothness like cool flesh.

He drew back his hand instinctively, then reached in again and pulled free a leather boot. The boot's condition made it obvious to Wintone that it had been in the lake for a long time. He released his grip on it and continued his systematic searching, ignoring everything else around him.

Wintone searched until noon, then he sat discouraged in the shade on the bank and ate the bacon sandwich that he'd packed. He rested awhile, sipping iced tea from his steel thermos bottle and gazing out at the lake. His oxygen tanks held only enough air for another twenty minutes submerged, and he decided to use those twenty minutes to search before giving up.

When Wintone was rested, he rose, capped the empty thermos bottle and returned to the boat.

Down again, into dimness and coolness, familiar in the pits of his subconscious. What had Holt said? "Our own primal past come to claim us."

The gloom about Wintone darkened, as if above in the other world a cloud had intersected the sun.

Within five minutes on the lake bottom, Wintone found what he'd been seeking. He surfaced with it, placed it in a plastic bag, then struggled out of his diving gear and headed the boat toward the bank where the patrol car and trailer were parked.

On the drive back to Colver, he felt an excitement, an anticipation, that surprised him.

THIRTY-TWO

Craig Holt was waiting for Wintone in front of the office.

"I'd like to see whatever photographs Alan Greer's camera contained," he said to the sheriff. "I've checked with the State Police and know you had them developed."

Wintone was still wearing his swimming trunks beneath his tan uniform pants, and his entire body itched either from too much sun or from something in the lake water. He wanted very much to get rid of Holt so he could shower and change clothes.

"You're talkin' like I don't want you to see 'em," he said to Holt, crossing to the file cabinets.

Holt reached for his pipe and drew it slowly from his shirt pocket, as if he needed a prop for security. "I thought you might let personal matters interfere with your job. I mean, Sarah and me . . . the fight." His fingertips rose to dance tentatively over his still-damaged face.

"I told you once before," Wintone said, "anything between you an' Sarah's no business of mine." Wintone meant it now. He had no choice but to mean it. He removed the photographs from the file folder and laid them on the desk in front of Holt.

Before looking at any of the photographs, Holt counted them by their upper right corners. "Eleven photos? Is that all there was?"

"I returned some to Mrs. Greer. They were personal."

"You shouldn't have done that."

"They had nothin' to do with Bonegrinder. If you want to see 'em, she took 'em home with her to Kansas City."

"What about the negatives?"

"Gave her those too."

Holt shook his head, then sighed to express tolerance for Wintone's incompetence.

Piss on him, Wintone thought. "Unless there's proof some crime's been committed," Wintone told him," she could have demanded all her husband's effects."

Holt ignored him, stood examining the photographs one by one.

"The only one that'll interest you is the last one," Wintone said. "But you won't be able to tell much from it."

Holt took his time leafing to the last photo, but when he reached it his body was still and his long neck craned with concentration. "He actually photographed it . . ."

"Some part of it."

"There doesn't appear to be any fur," Holt said, still staring at the photograph. "And the flesh appears dark, though that could be in the light or the development of the picture."

"Kelly Greer described what she saw as bein' dark," Wintone reminded him.

"It's strangely textured." Holt was still studying the photograph. "Not scaly by any means, yet not exactly smooth." He raised his eyebrows and looked at Wintone without raising his head. "May I have this photograph?"

"I'll have another one developed an' you can have it," Wintone told him.

Holt continued to stare at him for a moment, then the thick eyebrows dropped to conceal the eyes. "Good enough." He placed the photographs on the desk.

Wintone picked up the photos by their edges, put them in their thick file folder and returned the folder to its steel drawer. When he turned, he saw that Holt was nervously tapping the shallow bowl of his unlit pipe in his palm, making a sound like dripping water tattooing something hollow.

"I'm glad you feel the way you do, Sheriff," Holt said. He placed the pipe stem in his mouth, as if he could speak more comfortably that way. "And I shouldn't have said what I did the other night. I was . . . well, drunk."

Wintone didn't feel like arguing with him and stood silent.

Holt extended his right hand. "No need for hard feelings on the part of either of us. There are winners and losers."

"There are those in everything," Wintone said, putting out his own right hand. Why shouldn't he shake hands with Holt?

Holt seemed satisfied that he'd successfully manipulated Wintone and left. Wintone was glad the patrol car and boat were parked out of sight behind the building, and that he'd driven them there the back way, out of Holt's vision. The last thing he wanted right now was Holt's interference.

After locking the office door Wintone took his shower, carefully rinsing every trace of soap from his body. He applied nothing scented to himself, and when he dressed he put on a dark tan long-sleeved uniform shirt despite the heat. Then he went into the office and unlocked the gun cabinet.

Wintone had a theory now about Bonegrinder. "When everything likely's been ruled out," he recalled someone saying, "whatever's left has to be true even if it's unlikely." Unless it's something else unlikely, Wintone cautioned himself. He got down his twelve-gauge Ithaca shotgun and loaded it with deadly deer slugs, solid projectiles fired by overcharged shells. Whatever else he needed and could supply himself with was in the trunk of the car.

Wintone left by the back door, unhitched the boat trailer and rolled it into the shed. He jiggled the padlock on the shed's double doors to make sure it was locked. Then he got in the car and drove toward Helen Borne's farm.

He stayed at the Borne farm only a few minutes, then drove through fast-lengthening shadows toward Big Water Lake. Through the trees along the lake road, he could glimpse the fire of the low sun on the water, and beyond that the red sky making its promise for tomorrow. The temperature was still in the eighties, and in the failing light there seemed to be a dusty haze hanging in the air.

It was just after sundown when Wintone parked the patrol car at the top of the rise, near the point on the bank where the Larsen boy's death had occurred. From the car's trunk Wintone got a large, wrinkled paper sack and a battered Coleman two-mantle gas lantern. One arm beneath the heavy sack, he hooked a finger through the wire handle of the lantern, slung his shotgun beneath his free arm and walked through the slope of trees down to the bank.

Within minutes the lake was almost completely dark, quiet under a half-moon. Wintone struck a match and held the flame to the mantles of the gas lantern until it spread its yellow glow. Black water lapping at the bank and the crickets' endless scream: those were the only sounds.

Wintone set the lantern on a stump, carried something down to the mud bank outside the yellow glow of light and returned. His skin felt prickly with the heat, and he drew his damp shirt sleeve across his even damper forehead. Huge shadowed night moths were circling the lantern. Wintone leaned down, brushing some of the flitting forms aside, and twisted the lantern's valve to off. In the closing darkness the scream of the crickets seemed almost enough to deafen. Wintone gripped his shotgun, checking by feel to make sure the safety was off, and crouched by the stump.

For over an hour Wintone hardly moved, staring out at the lake. Beyond the black and reeded water near the bank hung the yellow moon and a wisp or two of cloud. By day at this point he might have been able to see the distant opposite bank of the big lake, hazy tree-grown hills and stands of cedar. Now there was only blackness under the moon.

Wintone had an older jug of Claude Borne's cider at his side, the hard cider. From time to time he sipped on it as the night gradually grew cooler, his right forefinger hooked through the jug's glass loop. The cider helped him to be patient. This might be the first of many long and lonely nights at the water's edge.

Wintone's blood drew into him.

The crickets had suddenly stopped, at once. Now the only sound was the lapping of lake water at the bank.

As Wintone crouched listening, the time between the gentle lapping sounds became briefer and the lapping itself seemed to grow louder and to reach farther up onto the bank. From off the dark water came a drawn-out moaning sound, like wind through the low strings of a bow fiddle.

Wintone's cramped legs began to tremble and he had to stand up for fear they'd give out. He felt suddenly exposed as if, even in the darkness, by standing he'd revealed himself.

The eerie moaning came again, closer, and Wintone's fingers edged along cool steel to double-check the safety of his shotgun. Something dark, something huge, was moving just off the bank.

Wintone took slow and careful aim and fired.

Black water exploded with the blast of the shotgun, and the thing stood up against the night sky. Moonlight glistened off its sleek, shining body and off ivory fanglike teeth, and it moved toward Wintone as if the shot had only got its attention.

Wintone backed a step, heard the lantern clatter to the ground behind him. The glistening thing was moving fast toward him now, over nine feet tall and lurching with a grotesque, desperate waddle, as if unused to moving on land.

The shotgun in Wintone's hands weighed a hundred pounds as he strained to raise it to his shoulder.

The gun held six more rounds, and Wintone used them all in as many seconds.

While the sound of the shotgun still throbbed in the air, the dark thing lurched to the side with surprising agility, crashed into the black woods.

Wintone stood trembling, not knowing if what he'd seen was real or illusion. He took a step forward, stopped, stared into the dark woods. What he'd shot was real, all right. And it had to be what he'd hoped.

He leaned down, still staring at the silent woods where the thing had disappeared, and picked up the cider jug by feel, took a long pull on it. His hands were calm enough now to reload the shotgun. He worked the shells in quickly, glancing around him, his senses alert. Then he relit the gas lantern and set out to examine Bonegrinder's trail.

Wintone was reassured when he saw bright splatters of blood on the wet, bent grass. He stooped low, touched his fingertip to the scarlet wetness as if to confirm that the blood was genuine. His heart was still pounding, causing his extended arm that held the lantern to move slightly with each beat. He entered the woods.

A trail of blood and bent and broken tree limbs lay plain before Wintone. He knew that at such close range most of his shots must have struck. Bonegrinder had to die soon.

As Wintone moved head-down and cautiously through the woods, the splatters of blood became larger, merged into a glistening scarlet trail. The fear slipped from Wintone then, to be replaced by a hunter's eagerness, a hunter's lust. Energy surged into his body, and he lunged swiftly and noisily through the thick, wooded underbrush.

The bloody trail ended at a dark finger of lake water, narrow and overgrown with algae and reeds. His feet set wide, Wintone stood panting, peering out past the wavering edges of the lantern's glow. The black-green water seemed disturbed, but in the darkness Wintone couldn't see if the thick reeds had been parted or bent to reveal recent passage. There was no sound in the woods here, only a stillness as solid as the tree trunks.

Holding gun and lantern high, Wintone waded into the cool water.

Quickly the water was well above his waist, and he was entangled in the tall reeds that not only hindered his movements but obstructed his vision. He parted the reeds before him with the long shotgun barrel as he waded. What felt like a large insect crawled across the back of his neck, and unseen things plopped into dark water to avoid him. He lost his sense of direction and was soon wading in a pattern determined by the ease with which he could move through shallower water.

Eventually the water was below his waist, then to his knees, and the growth of reeds became sparse, then disappeared. He was on the opposite bank.

Holding the lantern low, Wintone walked in a crouch,

skirting the marshy line of the bank, ignoring the vines that tried to snake his ankles, the whiplike branches that brushed his face and upper body. The cold lake water had apparently stemmed Bonegrinder's bleeding, at least temporarily. Or perhaps Wintone had lost the trail in the shallows. He could find no trace of blood on the bank, no sign of Bonegrinder's exit from the water.

Wintone turned suddenly toward the tall reeds, toward the dark width of water he would again have to cross. Shadows and silence there.

Slowly, involuntarily, he moved backward with uncoordinated steps, up away from the bank.

Then, on the rough bark at the base of a tree, he saw a small drop of scarlet. He went to it and examined it, touched it and found that it was half-dried blood. With a whispering rush of air, he let out the breath he'd been holding.

Eagerly Wintone searched the woods in the area of the blood, but he found no other sign, no second marking of blood to establish direction. He extended his search to include a wider area, but without result.

For now, he would have to give up.

Turning away from the woods, Wintone walked along the bank until he reached a spot where the passage across looked easiest. His shadow trailing him like a wake, he held the lantern before him and entered the dark, still water.

On the opposite bank he had no trouble locating the trail of blood he'd tracked along to get there, and he followed it back the way he had come.

It was almost eleven o'clock when Wintone returned to Colver. As he climbed out of the patrol car in front of the office, old Bonifield and Frank Turper approached him.

"We been lookin' fer you," old Bonifield said. He spat chewing tobacco very near Wintone's boot toe.

"We'd like to know if you come up with some plan of action," Turper said. "Time keeps passin' an' nothin's gettin' done." His voice was high with exasperation.

Still dazed from both his confrontation with Bonegrinder and the cider he'd drunk, Wintone pushed past the two men, walked unsteadily to the office door and fumbled with the lock. The key seemed to fit only halfway.

"Least he could do is answer," old Bonifield said.

"Tomorrow . . ." Wintone said thickly.

Turper cursed. "Now listen, Sheriff! . . ."

But Wintone had the door open and was stepping inside, swinging it shut.

"Least he coulda done was talk to us," he heard old Bonifield say. "Whatever his condition."

Wintone didn't bother to turn on the lights. He made his way through the familiar, dark office to the back room. He shed his clothes, let them lay formless where they dropped, and stretched out on the groaning cot. The cot seemed to sway soothingly, as if riding gently undulating water, but the sensation was soon lost in sleep.

In the morning Wintone returned to where he had lost Bonegrinder's trail, this time skirting the finger of water to reach the opposite bank. It was all much simpler by daylight.

But he had no more luck than the night before; he couldn't even locate the blood he'd seen near the base of a tree.

Wintone stood in the shaded woods with the shotgun propped trigger up on his shoulder. He was sure Bonegrinder was dead. He'd seen enough lost blood to guarantee that. Most of his shots had to have hit, even fired as they were in stark panic.

The only doubt in Wintone's mind was as to whether the thing he'd slain conformed to his theory. He told himself that it must, that the only thing to do was to proceed as if it did. Verification would come. Eventually word of last night would get out, and Baily Howe's reward seekers would be more numerous in the woods than squirrels.

Wintone returned to the patrol car, unloaded and broke down the shotgun. Then he drove toward Higgins' Motel to talk to Bill Peterson.

THIRTY-THREE

Peterson had been lying on the double bed in the motel cabin with his head propped on the pillows, watching a game show on television. From the doorway Wintone looked over Peterson's shoulder into the room, saw the fresh indentation on the fluffed pillows, heard a feminine scream of glee as an announcer whose voice fairly dripped syrup kept up a steady yammer about everything the contestant had won.

"It's about your wife," Wintone said to Peterson, who was looking at him with guarded curiosity from the dimness inside the doorway.

Peterson stepped back so Wintone could enter, turned off the TV. He was barefoot, wearing only slacks and a sleeveless undershirt, and he hadn't yet shaved. "You're lucky you found me in," he said to Wintone. "I'm leaving this afternoon. The autopsy was yesterday, and I'm returning with Cheryl . . . with my wife's body to Saint Louis."

"I know," Wintone said. "I checked."

The faintest light of alarm glimmered in Peterson's eyes. He raised a hand to smooth his uncombed hair. "What exactly do you want, Sheriff?"

"I found somethin' in the lake, Mr. Peterson."

The glimmer returned, stayed longer.

"On the bottom, right below where your wife was killed, I found what you used to kill her."

Peterson's mouth opened, remained open. Stunned, he sat on the edge of the bed, but rose almost immediately. He stood with his arms hanging limply, his hands fluttering at his sides. "Do you realize what you're saying? . . ."

"What I found," Wintone said, "is a lead-weighted glove fitted with four sharpened bone claws. Homemade. Must weigh eight or ten pounds."

Peterson had recovered most of his composure. His face was hostile. "Coincidence. I don't know anything about what you're saying."

"You figured all you had to do was kill your wife with that weighted glove, toss it overboard and blame her death on Bonegrinder. It'd be just like the other cases you seen in the newspapers."

"I don't have to listen to this and I won't," Peterson said, but he made no move to stop Wintone.

"The glove itself mightn't convict you," Wintone went on, "but together with your account of the attack an' description of Bonegrinder, I'd say there's a plenty strong case. What happened is, I killed Bonegrinder last night, an' soon as the body's tracked down it'll prove that nothin' resemblin' what you described coulda been in deep water or anywhere else that day. Among other things, Mr. Peterson, the attack on your wife was the only one that took place in deep water. Her death was the only one I couldn't make fit the pattern, the reason bein' that you killed her."

Peterson had balance. He knew now where he stood, and

he was actually grinning at Wintone. "I deny that, of course."

"'Course you do, but that don't alter the fact you killed your wife."

"You're getting me confused with yourself, Sheriff. Maybe your problems have affected you mentally, interfered with your ability to do your job."

Wintone took a step forward and Peterson seemed to get smaller and farther away without budging, but the desperate grin stayed glued to his face. Remembering his run-in with Holt, Wintone clenched his teeth, forced calm on himself.

"Oh, it doesn't sound so good when you're the one being told you killed your wife," Peterson said, picking up confidence. "But I'd like to know what the hell's the difference. You're a county sheriff, is that it?"

Wintone surprised himself with the readiness of his answer. "The big difference is you planned and executed the murder of your wife."

"Well, you don't sound so convinced yourself, Sheriff. And if you're telling me the truth about Bonegrinder, if you did kill something, I suggest you wait until it's found. Otherwise I'm afraid you don't have a very persuasive case."

Wintone knew Peterson might be right. He'd hoped that when confronted with the evidence of the deadly glove, Peterson might confess, but Peterson was grittier and wilier than Wintone had thought.

"I don't know anything about this glove you described," Peterson went on, " and I'm sure that where you found it isn't exactly where my wife's death occurred. Anyone could have made that glove, dropped it in the lake. Anyone at all." Peterson had passed beyond confidence now and was working up anger.

"I think," Wintone told him, "you'd best come along with me."

Peterson's building anger faded; he gave Wintone an incredulous, wide-eyed look. "For what?"

"As of right now," Wintone said, "you're under arrest for suspicion of murder." He drew a rectangular card from his breast pocket and began to read Peterson his rights.

"Jesus!" Peterson said. "You do that out here in the sticks?" He bolted across the room, tried to push Wintone aside so he could make the door. With a sweep of his huge arm, Wintone hurried Peterson along, but not in the direction he wanted to go. Peterson slammed into the wall two feet to the left of the door frame, danced sideways out the door and walked in an aimless circle holding both hands to his head. He was dragging his feet, raising a surprising amount of dust. Almost gently, Wintone pulled Peterson's hands behind him and clamped the handcuffs into place.

Then he stood Peterson in the sun and finished reading him his rights.

"How could you'a figured it out?" Frank Turper asked Wintone the next evening at Mully's.

"Talked to Claude Borne's widow," Wintone said, sipping the beer Luke Higgins had bought him, "then I recollected how it was where the Larsen boy got killed, and I knew somethin' had traveled south besides the tourists."

"You best explain yourself," old Bonifield said.

Wintone didn't bother to look at him. "What I remembered was that the bait on the Larsen boy's fish hook was covered with ants. When I'd examined it I saw it was somethin' he'd made up himself with sorghum or molasses—somethin' sweet. Then I talked to Helen Borne an' found out Claude had taken sweet cider the night he was killed. Soon after, Alan Greer was killed an' young Kelly told me he'd had some sweet wine in a goat bladder, spilled it on himself an' his backpack. I got to thinkin', maybe the jug Claude had with him hadn't got cracked when he was attacked, maybe it was cracked before an' the sweet cider was leakin' off into the lake water.

"That meant the only death I couldn't make fit was the Peterson woman's. Her husband's account of what killed her an' the fact it happened in deep water threw me. An' when Peterson told me what they'd had with them that day in the boat he mentioned nothin' sweet.

"Then I remembered Peterson had said somethin' about him and his wife not gettin' along lately."

"He did say they'd made up, though," Luke Higgins pointed out.

"Said it after she was dead," Wintone told him. "I got to figurin' maybe Peterson had used Bonegrinder to cover up his own murder of his wife. So I searched the lake bottom an' found the weapon he used. I knew then that once I'd killed Bonegrinder an' proved my theory was right, it would cinch Peterson's guilt for his wife's murder."

"Can't prove it now, though," Bonifield said. "That's why you had to let Peterson go."

"That's true," Wintone admitted. "But it'll be proved if Bonegrinder's found." But he knew himself that if Bonegrinder hadn't been found yet, it wasn't going to happen. The woods in the area where Wintone had last seen Bonegrinder had been teeming with reward seekers; they had found nothing but more blood markings. Whatever scent there had been for tracking dogs had faded. Bonegrinder might have traveled for miles before dying, and Wintone knew the deep wild had a way of keeping its secrets. There were woods simply too thick for searchers to comb.

"Peterson'll stay free," Bonifield said. "Man kills his woman, walks around like the rest of us—it ain't right, in God's eyes nor no one else's."

"So after eliminatin' the Peterson woman's death, you figured it was sweetness," Mully cut in on Bonifield from behind the bar, "an' you used sweet cider to bait the thing."

Wintone nodded. "An' sweetness drives bears crazy, especially starvin' bears like this big one that couldn't get his usual food supply 'cause of the way the forest fire up north had burned an' deformed him, burned most of the fur off his hide an' ruined that back paw—the one that left the print—so he could hardly walk on it. Animals are prone to habit, even if they're hurt an' bedeviled. Bonegrinder took to the lake first off probably 'cause the water eased the pain of his burns, comin' outa the shallow water only to search for food till the pain drove him back. He could only snag a fish to eat now an' then there in the shallows, so he was probably gettin' hungrier by the day. Larsen boy likely had more of that sweet bait on him, maybe in his pocket—which would explain why the bear mauled his hip an' leg—an' we didn't find it 'cause it was eaten."

Bonifield cackled and shook his head. "If it were a bear, how come nobody's found it?"

"Had to be a bear," Wintone said. "You seen the blood yourself."

"Remember you was drinkin', Sheriff. An' we know how you are drunk. Maybe you was so scared you wanted what you seen to be a bear."

"I wasn't drunk," Wintone said flatly.

"Maybe it ain't dead," Frank Turper said. "Or crawled off in a cave an' died, or to some deep part of the woods where nobody's been."

"Or maybe it weren't a bear," Bonifield said.

"Bear or not," Luke Higgins said, "it was somethin' an' it's most certain dead. Them that wants can believe it was a bear. Thing is, far as we're concerned, it best have been a bear."

"It best have been," Frank Turper put in, amidst other murmured agreement.

Old Bonifield lapsed silent.

Mully set up another cold beer for Wintone, but the sheriff shook his head and slid off his bar stool. He'd spent a long day full of questions, congratulations and nosy reporters, and he was tired and wanted to go to bed. Wintone hadn't told anyone he didn't feel good about what he'd done, not like he'd expected. He felt a loss.

"So it was only somethin' wounded an' tryin' to survive," Mully said, slowly gliding a rag over the bar where Wintone had been drinking.

Wintone pulled the weight of his sweat-soaked shirt away from his body as he started toward the door. "Ain't we all now?"

"Speak fer yourself, Sheriff," old Bonifield said, swigging hard at his beer.

Wintone stepped out into the hot night and hesitated, wondering if he should go home to sleep or bed down in the back room at the office. Not that it made a difference.

Had it been a bear he shot? Already the memory of that night had become less vivid, touched by time, taking on new images and new meanings in the darkness at the base of his mind. He remembered what Higgins had said: "Them that wants can believe it was a bear." But would they ever really, completely, believe?

It had to have been a bear, Wintone told himself, but he knew there wasn't much that had to be. He'd never be sure, not really sure. There was so much he'd never be sure about.

Wintone stood for a time in the heat not knowing why, beneath Mully's buzzing electric sign and the circling night moths zigzagging their way to frantic, silent death. Then he turned and walked toward his office.